BIRD OF PREY

BIRD OF PREY

a novel by

COLLEEN TOOMEY

based on the BBC-TV serial
scripts by
RON HUTCHINSON

British Broadcasting Corporation

Published by the
British Broadcasting Corporation
35 Marylebone High Street
London WIM 4AA

ISBN 0 563 20063 4

First published 1982

Printed in England by
Love & Malcomson Ltd.,
Brighton Road,
Redhill, Surrey.

PART ONE

Chapter One

Louis Vacheron sat impatiently in the cathedral-sized hallway of the National Credit and Commerce Bank, his long, bony fingers playing scales along his briefcase perched on his lap, his toes marking time secretly inside his Gucci shoes. He stared, unblinking, at the three uniformed commissionaires, who were gossiping quietly among themselves in the giant rosewood pulpit which rose up from the centre of the hall. Occasionally, their conspiratorial banter would be broken by a loud croak as one of them buckled up laughing.

Gripping his empty briefcase, Louis approached them, 'Excuse me, I'm waiting to see the manager and I'm growing a little sleepy,' he said and looked at the old commissionaire with a disgusted expression.

The man propped himself up with his elbow.

'Sorry, sir. I'll try the extension again for you. Who shall I say it is, sir?'

Louis gave him his card, tapped his nails on the rosewood top, waited until he heard the commissionaire speak then returned to his seat.

The entrance hall was a splendid showcase for the bank; giant pillars of dark-green marble stretched high, supporting the elaborate domed ceiling. Louis watched streams of dark-suited men clatter across the marble floor – clerks with files, analysts, directors, foreign exchange dealers. It was to his credit that he hadn't panicked. He had an aversion to hanging about in security-conscious areas, particularly banks. But, today, he had told himself, he would be relaxed, laid-back. He glanced at his watch. A Patek Phillipe. He picked at his jacket. Piero de Monzi. Louis, my boy, he gloated, you've done all right for yourself. Here you are, in the shadow of the Old Lady of Threadneedle Street in London, adorned in the kind of attire these colourless creatures here can only dream of. What was more, he told himself, you've paid for it all, legitimately. Louis was proud of this rare fact.

Pangs of conscience never troubled Louis. He figured that his sins – and there were many – had been well dry-cleaned by serving time in the nick. Nowadays, the odds against a long stretch were slim, his friends had seen to that.

This maxim, held by one so well-doused in crime, plus the fact that Louis possessed considerable Gallic charm and style (being the kind who preferred BMWs to Cortinas) made him the perfect candidate for small, élite swindles. Louis carried diamonds to Amsterdam, gold coins to Zurich, delivered documents to Washington, played the role of arms dealer to Chile. This morning, he was a successful Swiss businessman in London and today, people would call him Louis Reims. It was a nostalgic choice. Reims was the town of his birth, where in his youth he had run wild. A petty thief, picking off wallets and swiping from stalls the sort of food which never normally appeared on the table at home, Louis had started small. But he had grown lucky. Now, he was in the big time.

'Monsewer Rhyme?' The commissionaire trampled all over his name. Louis had been miles away. He stood in acknowledgement and silently followed the man into the lift. It groaned to a halt on the sixth floor. Louis allowed the old man out first, walked behind him up the sleek corridor which arched around the boardroom to a small waiting room at the end.

'Here we are sir. Take a seat. Mr Blennerhasset won't be long.'

Louis flashed a look of indignation and fury – but the old man had already shuffled his way back down the corridor. He sat, nervously tugging at the knot in his tie, licked his dry lips.

'Good morning, Monsieur Reims. Sorry to have kept you waiting.'

It was Blennerhasset, sub-manager of National Credit, a stocky, jovial man in his late fifties with greased black hair and a well-defined stomach. Louis jerked to attention and mustered a thin smile as he stepped into the office.

'Is it normal,' he enquired, 'to have to sit in waiting rooms in English banks? As though one is waiting for a train, or a dentist?' There was an edge to his voice and he warned himself to stay cool.

'Not usually. Again, I apologise for keeping you. But Turin was very busy this morning.'

Louis reached into his breast pocket and produced an envelope, he said: 'The written confirmation you required – and my passport.'

It was Swiss, a good forgery in his opinion.

Blennerhasset hooked his spectacles behind his ears and began reading the documents on his desk. Silence. Louis broke into a verbal canter; he denigrated waiting rooms, questioned the efficiency of British banks. Blennerhasset ignored him, studied the documents thoroughly. He removed his glasses and smiled.

'Everything seems to be in order. I'll have the £50,000 brought in directly.'

He made a phone call, passed several sheets of paper across the desk.

'Would you mind signing these . . . just here,' he said, briskly pointing. Louis signed. A few minutes went by in silence, Louis clicked his pen impatiently.

'Ah, splendid,' Blennerhasset beamed as a young clerk appeared with a square black box which he placed on the desk. 'You will naturally wish to count it.'

'Thank you, no. I have a plane to catch – that is, I have to join one of your English queues to catch a plane,' said Louis sarcastically. He piled the crisp bundles into his briefcase, paused briefly to admire the cash. The locks clicked, signalling the meeting was over. As he descended in the lift, Louis couldn't resist smiling to himself.

Blennerhasset sank back into his armchair. It was still early in the day. He checked his diary to see how many more appointments were scheduled, then shoved the black leather book to the edge of his desk. There was a gold pen there, not his, so probably the Swiss businessman's he assumed, and called for the junior clerk.

'Take this to the commissionaire, immediately – on second

thoughts, take it yourself – and be quick. He's only just left.'

Louis strode confidently out of the bank towards Moorgate. He stopped to buy *Le Monde* from a wizened news vendor, held out his hand for change and glanced back casually at the bank. A young man waved frantically in his direction. Christ! It was Blennerhasset's spotty clerk. Louis turned and walked away briskly. The clerk broke into a trot, dodging the morning crowd. Louis scanned the clogged streets, began to panic. On the far side of the road he spotted a taxi with its yellow light shining. He looked back – the clerk was closing in. Without hesitating, Louis waved his free arm above his head and ran towards the black cab.

Brakes screeched. Louis screamed as the unseen car slammed into his abdomen, dragged him along on the bonnet for several yards before flinging him backwards into the gutter. The briefcase spun into the air and bounced against the railing. The locks kicked open, the banknotes spewed out into the street. It was all over in seconds.

Louis lay in the kerb, clutching his stomach. His body crumpled, his jacket torn. Cars had come to a halt, horrified passers-by gathered around him, mouths gaping. Disaster always brought its audience out on cue and today in the morning rush hour, spectators were in bountiful supply. Hovering on the edge of the hushed crowd was the bank clerk, in his hand, Louis' gold pen. He stood there, indecisive. Then, quietly he tucked the pen into his top pocket so that it was hidden beneath his lapel, and sauntered back the way he had come.

Chapter Two

By the hundreds, they poured out of Blackfriars Station, great clumps of commuters moving through the ticket barrier in mindless unison, out into the dull morning. There, they dispersed, according to their destination: Fleet Street, the City; down Upper Thames Street, New Bridge Street, Queen Victoria Street. It would be the same in the evening, floods of people, homeward bound, like a movie being run in reverse.

It was a damp morning in October and Henry Jay walked purposefully out of the station, stopping to buy a packet of Tic-tacs from the confectioner's in Queen Victoria Street. It was a time-honoured habit. The packet would last him the day – provided he sucked them, that was. It was nine twenty-four and Henry was in a black mood, stabbing at the cracks in the pavement with his lean, black umbrella. Henry Jay tried to dress smartly. But, despite everything; neatly-pressed suits, clean shirts and shiny leather shoes, he somehow missed the mark. His waistcoat rippled over his large stomach, revealing a little too much shirt at the midriff. His trousers were, perhaps, too short. And his ties were a kaleidoscope of colours, a never-matching array of patterns.

He was nearly there. As he reached the point where St Paul's Cathedral looks majestically down through Peter's Hill onto the bland Government buildings where he worked, a police car roared past. Probably just a couple of young cadets in their first patrol car, he scowled as it disappeared from view. Then an ambulance screamed up behind. Henry hated their sound. They heralded untimely death. It followed the police car, turned inwards to the City. Some poor bugger, Henry thought, as he counted the steps which led to the monolithic building containing the staff of the Department of Commercial Development. He had started working for the Department sixteen years ago, when the offices were tucked behind Waterloo Station. Fresh from university, Henry had arrived with a personal aim; he wanted to design a computer system which would operate in every government department, which would break down numerous bureaucratic layers and save millions of pounds. Such a project was not to be. His first task was to analyse technology in the carpet industry and to project its future. Henry toiled on, from one laborious task to the next, year in, year out. Occasionally, he was permitted to implement his own projects. Many of those were imaginative, and occasionally words of congratulation winged their way from the House of Commons, from a junior Minister. Promotion came quickly at first. But Henry was thirty-eight now. He was a Principal Scientific Officer and had found himself stuck at PSO level too long. There had been whispers that promotion was on the cards. But competition was stiff and included the PSO he had shared an office with for the past six months – Harry Tomkins. Henry knew very little about his colleague. He had once thought how strange it was that, even though they probably spent more time with each other than they did with their wives, they never talked about their private lives. He realised then that he didn't even know if Tomkins had a wife.

Harry Tomkins seemed deep in thought when Henry walked into the office, shed his coat and umbrella and sat down in the desk opposite. In fact, Tomkins was thinking of nothing much at all, his eyes were glued to his Stationery Office ballpoint pen, which he was taking apart, studying and putting back together.

'Morning Harry.'

'Morning Henry.'

They looked at each other and smiled cordially. Tomkins returned to the autopsy of his pen while Henry unpacked his briefcase. The Tupperware lunch-box was dispatched to his top drawer and the thick folder onto his desk. He sighed.

'Anything happening?' he said leaning forward.

'Nothing. Dead as a doornail.' Tomkins kept his head down.

Henry rested his chin on his hand and stared despondently down at his file. The EEC's draft directive on data protection – the British approach. Since the Government remained on the fence and refused to draw up any legislation to protect confidential data while bickering and eye-scratching continued in Brussels, Henry didn't suppose for one minute that he could raise any enthusiasm for his report. He turned despondently to the first page, though. Was it really more than a week ago since he last sent off a memo requesting an investigation into cryptography? He couldn't remember. There had been so many. He yawned, stretched his arms and tried to read. It was no use. He couldn't concentrate. He began doodling in the margin, patterns of no great distinction. Suddenly, he heard a man clearing his throat beside him. Startled by the intrusion, he looked up.

'Ah, sorry, Mr Hendersly. Had my head down.' Guilt crawled across his face and he edged his hand over the file to cover his pencilling from his boss. Tomkins had begun to write feverishly, pausing only to shoot a sarcastic glance at Henry.

'What's this about?' said Hendersly, dangling a piece of paper in front of him.

'What? Oh, the memo,' Henry replied. 'Apparently, the Americans are considering new ways to restrict the publication of research into cryptography – computer codes to protect information.'

'I know what the word cryptography means, Mr Jay.'

Henry, oblivious of the acerbic tone in his boss's voice, continued.

'Telephone networks are now more or less computer networks – as are modern office accounting and money transfer systems. Anyway, American intelligence agencies are concerned by security aspects of unregulated publication of cryptography research. I've done some more work on it this week,' he said, drawing in air.

Hendersly raised his eyebrows.

'And you think we should investigate the matter and how it affects the United Kingdom?' He made it sound more like a challenge than a query.

'Absolutely.'

'Your previous report, the one with the long title . . .'

'Fraud and Related Security Problems in the Age of Advanced Computer Intelligence and Electronic Accounting.'

' . . . is certainly very thorough. I would have thought complete. We should be thinking of entirely fresh topics for your detailed attention. Yes?'

Henry protested. 'But that report was centred around frauds perpetrated by experts using technology. This report would take it further, it would examine international systems, government agencies, legislation abroad . . . anyway, there are always finishing touches to do on my last report.'

'Yes, I see. Still, we should be ever-ready to sense when a job is well done and best left alone. I'll come back to you on this matter.'

Bloody typical, thought Henry as the door slammed. The Americans were sailing ahead, the Germans were taking a keen interest, British companies were already using cryptography and here, in the epicentre of power, otherwise known as Whitehall, was a Departmental head, a Pinhead, who continued to prevaricate. Henry also admitted privately that his feelings on the report were buried deep in his gut – he needed that investigation to help clinch his promotion. It would convince them he was the right man for the job.

Tomkins had watched the verbal tennis match between Henry and Hendersly, fascinated; the warning glint in Hendersly's eye, the tiny bubbles of sweat on Henry's top lip forming as he drummed out his argument. He revelled in such sparring, not because he disliked Henry – he rather admired his colleague, the ideas he put up were good and they flowed regularly from his out-tray, his reports were thorough. But that worked *against* Tomkins. No one doubted he was intelligent – it was just that his adrenalin had packed up a long time ago. The days when he produced a dazzling report (dazzling in Civil Service terms) had passed, his imagination had gone flat. Instead, he accepted work from his in-tray, devouring reports on bilateral trade, anything he was asked to, in fact. And in doing so he'd dug himself into a hole. He looked at Henry and felt a twinge of jealousy. Promotion isn't much to ask, he told himself. No, but promotion will not come handed on a plate. Henry has the edge on you, not just because of his work output. He presents an all-round package, as a married man. He has a wife who can entertain guests, small troops of executives, government contacts; much more than you could offer. Yes, but things are different for me, Tomkins argued with himself. I'll say they are – for a start you're not married, never have been. Still live with your mother, doesn't sound all that impressive; downright dodgy, in fact. But I do my job well, he continued his silent debate. Nobody has cause for complaint; and surely what I get up to in my private life is my own business! Not in the promotion stakes, dear Tomkins. Being a solitary man did not augur well for his future.

It had all begun years ago, when he built a small wing off the back of his mother's house in Surbiton – his father had died twenty years before. He moved all his photographic gear into it – Tomkins was a camera buff. He had a dark room, numerous cameras and just about every lens and filter on the market. He spent hours there, often not emerging for almost the entire weekend. It was like that, every weekend. A routine he followed faithfully, a routine that was as regular as clockwork and just as predictable. Just like his work.

The tea trolley rattled outside the office door, diverting Tomkins' attention from his home and career prospects to the needs of his stomach. He settled down with a ham roll and a mug of tea and watched Henry effortlessly plough his way through two ham rolls.

The two men were physically unalike. Henry looked like a sort of Billy Bunter character, as he sat with his stomach pressed up against the desk, his fleshy pink face with its button nose, so ill-equipped to hold his glasses at the appointed place. But, in fact, there was nothing of the buffoon in Henry, who was serious to the point of being dull. And as for Tomkins, he gave the impression of possessing a wily charm. His face was sharp, remarkably unlined for his thirty-six years, he would have looked young for his age but for the fact he'd gone prematurely bald. His cranium stretched back into a shiny dome, curtained from ear to ear with thick brown hair and his grey-green eyes sparkled. But it was *Tomkins* who was life's plodder and not Henry, as so many assumed.

'Erm . . . Excuse me,' Henry peered tentatively at Tomkins. 'Couldn't swap lunch-hours today, could we, old man?'

Tomkins yawned. It was a regular request and one he always responded to with a grudging, 'Oh, all right.' He slumped back, bored, his eyes following Henry's laboured movements – unlocking his top drawer, removing his Tupperware lunchbox, slipping an envelope furtively into his top pocket. When Henry had left, he leaned forward and, slowly, dismantled the stapler.

Chapter Three

'This it?'

'Yes.'

Henry watched indignantly as Chief Superintendent Stanley Richardson weighed up the sealed envelope. He'd gone to some trouble to get the information and felt hurt by the scant regard with which Richardson seemed to regard it. Sulking, he lifted a sandwich from his Tupperware box and stared at the contents bulging from the thick white slices. Beef, pickle and mustard. With peanuts! How on earth did Anne dream up such strange concoctions? He rummaged about for another and, satisfied with his second choice, began munching.

Richardson had opted for a liquid lunch, as usual. And it was the Founder's Arms, again. Richardson sank his pint in one motion, his Adam's apple jumping furiously in his throat. 'Needed that like I need a good poke,' he slapped his glass onto the table and burped. Henry winced.

Richardson was a successful copper, a respected operator, young for his elevated position. He had the chewed-up face of an SPG man and lacked the sophistication to improve on his rank. He liked it that way – popular with his men, daggers drawn with his superiors. His eyes, flecked green, were hard and his mouth never relaxed, even when he smiled.

'Right Henry, listen. It's summarised in the notes I've got, if your brain flags . . . This team's been working the same bank fraud for two years, see. Always the same story – they create a diversion, whip into the telex room, feed in the correct cash authorisation codes to at least half-a-dozen banks round Europe. The funds are shifted and they have collectors at the other end. They pick up a million quid's worth, in different currencies, in one go. This time round they screwed up in Turin and had to shoot their way out. Their fella – a bloke called Louis Vacheron – at the London end wasn't so lucky, he got nabbed. Anyway, thought you might be interested, even though it's not strictly computer fraud.' He reached inside his coat pocket and pulled out a squat envelope.

'What some people will do for promotion, eh Henry?' He began picking away at one corner.

'Not here,' Henry hissed.

'Suit yourself,' said Richardson stuffing the envelope back in his pocket.

There was hardly a soul brave enough to sit out on the patio of the Founder's Arms. It was freezing. Most of the lunchtime drinkers peered through smoked glass from the warmth of the bars. 'Probably think we're testing asbestos underwear,' Richardson chuckled. 'Wanna half?'

'Thanks, Stanley. I have to be off. You couldn't give me the envelope now, I suppose?' his eyes drifted down to Richardson's coat.

Richardson pretended not to hear him. 'Did you know, if you jumped off Blackfriars Bridge over there, any bridge into the Thames come to that – you'd last seventeen seconds; fair do. The undertow would suck you down. If *that* didn't get you, the temperature would. Freeze to death in no time. And if you were *still* kicking about, a few gulps of the old Swanee Thames would send you reeling into the next world. Fascinating river this, eh?'

'Very,' said Henry testily. 'But have you got anything for me?'

Richardson sighed, handed Henry his envelope, and pocketed the one lying on the table.

'Anything on those Inland Revenue Special Investigations Unit enquiries?'

'Not so far.'

'Keep me posted, Henry.'

'Sure . . . I was wondering. Do we have to meet in such public places? Our contact is highly irregular.'

'But necessary. You can't fight a thousand millions' worth of fraud keeping to the rules.'

'I know, but –'

'Why fight it at all, I sometimes ask myself. When you land them, what happens? Months of preparation to get to court, the expense of Queen's Counsel, and a bloody lay jury who get totally confused inside two days; two in five acquittals, not that being found guilty cops a fine or a stretch inside that means much. And here's you and me, Henry, on the same side – City of London Fraud and the Department of Commercial Development – passing each other notes under tables like schoolboys.'

However right Richardson was, it didn't make Henry feel any less uncomfortable. 'Do we have to keep meeting in pubs, though?'

'Good cover, pubs. Also, they sell beer.'

'But this is at least the sixth time we've used the place. Despite what you say, we can't afford to become complacent,' Henry protested.

Richardson leaned back, rocked his chair back and forth with a casual disregard for Henry's paranoia. 'I like it here,' he said, waving his arm. 'I like the river, it's been around a long time. It goes all the way down there, turns to the right, past France, Spain, Portugal and Africa. And the other way it curls round Norway – all the way to Russia. The river keeps me humble, Henry. Reminds me there's more to the world than the stinking, sweating mass they call the Square Mile . . .'

'The City happens to breed some diligent, hard-working men who –'

'I know what you're going to say. Rose-tinted glasses, Henry, you should try another pair.' His voice became harsh. 'Now piss off back to the missus . . . and keep those photostats safe or I might have you over that bridge one day – another one of those Civil Service cutbacks.' He stayed to watch Henry scuttle off, his mac flapping behind him. Checked his watch.

'Jesus Christ!' he leapt to his feet. He'd better get cracking if he intended to get to St Bartholomew's Hospital to break the news. And he wanted to be the one, so he could see Louis Vacheron's face for himself.

By the time Henry reached St Paul's Court, Anne had finished her lunch.

'Sorry, dear. Something came up,' he panted. She finished packing her lunchbox into her shoulder bag and looked at him, without malice. 'These things happen.'

They began walking, their arms touching. In all the years she'd been married to Henry, sixteen to be precise, she had rarely known a time when he'd let her down without good cause. Naturally, she begrudged the time he devoted to his work and to his hobbies. It was just that Henry's idea of a good reason didn't always tally with her own and jealousy of time stolen by whatever source, human or otherwise, was an emotion she had never been able to exorcise. At least she had learned to find a strange comfort in her possessiveness – a reassurance that she still loved him.

Anne tossed her head, her long soft brown hair falling back over her shoulders. 'I thought we'd go to the caravan tonight, for the weekend,' she said. 'It seems to be clearing up and it'd do us the power of good.'

'Sorry, dear. It won't be possible – not this weekend, I'll be working late; it's the report, something else has come up on it.'

She showed no sign of disappointment. 'I thought you'd finished that weeks ago.'

'Files are never finished . . . I'm hoping to add extensively to it. If that doesn't clinch promotion, I'll stay a Principal Scientific Officer all my career.'

'I know, darling,' she said. 'See you later, then.'

He gave her a light peck on the lips and made his way down the steps towards the Embankment. Anne disappeared into the shadows, back to her office. She knew how badly Henry would take it if he didn't make the grade, if he watched promotion pass him by. He had worked so hard; harder than she had ever seen him work before, and the harder he worked, the less he talked about it. She supposed that had something to do with their marriage. After sixteen years, communication between them had been reduced to a shorthand of looks, key words, signals which often said far more than elasticised discussions they had had in their youth when they would sit about for hours and talk about every subject under the sun. Sometimes, she worried, their 'shorthand' had gone too far, and they didn't talk enough. She supposed all marriages went that way, after a while.

She had met Henry when she was nineteen and two months; she remembered that because ten months later they got married, on her birthday. She recalled the wedding photographs, how dreadful they looked now. Henry squeezed into a morning suit (hired), looking itchy, bothered and unsmiling. She had spent hours flouncing out her full taffeta skirt overlaid with white tulle, ended up like a dowdy ballroom dancer. The bodice didn't fit, floated around her breasts and waist, her hair was short, teased and lacquered, with two curls on either side pointing at the camera. Her veil frizzed around her head like an electrocuted halo, her white satin stiletto shoes turned awkwardly inwards. Everything jarred. It was conservatism at its worst. While everyone else was wildly leaping into the tidal wave of sexual freedom, flower power, drugs and burning bras, Mr and Mrs Jay were quietly sealing their fate with a marriage that mirrored, in almost every respect, their parents' wedding some half a century before.

They were happy then. Still were, she supposed. They had

their own home, their own garden, their own hobbies, their own jobs. Yes, their careers. That had been the major snag. Anne was every bit as talented as Henry, even though she was a couple of years younger; her job with the Department of Energy was more than just bringing in money to pay the mortgage. She often thought of the family they could have had, and didn't, because she wanted to pursue her career. Now, it was too late and she couldn't bear children. A hysterectomy had seen to that. She didn't regret her earlier decision; just wondered how things might have been if they had had kids. But now, her career was taking off. There was an excellent chance of promotion. That was something Henry didn't know, yet. And she wouldn't tell him until she was successful. Right now, Henry had his own career problems to attend to.

'You've had it, Louis, mate,' said Richardson drily. 'They've decided to do you for accomplice to the Turin murders, rather than for the fraud this end.' His eyes were pinned on Louis' face. Nothing. Not a flicker of anger, surprise or resignation even, passed across his face – it was inpenetrable. It was a studied coolness Richardson only partly understood. He knew he was tough – Louis had to be, to survive. Toughness was inbred, it could not be destroyed by a botched raid in Turin, by the death of friends or colleagues, by the fear of being cut out of a deal, or being cut out of life itself. Louis was ruthless and like courage it was a powerful force against adversity. He knew how to play the system, hopefully without having to pay for it. Still, Richardson was a little taken aback to find *no* reaction when he sprang the murder rap on him. He stared hard at the Frenchman – his face bore all the hallmarks of an extremely good-looking man, its symmetry guaranteed beauty; an asset Louis was not slow to put to use, especially with women. But now, his olive skin threw up a gamut of shades from purple, blue-black to iodine brown. His left cheek was speckled with tiny scabs, his eyes, usually a rich nutmeg brown, gazed up at Richardson through black and puffy lids.

Without a word, Louis lifted a glass from his bedside table, drew in a mouthful of the minty green liquid and began swirling it around his mouth. Unable to speak he beckoned Richardson to hand him the metal bowl. It was within Louis' easy reach and they both knew it; he was challenging his opponent. Richardson complied. Triumphantly, Louis spat out the mouthwash and passed back the bowl. A small dribble hung unceremoniously from his bottom lip. With an adept swipe, he removed it with his index finger and slumped back into the stiff white pillows.

'You know what I like about you, Louis? You've got style. All I get from the home-grown villain is grunts. But you, facing twenty years of cold spaghetti and still coming flash.'

Louis smiled at him, 'I'm not one of Mother Nature's worriers, Stanley. I shall spend two, possibly three months in a Turin prison. And then, like an assistant at the end of a magic trick, I shall be released, to prepare for the next performance. And when we carry out a fraud like this one again, be it in London, Paris, Athens, wherever, I shall cross the road *extremely* carefully with my laden briefcase.'

'Be a next time, will there?' Smart-arsed Frog, thought Richardson.

'We have very high connections, Stanley. I know something about someone in Le Pouvoir. That's why I can rely on assistance.'

Richardson looked more sceptical than he felt. Louis might be just a small cog in a very big wheel, even so, he could be very useful, he guessed. All the more reason to make sure he was given safe passage to Turin.

Outside the door of the private room, a uniformed police constable sat, picking his nails unselfconsciously. He yawned and crossed his arms. He couldn't see the sense of wasting his time and police money on protecting a petty criminal who, judging by the state he was in, was hardly likely to nip down the corridor and out of the front door. Oh, well.

Richardson nonchalantly reached over to the bedside table and stuffed a large white grape into his mouth, crunching the seeds loudly between his teeth. Louis had probably flattered a nurse into bringing these from a neighbouring ward. He wouldn't put it past him.

Louis stared at Richardson who was eating his way through the fruit ball, at the end of the bed. Disdainfully and without warning, he tossed his mouthwash bottle at Richardson and smiled as he juggled it in his hands. 'You should use the stuff.'

Richardson glanced at the label, threw the bottle on the bed and without smiling, asked 'Where?' Then he turned his back and walked out, stopping at the door. 'Be seeing you soon, son.'

Louis seemed determined to bypass a farewell and ignore him, his head down, reading yesterday's *Le Monde*. Richardson extended a friendly wink to the duty policeman and marched soberly on down the long, echoing corridor. The hospital was quiet. Three visitors sat in plastic chairs along the wall: an old woman in a worn vermilion coat and two small girls in their Sunday best, their legs swinging, unable to touch the floor.

'Hey, Gran, look,' cried one of the children, 'he's got a boxer's nose like Uncle Bernie.' They giggled as Richardson approached them.

'And I've got a mouth which gobbles up little girls like you for breakfast.' He tried to sound kind but his voice came gruff. In unison, the girls began blubbering. Uncomfortable with his helplessness he walked on, out into the courtyard at the rear of the hospital. Richardson didn't like children much. He remembered a time when he thought having a family would be a terrific idea. But that was a long time ago and before he and Gail got round to having any, she walked out. Two years was all she could take, she said, of being a squaddy's widow. She'd had it up to there, she said. So Gail went back to her parents. The divorce went through smoothly, he didn't fight it. Later, he learned, she'd moved in with a bloke from the Met. That really stuck in his gullet. Bloody women! Silly cow, kept her brain between her legs. He still felt bitter about that episode in his life and cursed the thoughts he'd so easily let slip into his mind. He bet Louis never regretted anything like that.

Chapter Four

Henry was upstairs in his study, stirring his tea thoughtfully with his left hand and holding his stamp catalogue open with the other. Carelessly, he shook the spoon and sucked it, placing it on the uncluttered part of the desk. It was Sunday, Henry's favourite day in the week, a day he devoted entirely to his stamp collection and writing articles about POW cards and postmarks for *Stamp News,* a subject he was regarded as expert on and for it he was paid £13.25 an article.

Sunday routine never changed. After lunch – usually moussaka or some other dish which would disguise yesterday's leftovers – he would plod up the carpeted stairs, replete, to his book-lined room, ease himself with a grunt into his battered armchair and stare out of the window for five minutes. Then, he would hoist himself up and feed a cassette into his stereo. Today, as usual, it was Elgar's Concertino in E Minor for Violoncello and Orchestra, Op 85, because it soothed him and helped him think. Henry played only music by English composers – except for Britten whom he considered too modern – because he was patriotic and because he considered them grossly underrated.

He had decided to catalogue his new purchases – an envelope from W/O S Brown No. 54. Stalag 357 with the rare cachet 'This letter has been returned by the Swiss Post Office who were unable to reforward it to Germany because of the interruption of communications'. He'd got that for £30 and was well pleased. He'd also got another find – a letter from the most notorious concentration camp of them all, Auschwitz, which had cost him £80. He read the letter again – translating it roughly –

> 'Dear Mum and Dad, Everything is fine . . . I do not wish to receive any tobacco as I can buy all I want here . . . and don't bother about food, I get all that I could wish for . . .'

It had been written by a man about to be exterminated.

Henry felt the food in his stomach collide. Sometimes his collection induced great passion and anger.

The telephone jangled in the hall downstairs.

'Anne!' he yelled. He heard her curse him as she ran to answer it.

Clump, clump, clump, she came up the stairs.

'For you. Someone from the office wants you.'

'Don't be silly,' he retorted. 'It's Sunday. I'm a Principal Scientific Officer in the Department of Commercial Development and God would not permit me to work on a Sunday.'

It made her smile.

When he came off the telephone, Anne had gone back to her studio, the only uncluttered room in the house. It was a repository for her thoughts, a room filled with plants, boxes of paints, a pottery wheel, plastic bags of clay and in a corner by the back door, shelves displayed her finished work. After struggling through night classes and failures, she had developed a flair for composition and colour, though her talent was confined to weekend daubing. She looked up from her easel as he came into the room.

'You know what *you* want, Henry? A job that will work you on Sundays – something to stretch you.' She said it without irony. 'The Civil Service isn't meant to provide the answer, you know, with its annual increments, steady promotion, a good pension at the end of the day. Makes you dull. Haven't you ever wanted to use yourself more?' she challenged him.

'I have to go out.'

'What? Straight away?' How typical of Henry, she thought, to ride rough-shod over her question, without even knowing it.

'Yes, I'm afraid so.'

'Good, I'll come along for the ride. I'm getting a bit stale with this painting, anyway.' She set down her brush and wiped her hands on a turpentine rag.

'Sorry, darling, this is business. I have to see someone on my own.'

'On a Sunday? It's the Civil Service, you know – never on a Sunday, it's our Golden Rule. Why?'

'Look – did you not answer the phone? And did I not just come through this door and say I have to go out to see someone, someone who has asked to see me – even though it is Sunday,' he bickered. Henry took a deep breath, trying to contain his frustration. 'It'll only be for an hour or two. I promise.' He put his arms around her and kissed her gently on the cheek. He wanted to explain why he was dashing off so quickly – but he wasn't really certain. It was just like Anne to ask him 'Why?' and not 'Who?' he mused as the Renault sputtered indignantly to life. To her, 'Why?' anchored all other questions to it, it interpolated motives, priorities, loyalties, it demanded analysis. They had discussed this often when they were students at Manchester University where she used the Socratic elenchus often. At that age, everything seemed more open to elaborate discussion. Not any more. As he drove off down Woolwich Road from Westcombe Park, he pulled his mind back to when they were still single . . . He parked the car and glanced at his watch, it was much later than he thought. He had been so engrossed with the past that the present hadn't even figured in his mind.

He crossed the muddy track behind the derelict corrugated iron shed which rattled eerily and headed towards the river. Debris piled up along the embankment, rusty cans tangled with muddied plastic. He scrambled over the boulders and stood at the edge of the jetty. It was full tide and the water lapped pleasantly about the stubby wooden poles. Half-an-hour had passed and still no sign of Richardson. He would give him just a few minutes more, then leave. Henry felt uneasy. It was a strange spot to pick for a rendezvous, Woolwich Dockyard. And Richardson had given no clue as to the reason or the urgent need for such a Sunday meeting. He stared out ahead, wondering.

The Thames reminded him of tinfoil, its silver crinkles catching the shades of the afternoon sky. Across, on the north bank, were London's docks, King George V, Royal Victoria and Royal Albert, once undisputed giants in their heyday. Before him the Thames Barrage, like a dismantled Sydney Opera House, its vast domes gleaming. A bevy of welders were hard at work on it, sealing fast the rivets to hold back the river from bursting its banks.

The dead grass behind him snapped. Somebody was right behind him and moving in fast. His blood thumped fast through his body, he turned, abruptly. It was Richardson.

'Oh, it's you,' he breathed a sigh of relief.

'Were you followed?'

'What?'

'Did anyone follow you?' repeated Richardson.

'Why should anyone want to follow me?' Henry said looking at Richardson incredulously. Coming from him these questions were quite out of character, caught Henry unprepared. Richardson's face looked strange, too. It usually looked as though he'd slept on it, but today it was even more pinched and drawn than usual. His tie, knotted around his neck, hung loosely to one side. They stood, side by side, watching a large ship pull by and said nothing as their eyes traced its journey towards the estuary.

Then Richardson spoke: 'I think I'm being rubber-heeled. That's why we're here. They'll either have to take the next ferry or do it by road through the Dartford Tunnel.' Richardson paused. 'Louis has been killed,' he added quietly.

'Louis?'

'Louis Vacheron, the London end of the Italbank fraud – remember, the raid on that Turin bank I told you about, Louis was their London collector.'

They walked on in silence, stumbling over the rocky landscape. Louis' death had hit Richardson hard. Professionally, he'd wanted the Frenchman alive, to keep tabs on him; they could have helped one another. But Richardson had also warmed to the arrogant Louis. He stared into the distance, murmured softly: *'Hibou et Minou allèrent à la mer dans une barque peinte en jaune-canari. Ils prirent du miel roux et beaucoup de sous . . .'* He turned to look at Henry. '*Owl and the Pussycat.* Taught me that he did. As he was being bundled into the police car going to Heathrow he slipped me a bit of paper with the words on. Said he'd taught it to his girlfriend in Brussels – an English bird called Hannah Brent. Said if I ever went there I should look her up in the EEC's legal department and to use the poem as a sort of check that I was a friend. Louis promised to show me another world, to open my eyes!' Richardson let out a choked laugh. 'Fancy a copper bandying French, eh? Time was you got a car ride up the M1 and it was an event. In the past ten years I've been to Germany, Switzerland, the States, South America – I blame it on Skytrain, myself. I mean, why pull a job in Rotherhithe when you can get to New York and back in time for News at Ten?' He stopped, his mind had clicked into another train of thought. 'Louis thought I was a mug, thought he could use me . . . I liked him, don't get me wrong . . . we could have used each other. But *he* was the mug. He thought *Le Pouvoir* would get him off – we call it The Power – but it shut him up instead. Just like that!' Richardson placed two fingers to his head. 'On the way to Heathrow, a wagon pulls out – big job, one of the Italian haulage firms. Police car brakes sharply, gives him a mouthful. Then up comes a BMW on the other side. Two shots in the back of the head, coppers untouched, Louis leaking all over the back seat. The Power took Louis out as cleanly as a tooth extraction.'

'You go on about the Power, what is it?' he ventured.

'The Power, Henry, is what protects our Lords and Masters; politicians, rulers and betters, when they find they have to do business with crooks, with big money, with people who have something on them.'

'I don't understand.'

'Not many do.'

'You mean, Louis knew something about someone involved with the Power – someone in business, politics, whatever – and he was depending on using that information as blackmail to get off the Italbank charges?'

'Yeh, a politician, in fact. Nice work, Henry.'

'Presumably Italian?'

'Wrong – British.'

Somehow Henry had always thought of other countries' politicians falling prey to bribery, shady deals, corruption; it had never dawned on him that home-grown politicians were every bit as susceptible. His face betrayed his thoughts.

'Yes, Henry. Louis had something on one of the "untouchables". I don't know what it was and I don't know who. But if Louis is right about the Power, his friends, the organisation, the people who work for it, wittingly or unwittingly, will try to rub out every reference to Louis Vacheron just as neatly as they rubbed him out. And just in case it's slipped your memory – one of those references will be in your computer fraud report.' Richardson's worn face turned on Henry. 'In which case you'll realise it's important to check the file – to see how far the network has infiltrated.'

'No way.'

'I think you ought to check the file, Henry.' There was a threatening tone in Richardson's voice.

'I've done enough for you.'

'No you bloody haven't. Not for me – you did it to catch your boss's eye with your report.'

'I'm no longer involved, Stanley.'

Richardson clenched his teeth, said: 'I don't think you quite understand, Principal Scientific Officer Jay. I've a note of all the confidential information you either dug out of your own files or passed on from Inland Revenue Special Investigations Unit. I don't know if there's a grade lower than Paper Keeper, Grade Ten, but if there is, you'll be it, my son. Of course they might just decide to make you the scapegoat and stuff the Official Secrets Act up your backside.' His eyes were burning, 'I don't mean to be crude, but I liked Louis you see. I liked him a lot. You get my point, Henry? You know what to do?'

Henry knew what to do. He stood facing Richardson, so close he could feel the copper's breath on his cheeks. 'I can't do it. It'll be too difficult.'

'Choices are what make things difficult and you, Henry haven't got a choice.'

That was it. No goodbye, be seeing you, call you tomorrow. Richardson turned his back on him and went.

Chapter Five

It was just after eight o'clock in the morning. Henry was already at his desk, hunched over a copy of the *Financial Times*, eating a currant bun. As he bit into it, the crumbs tumbled into the crease of the paper, opened at the Technology Page. With the ball of his dampened finger he squished them up, drawing the crumbs into his mouth. He had arrived early especially to check the references to the Italbank fraud in his file. But he had failed. The combination to the lock had been changed over the weekend. The cabinet door wouldn't budge; now he would have to wait until Hendersly's secretary arrived before he could discover the new three figure combination. He looked up at the clock. It was now eight thirty-five. Only twenty-five more minutes to go till the rank and file marched onto the production line of Whitehall, to the lack-lustre Department of Commercial Development. At that moment, the door flung open and Harry Tomkins walked in.

They both stared, surprised to find each other in the office so unusually early. Tomkins slapped his briefcase on his desk and spoke as he removed his coat.

'I suppose you're working on that blessed report of yours again? You'll stick your neck out too far one of these days for information, you know that. What's it this time, another whizz-kid programmer diverting the odd pence from every account into his own?'

'No . . . I mean, I'm not working on the report. But do you know what I've come up with – an international bank fraud, it's a cracker.' Henry loved relating to Tomkins the cases he dug up – his enthusiasm over them always rattled Tomkins.

'If it's a big case, why not go direct to the bank's security people?'

'What for? The banks would rather collect the insurance and deny it ever happened. Wouldn't do for Mr Average to lose faith in the security of the banking system now would it?'

Tomkins flopped into his chair and leaned across the desk, his pencil aimed at Henry.

'You know Hendersly and the Department would disown you if it ever came to light?'

'To do a job well, one sometimes has to take risks, you know.' This was a dig at Tomkins who he knew had never risked a thing in his professional career.

'Asking under-the-counter favours of the police, Henry,' Tomkins retaliated, 'has the drawback they might ask them of you one day.'

If only he knew how percipient his remark had been, Henry thought. If he only knew about yesterday.

After that brief contretemps they ceased talking. Tomkins embroiled himself in a report on the export of technological equipment to Soviet Union chemical plants, refusing even to take refreshments offered by Mrs Peach, the veteran tea lady. She'd looked quite indignant – he might just as easily have insulted her.

Henry was paper-deep in company brochures and reports. One of his side-lines was office automation and for once the British were ahead of their American counterparts. Plessey, one of the leading telecommunications companies in the UK had already announced its strategy for fully automating offices; Wang and IBM in the States had only recently brought out their systems. They all had the capability of six technologies – word processing, data processing, image processing, audio processing, networking and the conciliatory 'human factors'. Henry's task was to analyse each of the companies' strategies and to put forward a proposal – in the unlikely event that nationalised industries or smaller Government divisions would adopt such a strategy. It was the dream of every computer – and thus Henry's dream. The very idea of fully-automated offices becoming a reality within a matter of years enthralled him.

He wouldn't have budged from his work only he was disturbed by shrieks of laughter from the next room. One of the girls in Zone D's typing pool was celebrating her birthday with sparkling wine and gifts.

'Here, open mine . . .' The sound of paper tearing, 'Cor he won't half go for you when he sees you in those!' trilled one of the girls.

His concentration ruined, Henry replaced the cap on his pen. It was nearly lunchtime anyway. He stacked the papers into a neat pile, locked his draft report up in the top drawer and looked expectantly at Tomkins.

' . . . Erm . . .'

'Got someone to see. Yes, I know.'

Henry looked grateful. He stuffed an envelope and his lunchbox into his briefcase and eased back the chair just far enough so he could stand. Tomkins' eyes followed him through the door with suspicion.

Henry's legs, stiff from a morning's inertia, now moved effortlessly as he crossed Blackfriars Bridge. The Founder's Arms was easily visible. On the whole, Henry conceded, it was an attractive pub considering it was new and frequented by thirsty German and American tourists on the last leg of their trek along the South Bank. Richardson wasn't there when he arrived. In fact, hardly anyone had arrived, save for a few hardened regulars propping up the bar inside. Henry chose a table on the patio away from the others; it was nudged into the farthest corner by the wall. From there, if you stood, you could see the Department and the bricked-in corner of Henry's office. Henry sat down, removed the lid of his lunchbox and began to eat.

Richardson would not be pleased – not when he told him he hadn't had a chance to get his report. At least he would pacify him with a few titbits he'd obtained from the Inland Revenue Special Investigations branch. That is, if Richardson ever arrived. Other tables were quickly being taken by the scores of office workers from both sides of the Thames and three dowdy girls were eyeing his table. He placed his briefcase on one chair, a newspaper on the other and finished eating his sandwich, turning his back to their scowls and pouts. Placing the now emptied Tupperware box on his seat, Henry pushed his way through to the bar, emerging after a short wait with a half of Special Brew. Richardson can buy his own, he sulked. Returning to his 'exclusive' corner, he spied two men sitting at his table; his briefcase, newspaper and lunchbox were now stacked on top of each other on one chair.

His neck and face puffed up like an adder, with indignation. But there was nothing for it but to join them, grudgingly. They were indifferent to his presence and continued without pause to argue the pros and cons of raising advertising rates in IPC. One of the most boring conversations I have been ill-fated to overhear, Henry decided. He directed his attention to the river. A helicopter droned above, hovering like a water insect above a barge on the north bank which had been converted to a helipad. The chopper landed, disgorged its passengers and rose into the air, to follow the curvaceous path of the south-bound Thames.

It was all very well, passing the time like this. But he was only here, drinking, because Richardson had arranged it. I'm not going to be *his* blasted patsy, he protested to himself. He got up, scraping the iron chair along the concrete. It was as if he'd run his nails down a blackboard, to observe the portentous looks of the two men at the table. Miserably, Henry retraced his steps, back over the bridge to the Department of Commercial Development. He shook a Tic-tac into his palm and pressed it between his lips. Two hours down the drain and a grovelling apology to Tomkins on his return.

Richardson was sitting on his desk, one foot resting on his chair when Henry returned to his office. He looked at Richardson flipping through a magazine, as if he owned the place.

'What the hell are you doing here in my office?' Henry hissed, one eye on Tomkins. To be stood up at the Founder's Arms was bad enough. To then find his 'secret' contact inside the Government building sitting as cool as a cucumber was the limit. Richardson got lazily to his feet, threw the magazine into the wastepaper basket and followed Henry into the corridor. Tomkins watched the scenario impassively, his face like a piece of blotting paper, it absorbed everything and gave nothing away.

Richardson leaned back against the wall, crossed his arms. 'Got tied up at lunchtime. Thought I'd better get on over here instead – you've got something for me, haven't you?' Henry opened his mouth to protest, just as Hendersly stepped brusquely out of his office, within feet of the covert pair. Henry slammed shut his mouth, gulped and smiled weakly at his boss. Hendersly gave Richardson the once over, shot a withering look in Henry's direction and disappeared down the corridor. What little composure Henry had left completely disintegrated. He stammered: 'That's why I didn't want you here – to be seen by Hendersly.'

'Give me the envelope,' said Richardson temperately.

Henry delved into his coat pocket and withdrew a manila envelope, crinkled at the edges.

Richardson casually stuffed the envelope under his jacket and spoke. 'Almost forgot. Did you check your report?'

'Ah . . . no. Impossible this morning. But I'll let you know as soon as I can tomorrow.'

'Better have. Won't be seeing you for a bit. Something's come up. Something even bigger than helping you get promotion in exchange for leaks of what your Department's up to.' He rocked forward, began walking down the corridor, Henry kept pace beside him. 'You'll have to phone me from now on,' said Richardson. 'Here, take this number. Don't speak to no one but me and be your usual oblique self. I'll catch up with you soon. Sorry about that.'

'Well, I'm not. Not if arrangements have come down to being as slapdash as this,' said Henry petulantly.

Richardson ignored the remark. He pressed the lift button and winked at Henry. 'Don't you ever change. And don't get in touch unless it's really important. Or unless you come across the Pouvoir.'

'Pouvoir?'

Richardson closed his eyes, opened them, as if the movement would contain his exasperation. 'The Power, Henry. Remember? And if you ever hear of it in connection with Common Market stuff – that's when I'd like to hear from you – and fast. Get it?'

The lift doors jarred open. Richardson stepped in.

'Be seeing you around, Henry,' he said as the doors closed.

It took the whole night for Henry's suppressed feelings of confusion to dissolve. He had been let down, he felt, by Richardson's offhand manner towards him. Added to that, he was overcome with guilt. In the darkness of their bedroom he groaned. Anne slept, undisturbed in the adjacent bed, the duvet rising and falling with her breathing. She had never liked the proximity of a double bed. Even in sleep, they did not encroach on each other's privacy. Henry lay on his wide-eyed. He contemplated a confession to his superiors that he was passing information to Richardson. But he guessed they already had a pretty good idea of what he was up to. More to the point, an outright confession would destroy any chance of promotion; it could conceivably knock on the head all hopes of a career in the Civil Service ever again. And he couldn't face that. Henry worried whether or not he should check the report for references to the Italbank fraud. Such a fuss over nothing, he thought. Yet Richardson was so adamant. As the dawn light marked out the slits in the bedroom curtains, Henry decided: he would pay his last debt to Richardson and that would be it. The finish. It was all for the best

Chapter Six

Tomkins was strutting around the office whistling a cheerful tune through his teeth when Henry arrived at the office. But Henry was in no mood to indulge his colleague, staring ahead with his chin on his hand, a frown stretched across his forehead.

'... of course, you may not understand the kudos attached to having one of your photographs shown on television ...

flashed up with the weather after the news,' said Tomkins, 'but it's a coup for me, for any amateur photographer . . .'

Tomkins' euphoria was lost on Henry. Shrugging off the snub, Tomkins began to read, humming to himself. Henry's thoughts were on a journey no one else could venture; he looked deeply troubled and Tomkins guessed there was no point in getting Henry to talk about whatever was on his mind. It was only when Henry felt the presence of somebody standing close by him that he snapped out of his reverie to find Hendersly hovering by his desk, staring.

'Miles away, sorry,' said Henry weakly.

'Just popped by to see how you were both getting on,' said Hendersly, beaming. He was obviously in a good mood. 'Everything all right? . . . Good.' He backed out of the room as he spoke.

Henry called out after him.

'Ah, Mr Hendersly . . . about my computer and associated frauds report. I wanted to check a reference to it this morning. It wasn't in the combi-lock cabinet.'

So that was what was bothering him.

'No?' said Hendersly quizzically.

'No.'

Hendersly considered the matter briefly, then his face brightened.

'Oh, yes. It's been reclassified. Taken off the general classification list and put on top security. Restricted circulation now. A compliment to you, Henry. It shows people are taking an interest in it.'

Hendersly managed a travesty of a smile and left, closing the door behind him. Henry didn't move, didn't say a word. But as if to exemplify his feelings his knuckles whitened and with a loud snap, he broke his pencil in two.

So, there was something in the report worth hiding. Why else, after all this time, change its classification? And without consulting him first? He was much more annoyed than he had showed. He evinced a great desire to storm into Hendersly's office and protest. Instead, he wandered along the corridor to the water cooler, gulped great mouthfuls of chilly liquid. He felt a little better after that. The report weighed heavy on his mind. It meant too much to him to ignore the matter. Tomkins was absorbed in the small print of a legal document, furrow browed, when he returned to his desk. Henry was sorry now he had so unkindly enveloped himself with his problems. He knew Tomkins had wanted to share his personal triumph. Now the moment had passed, it was too late.

Henry crossed the corridor and knocked discreetly on the door.

'In!'

He hesitated before turning the handle, then walked in straight up to Hendersly's desk.

'What is it, Jay?'

'I'd like to have authorisation to check that reference in my report, now that it's top security.'

'If you really must . . .'

'Yes.' Henry stood his ground.

Hendersly swivelled his well-upholstered chair round to within easy reach of a small wooden cupboard behind his desk. All the furniture in his room matched – dull wood veneer desk, cabinet, bookshelves, cupboards (including one for coats and other oddments), and a large conference table on the far side of the room. An original oil painting hung above the bookshelf, an ugly river scene in blues and yellows with a touch of the Bayswater Road about it. By the door there was a reproduction sketch of St Paul's Cathedral imprisoned behind glass.

Sighing, Hendersly hoisted himself back into an upright position, the red vinyl security folder from the cabinet in his hand. Henry cast his eye down the list of names of those who had enlisted access to high security files before him, it told him little. He signed his name, a jagged, illegible scrawl.

Hendersly closed the folder with a loud snap. 'There comes a time you know, Henry, when attention to detail becomes mere fuss, you know.'

'There would have been no fuss if the file had not been reclassified,' he responded coolly. If he thought he could elicit an explanation from his superior he was mistaken. Hendersly wished their conversation to end and sat waiting, one hand on the receiver of the phone.

'Right, Henry, talk. I haven't got all day.' Richardson wiped the beer froth from his moustache with his sleeve and waited.

'I'm sorry I had to ask you to meet me, but it's important,' said Henry.

'Well, get on with it then.'

Henry gazed around the bar of the Samuel Pepys to see if anyone was listening and began. 'You wanted to know about the computer and associated frauds references to your friend. Well, over the weekend the report was reclassified Top Security. The reference relating to the Italbank fraud in the Appendix has been removed.'

Richardson let out a long, low whistle. 'Who by? Any idea?'

'Somebody who obviously knows the office procedure. Getting access to Top Security files means signing the security register. I had to, to check the file. Whoever removed the reference from the report knew how to get at it without signing. No one had checked out my file since it was reclassified.'

'So, we're really up against a First Division team, eh?'

Richardson drained his glass, looked at Henry's half-finished drink with disgust and went to the bar for a refill. He leaned up against the bar, a good head taller than anyone else along the drinking strip, looked every inch a copper, so much so that Henry felt uncomfortable by his presence. Richardson made him feel like the school snitch.

Whatever he had said last night about not being involved, about cutting loose from Richardson, seemed irrelevant now. There would be repercussions and if his report was involved, there was no way he could duck out now. Just what kind of role he would play, he had no idea yet.

Richardson had obviously given the matter some thought already. Once his lager had safely reached the table between them, he resumed his speech.

'Now we know the top league's hovering just above, I want you out of this. You're no longer involved.' He said it without rancour.

'How can you say that?' Henry exclaimed.

'Because I'm flying to Brussels to see Hannah Brent, Louis' girlfriend, and I don't want you tinkering about here.'

'I have to be involved; it was my report, remember, that was altered.'

'I'm telling you, Henry. Forget it. You're a dull, boring, middle-rank civil servant and the most exciting thing that's likely to happen to you before you retire is you'll go bald. Keep it that way. I don't want to be callous, but you're out of your league. So, don't try and mix your mundane existence with that lot over there,' Richardson said, jerking his head back towards the City.

'Look, if it's got something to do with the Square Mile . . .' Henry pressed.

'Hasn't everything when you boil it down? Almost everything, anyway.'

Richardson bolted down his drink, smacked his lips, allowed a smile to creep across his face. 'Henry,' he said, 'forget me, forget your report. Put in your nine-to-fives and don't make waves. The recipe for a happy, if boring life. I'd thought you'd sussed that by now.'

'But all the same, it is my report!' he continued to argue.

'Let's go, son,' said Richardson as he stood and buttoned up his coat. 'We've said all we came to say.'

They walked, single file, back down the slim alley from the pub onto the main road.

'Take care, Henry, and remember what I said.'

Angry and hurt, Henry strode back to the office. So, Richardson thought him dull. No one had ever told him that to his face before, though he suspected that some people thought it of him. No one, that was, but Anne and she was his wife, so that didn't really count. And Richardson reckoned he was out of his league. Well, he would see about that, Henry fulminated.

'Someone's tampered with your report, Mr Jay?'

'Yes,' said Henry grimly.

He had marched resolutely back to the office, taken the lift to the fourth floor and breezed into Hendersly's room. Hendersly was dictating a letter into a small recorder and brushed his hand in the air, indicating Henry should leave. But he remained, standing close enough to his superior's desk to cause discomfort yet distant enough to allow himself an aura of positiveness. It worked. Hendersly abruptly ended the dictation.

'Tampered? I'm not sure I like that word,' said Hendersly, distastefully. '*Your* report. A report you collated on behalf of the Department of Commercial Development. The *Department's* report.'

Henry's hand twitched, a dead giveaway. He thrust it quickly into his trouser pocket to hide his confusion and fear. It was the way Hendersly had said it, each word clipped viciously; strung together they sounded insulting. But he couldn't back down now.

'When you agreed I should do the report you entrusted in me the responsibility to complete it using all my expertise, my thoroughness which never fall short of accuracy. I took on that responsibility because it is my job and because I enjoy the work. You cannot now absolve me of that responsibility, not lightly, and not without a proper explanation!'

Pearls of sweat gathered on his forehead and on the palms of his hands, his body was wired stiff with tension. He'd said it, the words had come before he could retrieve them. He shuffled uncomfortably, waiting.

'Please. Sit down.' Hendersly pointed to a low chair by his desk, his expression drawn tight.

'There is no mystery about your report, Mr Jay, no skulduggery. Merely that the Metropolitan and City Police Company Fraud Department, otherwise known as C6, are compiling their own report on international frauds involving computer or electronic funds transfer systems.'

'Why couldn't they photostat the appendix?' he asked curtly.

'Why was the index reference removed? When was the last time any document in this Department had its classification changed over a weekend?'

'You put these questions in rather an abrupt manner, Mr Jay.'

'I'm sorry if you think I'm being awkward but I take this matter very seriously . . .'

'Yes, you have made your point loud and clear. Allow me to continue – the Fraud Squad and the Met are jointly undertaking a major investigation. The Department's Security Adviser – Mr Chambers – was asked to trawl the files in this building to remove any reference that could give an early warning, if leaked. We have had one or two problems with leaks in the past, as you may know.'

If there had been accusing hints in Hendersly's voice, Henry seemed not to have noticed.

'This major investigation is into the affairs of a Member of Parliament and City figure?' He spoke slowly, deliberately, his eyes imparting nothing.

Hendersly's eyebrows darted upwards.

'A Member of the European Parliament . . . how did you know?'

'Other Departments also have problems with leaks.' The edges of Henry's lips curled with pleasure – touché.

'Well then, you'll appreciate how sensitive any reference, no matter how peripheral, to do with this man is, won't you. You'll leave the matter there.'

'It could be,' said Henry edging cautiously 'that the files are being sanitised to protect this man, rather than aid the investigation into his affairs.'

There was a long pause, the two men challenged each other with their eyes.

'That, Mr Jay, would be a very dangerous assumption for a civil servant of your middle rank to make. The matter is closed,' said Hendersly with cold finality.

At which point Henry stood. Hendersly assuming victory, also stood to show him out. But his subordinate was unmoved.

'The matter is not closed. I care too much about the Department, despite my middle rank position, to let it be closed at this point.' Henry drew breath, his heart thumping wildly. 'I wish . . . I demand an appointment with the Department's Security Adviser, as soon as possible.'

'If that, Mr Jay, is your wish . . . then so be it.'

He had totally underestimated Henry. To look at, he was the epitome of a man who had no need, no inclination to rock the boat. Yet, just a few minutes before, Henry had stood there, prepared to jeopardise his chance of promotion. Extraordinary, thought Hendersly, quite extraordinary behaviour for someone more renowned as a benign plodder than a firebrand.

Henry's eyes gleamed. He squeezed into his chair, thumped his hands on the arm rest. 'I'm going to see Chambers tomorrow,' he said to Tomkins. 'It'll be all right then. Be his problem, not mine.'

'What do you need to see him for?' Tomkins enquired, crinkling his nose inquisitively.

'My fraud report, the one Hendersly always forgets the title to . . .'

'Well, it's not the shortest in the history of Whitehall . . .'

' . . . has been classified Top Security and then mucked about with. Hendersly's given me a pretty flimsy reason why, but I'm unhappy about the whole affair. Left a bad taste in my mouth, you know.'

'You and your bloody report!' said Tomkins. 'By the way, got yours yet?' He leaned across his desk, waved a memo in his hand. It was his appointment with the Promotions Board, in six days' time. Henry recognised it immediately and scowled.

'No. Not yet,' he said, deflated.

'Oh,' said Tomkins, with a glint in his eye.

They sank into their work for the rest of the afternoon, not daring to look up, even when Mrs Peach's tea trolley squeaked by the office. At five-thirty, Henry rose, donned his scarf and coat, and collected his briefcase and umbrella.

'You don't fancy a drink do you, Harry?'

'What, straight from the office?' It had never occurred to Tomkins to linger on in town after work unless he went to the opera or theatre. Then he worked late or snatched a bite to eat in a West End snack bar.

'Yes,' said Henry. 'I've taken to having one on the way back. Now and again, two or three . . . come on, be a devil.'

'Okay. Just the one mind.'

The Cockpit was crowded when they arrived. Henry and Tomkins pushed their way to the bar.

'I suppose it's between you and me, really, this year's board,' said Henry above the din.

'Mmmm,' said Tomkins trying to avoid the issue head on.

'I think I may have ruined my chances, though, with all the dust I've been kicking up over my report,' said Henry. He seemed hellbent on airing the issue. Tomkins sipped his shandy and waited for Henry to continue. But the conversation ended there. Henry snapped his head around abruptly, scanned the faces of the drinkers at the bar.

'Are those people talking about me?' he turned towards Tomkins.

'Which people?'

'Those two in the corner, I think.'

Tomkins shrugged. 'No idea. I didn't hear anything. Why should anyone want to talk about you?'

Henry put his unfinished drink on the bar. 'Got to go. Can't keep the little woman waiting. See you tomorrow, Harry.' He patted Tomkins on the back and left by the side door. Tomkins stood, indignant. The bloody nerve!

Chapter Seven

Henry joined the swarm of commuters pressing through the barrier, flashed his annual season ticket at a disinterested guard and made his way down the concourse to the platform. Tomkins' scepticism had done nothing to eradicate his paranoia. His eyes shuffled through the myriad of faces belonging to his fellow travellers. There was no one he recognised from the pub. The train pulled in. Relieved, Henry clambered aboard, elbow-digging a pretzel-stick of a man in a bowler hat and navy serge coat. Henry squinted, suspiciously. The City gentleman glared, having lost his seat at the rear of the carriage to Henry. As the train jerked out of London Bridge station, Henry continued to gaze around him, nervously. Somebody *had* mentioned his name in the pub, somebody he didn't recognise; but he couldn't see anyone who looked remotely suspicious. He hugged his brief-case to his breast and recalled Anne's stern lecture which had dragged out over dinner the previous night.

She had yelled: 'I don't want to hear any more about this damned report of yours . . . I do a routine and boring job, too, but I don't manufacture drama and excitement out of it. Some people are born civil servants, others achieve being civil servants and others have being civil servants thrust upon them. You, Henry, were born.'

On and on she talked, her voice high-pitched, almost raucous.

'After all our years together, I accept the mundanities of marriage. But if you're trying to make your job sound desperately important and exciting for my sake – don't bother. When I said "yes" to you, Henry, I settled for cocoa and not champagne. I'm prepared to live with that. So don't glamorise what cannot be and not another word about it . . .'

He hadn't said another word.

As he ambled across the road from Westcombe Park station, an old Morris Minor and a police patrol car purred by slowly. He looked in the windows of the shops as he walked by, checking that no one was following him. Reassured and feeling less jumpy on his home patch, he turned the corner. The pub had just opened, he checked his watch. A quick one to calm the nerves; he didn't feel like heading straight home. The craggy heads of the regulars moved in silent unison to survey him as he ordered a gin and tonic, fumbling for the right change.

'Is there a phone I can use?' he asked the beefy barman who wiped his hands on a filthy tea-towel slung over his shoulder and pointed to a door marked 'Gentlemen'.

'Through there on the landing.'

Henry obediently followed the finger to find a coin-scratched phone on the wall. He fumbled again for change, balancing his drink on the coin-box where someone had etched 'Billy loves John' and somebody else had added 'Sore arse'.

. . . blip, blip, blip, blip . . . Henry wedged his five pence in the slot. 'Hello? Is Stanley Richardson there . . . oh . . . have you any idea when he'll be back . . . No, I've already left a message! Did he get it? . . . Who is this? . . . hello?' The line went dead. His eyebrows met in a frown, he replaced the receiver and took a large swig of his G and T.

''ello 'enry, Got something I'd like to ask you, Detective Constable Slater, Vice Squad. Like to take a ride? Car's outside,' he leered.

'What's all this about? Who are you?'

'Like I said. Come on Mr Jay, there's a good chap . . . after you . . .'

'But . . .!' It was no good. Shoving him in the back with his fist, Detective Constable Slater pushed him through the bar to a waiting patrol car outside, silently watched by the handful of old men drinking in the corner.

'What on earth . . . what right have you got . . .' Henry was more indignant than scared. 'There must be some mistake. Look, are you sure you've got this right?'

Slater just grinned. 'Hang in a tick. This 'im?' he asked an acned teenage boy sitting in the back seat of the car.

'Yeah . . . that's him. Dirty bastard.' The boy spat.

A red Cortina screeched up behind. Slater pulled open the door and jerked his head. 'Get in . . . forty-seven, driver. That's right isn't it, Henry? Why'd ya pick 'im, Henry, nasty little bleeder . . .'

Anne was reading, her feet curled under her on the couch when the doorbell rang.

'Mrs Jay?'

'Yes,' she looked surprised to find a young man, casually dressed standing there. He airily waved a plastic card before her. 'Detective Constable Morrisey. Concerning an enquiry re your husband, Henry Jay.'

'I'm afraid he's not back from work yet . . .'

The plain-clothes cop put his foot in the door, booted it open and squeezed roughly past her. He walked nonchalantly through to the living room off the hallway to the left, sniffed loudly and sprinted upstairs. Steeling herself against the wooden railing at the foot of the stairs she heard him rifling through Henry's papers in his study.

'What's going on? Is Henry all right?' she shouted up at him, trying to sound calm. There was no answer. A drawer slammed and Morrisey thumped down the stairs, cradling something bulky in his arms.

'Been acting a bit odd lately, has he? Something on his mind he can't share with you?' his eyes penetrated her face.

'Please . . . tell me what this is about,' she pleaded. Her hands raised, palms upwards, were stiff and shaking.

He stood there, a sneer spread right across his face. With a loud 'flop' he dropped one magazine, then another, and another, onto the smoked glass coffee table until it was covered.

'Not surprising wouldn't you think, that he'd want to keep it quiet if he's into all this?'

She looked down at the glossy magazines and gasped inwardly at what she saw.

'That's right, Mrs Jay, gay pornography. Your husband's. Quite an assortment, bondage, small boys . . .'

'Don't be ludicrous! You don't expect me to believe that do

you? I just know he wouldn't. Not Henry! He wouldn't.' Her voice was a mixture of anger and horror. Lurking at the back of her mind was the awful thought that, possibly, it could be true. She looked at the policeman. His eyes danced between the magazines and her face, his lips curled. He moved to the window, treading on her corduroy couch with his thick-soled boots.

'Ah! Here he is now.' He peered between the white mesh curtains, watched Henry angrily shrug off Slater's grasp. Henry was seething. 'I've never seen that young man in my life, I don't know what you're talking about.' He looked angry and bewildered as he entered the living room, avoiding Anne's questioning eyes, flanked on either side by Slater and Morrisey. 'I'm telling you you've got the wrong man!' he whispered hoarsely.

'Not a chance, mate,' said Morrisey.

'Bit of the cottaging passes the time between the office and the dutiful peck on the missis' cheek, eh?' Slater taunted him. 'Nice day at the office, dear? Dead quiet, says she. Oh, I picked a nice one up at the station bogs, dead quiet but tight little bum, says he. How nice dear, mince and onions all right tonight? . . . You're a right one Henry.'

Morrisey got down onto his haunches and flicked ostentatiously through the magazines. He was young with thick blond hair, with a face bereft of flesh, skin stretched tight over his bones, drawn in to pouting lips.

'You're a bit of a loner, Henry, so the wife tells me' he said. 'On your jack a lot. Claim to be working late at the office, important man, called in at short notice, big wheel in the Philately Club . . . stamp collecting,' he added, noticing Slater's nescient look.

'Who's this fella, Richardson, been worrying you?'

'Tell them who Richardson is, Henry,' Anne begged him.

'Be quiet,' Henry hissed, his pulse jumping at his temples, his hands clenched tight.

'Henry!'

He turned on her. 'You're to say nothing to them, understand? Not about Richardson, not about anything.'

Morrisey plugged on. 'Is he the fella you get these mags off? Your contract with the dilley-boys? Hmmm?'

Anne blurted it out before Henry could stop her. 'Richardson is a policeman. It's Richardson who got him into trouble about a report at work in the first place . . .'

'I said, keep your mouth closed Anne! Keep your harpie's mouth closed! We say nothing. Nothing. We sit it out and we listen to what they've been sent to say – that's right, isn't it. Well, isn't it?' His voice rose hysterically.

'Makes you sick, don't it,' said Slater. 'What your sort never think of is what you're doing to those around you. The wife. The kids. Got any kids?'

Anne shook her head. 'No.' But the sound didn't come out.

'You know, Henry,' said Morrisey, 'you ought to be specially careful, working in the Civil Service, handling sensitive papers and things in the Department of Commercial Development. This might have to be reported, you know.' He stood on the balls of his feet, his face closing in on Henry's.

Henry arched back, stared, loathing stamped across his face. Morrisey was exactly as Henry imagined a thug to be – with his light trousers, bovver boots, and old anorak. But it was his face – menacing, unintelligent, yet compelling, that grated on Henry's nerves most. Slater, in contrast, epitomised the ageing Detective Constable from the vice squad; a face worn round the edges, emotionless except for his mouth, a face that had seen many bars and a lot of action, a man so patently tired by his job.

Henry was agitated: 'How many more times do I have to say it – I have *never* met that young man before, those are *not* my magazines, I have never read one in my life. So *what* is going on?'

'A bit of private shirt-lifting's all right, it's Liberty Hall these days. Who gives a toss what you do with it in the sheets,' said Morrisey, coolly. 'But picking up young cherries in station bogs? Not healthy – never know what you might catch.'

'Breach of the Peace, section five, Public Order Act 36 –

publicly exposing the naked person, Criminal Law Act 77 – Wilful Indecency 1847, commissioning an act of gross indecency – Sexual Offences Act 36 and 37 – persistently soliciting or importuning in a public place, performing an immoral act, Sexual Offences Act 56 – loitering or soliciting in a public street, Offences Act 59,' Slater's voice reeled off the list from memory, with all the excitement of a Latin prayer recitation. Morrisey growled. 'This is a warning, Henry. Family man, no form, steady job.'

'Take warning,' chipped in Slater.

'Yeah, take warning. We'll be at your shoulder, mate.'

'This sort of thing makes a mucky little paragraph in the evening paper, and a fraught half hour with the boss.'

'Just watch how you go . . .'

As they opened the front door Henry found his voice. '*You* take warning. Tell whoever you're doing this for that I'm not to be shaken from my resolve. I will press more strongly for the Department's security to be tightened. My fraud file has been tampered with and they will not get away with it.'

'What the fuck are you on about?'

'Tell whoever you're doing this little favour for that I'm a glitch that won't be cleared up so easily.'

'Glitch?' said Morrisey. 'Have you gone soft in the head – or what? I don't talk Venusian, Henry.'

'Glitch is computer jargon for a hiccup in the smooth running of a programme. Despise me as you do, I promise to be more than just a hiccup.'

Morrisey pointed his finger threateningly. 'Hiccup, belch or big green fart – I don't understand a word you're saying – burk.'

'And stay away from young boys,' interrupted Slater, 'or we'll chop your disgusting perverted goolies off.'

They slammed the tiny gate behind them and clambered into the car parked on the kerb outside.

'Some pushover,' said Slater.

'What was all that about a copper and a fraud report?'

'Who gives a toss? We done our bit. A favour done is a favour owed. How about a pint?'

Chapter Eight

'Right, let's have him in.' Trevor Chambers brooded over a thin file lying open at one end of the long square table in the far corner of Hendersly's office. The rich green curtains were drawn and the light poured in casting his shadow larger than life across the papers. His right hand rested casually on the table's veneer surface a few inches from his treasured rosewood pipe. As he began abstractedly stuffing the bowl with moist tobacco he continued to read the internal file on Henry Jay. He was already familiar with most of the contents and a quick debriefing from Hendersly completed the picture. He struck a match and applied it to his pipe, blowing plumes of smoke into the air.

Hendersly acted even more formally than usual. He guided Henry with great aplomb to a lone chair on the far side of the table, then briskly marched to an armchair next to Chambers. The seating had been carefully mulled over by the department's security head to give him the best psychological advantage. There was no preamble. He smiled as Henry entered and once seated began, his bass voice resonating. 'Right. Let's get right down to the matter, Henry. I'll go down the headings first. Your initial contact with Richardson –'

'Who now can't be found,' Hendersly butted in.

'Richardson's belief that there was a connection between the London end of the Italbank fraud, Louis Vacheron –'

'Who you say is dead,' added Hendersly.

'And a European Member of Parliament whose name you don't know.'

Chambers continued smoothly, ignoring the interruptions. 'Richardson recruits you to check your computer fraud report, which in the meantime has been sanitised by me. Your concern that I may have been unwittingly used to cover up for this man.'

'Name unknown to you,' added Hendersly barely moving

his lips. 'Interesting . . . Does that cover all your points?'

'And the Power – don't forget what Louis Vacheron told Richardson about the Power,' said Henry, the words tumbling from his mouth.

'The Power . . .' boomed Chambers. 'Yes, the Conspiracy Theory.'

'That is the whole point. It's *not.* Nor is it one vast autocratic machine with a single control. It's scores of people, like me, like you, making up a huge cross-reference system, removing a file here, returning a favour to another department there and so on . . . it's everywhere. As the Community increases its ties, politically, economically, socially, with other countries, the more successful the operation becomes,' he said catching his breath.

'Hmmm,' was Chambers' only acknowledgement. He peered through the glasses onto the files, bitterly reading on through the list. 'And also last night's visit from two men claiming to be from the Vice Squad –'

'Who may yet try to discredit me with their fallacious allegations, or – blackmail me in some way.'

'Blackmail you? But your wife was present, so they're hardly likely to badger her – and you have confided in Mr Hendersly the outline of their allegations haven't you? That, I would have thought, should take the sting out of their tails.' He scribbled 'Blackmail Claims' in the margin of his page. 'Still, must have been rather frightening, eh?'

Henry shrugged, then nodded.

'So, you're quite happy to leave this matter with Mr Chambers, then?' Hendersly asked crisply.

'All I want to do now, believe me, is to get back to my desk and carry on as before – these excitements are just not for me.' Henry was sounding tired now.

'Well, in so far as returning to your desk is concerned –'.

'I wonder if you would excuse me, Tony?' Chambers interrupted. 'I have one or two appointments and I shall need to consider the best mode of investigation into the matters which are concerning you, Henry.' Chambers stood to leave. 'If you don't hear anything for a while, don't fret.

These things take time, I'm sure you understand. Goodbye, Henry. And thanks for the use of your office, Tony.'

'Any time, Trevor,' replied Hendersly darkly. He waited for Chambers to close the door, pacing the carpet. 'I have had a few words with the Treasury Medical Adviser and made an appointment for you to see him, on your behalf. I have to tell you now, Henry, that it will be merely a formality. I've watched you closely – your work performance has decreased measurably. Your usual attention to detail has slipped badly. When did you last have a holiday? . . . yes, some time ago. High time you took a break – a couple of weeks should do the trick, starting from now. Do you the power of good.'

'Why, in heaven's name, *now*?'

'There's no point in discussing the matter further,' said Hendersly curtly showing him the door. 'We've already made arrangements to see you safe home after your desk is cleared.'

Hendersly was right – there was no use in arguing with a steamroller. He accepted the appointment card like a sleep-walker, shuffled across the corridor to his office.

Tomkins was in Henry's chair, his feet perched on the desk. He got quickly to his feet as Henry entered. 'You lucky blighter – I've heard . . . a fortnight's special leave, eh?' he said a little too brightly. 'Um . . . I'm meant to be carrying on with the cryptography report in your absence – I wonder, could I have the key to the filing cabinet?'

Henry had to hand it to Hendersly – every last detail had been worked out in advance. So Tomkins was to take on his precious new report. An ominous sign. He bent down, opened his top drawer, removed the key and with all the dignity he possessed gave it to Tomkins. 'I wish you luck on it – if you need any help . . .' it sounded so final.

Tomkins wrapped his scarf about his neck, put on his overcoat and waved lightly. 'Off to the graveyard for lunch – see you in a couple of weeks.' He backed out of the doorway, colliding with a tall handsome woman. 'Sorry,' he mumbled.

'Anne – what are you doing here?' Henry asked, surprised.

She had been standing in the open doorway, watching her husband wretched in his misery. 'They phoned,' she spoke gently. 'It's for the best Henry.'

'Yes and it's all been sewn up before you can get a chance to do anything about it.'

'Seriously, Henry, it's just a short break – I've got two weeks off as well, we can –'

'This is the finish, not just a ploy to get me out of the office for a couple of weeks. They mean to get rid of me.'

'Oh darling, it's not like that.' She moved in closer to him and cupped her hand over his, noticing as she did it, the utter despair in Henry's eyes. 'We'll go to the caravan in Wales for the fortnight. We can relax, unwind, talk things over.'

'They'll arrange an adverse medical report, part of the "formality", indefinite leave, suspension on full pay and then quietly shunted out on health grounds – they've just fired the first round – as soon as I walk out of the door they'll prepare the ammunition . . . you know something? I can't believe I'm leaving this office for the last time – and I'm not fighting, or shouting. I almost did, but it was like being hit over the head with a blunt instrument. They cut me down professionally, made me out as though I was under the weather – totally demolished my morale . . . I suppose if I did do battle with them, they'd just make it awkward about the pension.'

'Henry –'

'This is what my life is made up of isn't it? Small failures of nerve.'

They resigned themselves to silence as Henry picked his belongings from his drawers, being careful to leave HMSO stationery and reports stacked to one side of the desk. He stared gloomily at two large cartons – he hadn't noticed them till now. How courteous of them to think of me, he thought bitterly. For once, the Commercial Development Department hadn't missed a trick.

'Come on – no point in hanging around now, they'll bring your boxes over in the morning.'

'When they've rifled through them to make sure they're innocuous enough to deliver.' He slid into his coat and paused to look around him. Metal rubbish tins, metal desks, metal filing cabinets, grey and dark green. Discoloured venetian blinds, the standard-issue camouflage pattern chairs, the noticeboard with its montage of postcards, yellow memos and samples of Tomkins' photographic work. The personal touches like the potplants brought in to bring life by a typist in the next office. He'd had only one personal touch on his desk and he'd tucked it safely in his briefcase; a photograph of Anne taken four years ago at a carnival.

They moved, hand in hand, along the corridor as Tomkins rushed by, glancing curiously at Anne. So that was Mrs Henry Jay. 'Forgot something – gotta get it out of the way before two,' said Tomkins lamely.

'That's Tomkins,' Henry explained to Anne. 'The chap I share – shared – an office with.'

'Excuse me for interrupting, Mr Jay.'

A man, tall, slightly balding, with bulky features stretching his two-piece suit to its limit, stood in their path.

'Who are you?' demanded Henry.

'Yes. Who are you?' Anne repeated.

The man's voice said: 'I'd like a private word with you, Mr Jay. We can use this office.'

'I'm his wife. Can't this wait? He's had enough for one day.'

'Please,' said the man firmly gripping Henry's elbow, 'this won't take a minute.'

He steered Henry through the door. 'If you don't mind, Mrs Jay,' he said, giving her a warning look.

'It's all right, Anne –'

The door closed, cutting off his sentence.

'Now what do they want? Haven't they done enough for one morning?' she said, staring at the closed door. She felt completely drained, her shoulders ached, she couldn't think straight. She walked down the corridor and sank into a plastic moulded chair. If only she'd supported him before, listened more solicitously to his complaints. She cringed at the recall of last night's furious argument. To her shame she had dumbly accepted the word of two constables who she'd never laid eyes on before; for all their uncouth ways they were the law, they had evidence, she'd assumed. And in so doing, she had betrayed Henry. It was a naïve assumption in the extreme, she now admitted, and one which had sparked off the worst row she and Henry had ever had. Cries of 'burn your bloody magazines and any more you've got secreted in that little haven of yours upstairs.' Hot tears, stubborn protestations of innocence from Henry, more cries of 'What kind of marriage is this – I thought I knew you', 'Well, I thought you believed in me'. Threats of separate bedrooms, Henry moving out, Anne moving out. Then him trying to calm her.

They had sat, side by side, each with a stiff brandy in their hands. He talked for hours, explained where he'd gone on Sunday – what Richardson had told him, word for word, explained that it wasn't just a simple tinkering with his file. It was a much bigger operation. What he said shocked her deeply. Had promotion meant that much to him that he'd passed information to the police? He told her he'd met Richardson at the outset of work on his fraud file. Richardson had gone out of his way for him, passing on interesting details of City frauds. Henry assumed the cases were confidential, Richardson had made that clear, but it had never occurred to him at first that favours would be asked in return. Promotion hadn't come into it then. Slowly it began to sink in, why Henry so vehemently insisted he was being set up. Sick with remorse and by then, slightly drunk, she had crawled to bed. Downstairs she heard Henry playing Elgar over and over and over again. Early next morning when she awoke, she found him curled up in bed under the eiderdown still dressed in his shirt and trousers. She crept downstairs to put the kettle on. His overcoat, shoes and tie, lay in a crumpled heap on the living room floor, the lights were still blazing. She gave him his tea, propped up the pillows behind him. He told her it would be all right, that he would be exonerated. She would see.

At any moment, Henry expected the man – who introduced himself to him as Detective Sergeant Vine from the

Metropolitan Police – to get to his feet and tell him it was all a big joke, that he had been the victim of a cruel prank. But Henry could tell by Vine's face that however bizarre the accusations Vine had come up with, he meant every solitary word.

'Let me get this right,' said Henry, sarcastically. 'Miss Callaghan, a typist in the general pool, has been receiving obscene phone calls and pornography through the mail. She has been followed home from work, spied upon, and one day in the office, chanced upon hearing my voice and recognised it as the culprit's. After complaining to the police you began surveillance and saw me follow her after work to her flat in Victoria. Have I got it?'

Vine nodded.

Henry looked hard at the puce-faced copper, pointed a stiff index finger at him.

'Then tell me how? *How* could I find the time to fit in my importuning of young boys in public toilets whilst pursuing Miss Callaghan?'

Vine stared, his mouth tight.

Henry leaned forward over the desk, and continued. 'Look, the vice squad has already tried to put the frighteners on me, my superiors have sent me packing. I would have thought that was quite sufficient. And, it has crossed my mind that these two events are not unrelated. But where do you fit in? Wires cross, I'd say.'

Vine still made no move, his big reddish face remained indifferent to Henry's taunts.

Henry said, slowly. 'In fact, I think I'll take the matter up with Chambers.'

'Who?' asked Vine, a little interested.

'Chambers – the department's security adviser . . .' Henry stopped short. Vine's expression had twisted into action, showed that he knew the name. He stood, rocked angrily on his heels. His eyes had a wild gleam.

'So!' he shouted. He hesitated then barged out of the room, kicking his chair to the ground with fury.

Vine knew Chambers! That was it. Henry's mind raced.

Would it not follow then, that Chambers had put Vine onto him? No, it was too clumsy. And it didn't explain the vice squad connection. Henry couldn't reconcile his thoughts. They bore down on him, suffocated him. He was still seated, transfixed, in the office when Anne rushed in.

She sounded frantic.

'Who was he Henry? What did he want?'

'It's not important who he was, what he said. What is important is that he knew Chambers – you should have seen his face! What's really horrifying is I know I can trust no one; certainly not Chambers.'

'So you'll drop the matter?'

Henry laid his hands flat on the desk. He said. 'Not a hope in hell. No, I shall go on; I'm even more determined now than before.'

'With no one to back you at this end?' she asked, incredulous. 'You can't possibly!'

Henry was insistent. He spoke evenly. 'I must, I have to, you know.'

'No I bloody well don't. You've suffered enough at their hands – and you know they won't stop if you won't. I'll be dragged into all this. What about me? Think about it,' she implored him. 'Henry, they'll destroy us. For both our sakes, please . . .'

Her eyes glassed over with tears. She stood by him, too afraid to blink in case her tears tumbled down her cheeks.

Henry put his arm around her waist, drew her down to him. She knelt beside him and whispered. 'What's happening to us?'

His head began to throb, his stomach was tied in knots. Please God, he said to himself, make all this end soon.

'Ah, there you are,' gushed Tomkins. 'Been looking all over for you.' He was still wearing his coat. Anne wiped her eyes with the back of her hand and stood up. Tomkins stopped suddenly.

'Sorry, I've intruded . . . um, Henry,' he flustered his words. ' . . . there's someone to see you, back in the office.'

'No!' Anne blurted. 'He's on leave now; we're on our way home.'

Henry sighed, and said.

'You deal with it, Harry. You might as well get stuck in right away; after all, you've got my file, my desk keys, my job effectively . . .'

'Don't be like that, old man,' said Tomkins, hurt. 'It's Richardson. He says it's urgent.'

'Henry, no,' pleaded Anne, spearing him with a warning eye. 'You're not involved any more. You're free of him now.'

Henry was torn. He looked at Anne looking at him, desperately not wanting him to go to Richardson. He looked at Tomkins, jiggling coins nervously in his pocket. Henry nodded.

'Let's go.'

They fell into step and walked briskly down the corridor. There was no sign of the policeman as they entered the room.

'Strange,' puzzled Tomkins. 'He said it was urgent – and looked as though he really meant it.' Tomkins gazed ineffectively around the office.

'Well, he's not here now,' said Henry walking towards his erstwhile desk. He spied an envelope which hadn't been there when he left. Bearing down on it he recognised Richardson's handwriting. Anne's footsteps came louder, heading for the office. Tomkins turned in anticipation. Swiftly, Henry stuffed the envelope inside his coat. It was as though the Almighty had caught him in the act – a loud wailing ripped out through the building. Henry jumped. Tomkins grimaced and held his hands to his ears in mock horror.

'Let me guess,' he groaned. 'Fire, or bomb drill.'

'Suppose this is our cue to leave,' said Henry to Anne.

They headed for the emergency exit to see Hendersly sprint out of his office.

'What's it to be then, Mr Hendersly?' said Tomkins cockily.

'Wipe that smile off your face,' said Hendersly. 'It's a general security alert – there's been a dreadful accident.'

He began running away toward the lift, like the Mad Hatter, legs in all directions. Tomkins raised his eyebrows. 'Take a look, shall we?'

A small crowd had already assembled around the lift when they arrived. Tomkins, seeing Chambers in the centre, jostled through the whispering huddle, trying to catch what they said.

'Excuse me,' Chambers turned abruptly on Tomkins. 'Yes?'

There was no need to enquire further, Tomkins could see for himself the reason for the emergency alarm. It was Richardson. His body lay slumped on the ground in front of the open lift, his head turned right, as though in sleep. There was no sign of a struggle, no blood. It was the job of a professional.

'He's dead,' said Chambers flatly. The words were so unnecessary.

Tomkins stared down at the body, horrified and fascinated by the proximity of death. He scrambled back out through the crowd, cried out for Henry. But Henry had gone, leaving Anne seated limply in the hallway.

Unnoticed and blithely unaware of Richardson's fate, Henry slipped away. Once he was safe in the stairwell, he began tearing at the envelope with urgency. There wouldn't be much time, he reckoned, and he had to see the contents before he left the building, to make sure. Already, excessive caution was creeping into his every move. On the gloomy landing wall above his head, the alarm bells screamed defiantly. He tugged at the papers, they were folded thickly and unevenly and would not part company readily with the envelope. His eyes moved rapidly over the first page – a ragged piece of paper on which Louis Vacheron had scrawled the French rendition of *The Owl and the Pussycat*. Beneath it, he had added Hannah Brent's name. Henry stuffed it indelicately into his coat pocket and continued reading, his eyes glued. Newspaper clippings, a good thirty of them. They perplexed him – no reference to the Italbank raid or to Louis Vacheron. He began reading. Suddenly, it was all clear to him. The press clippings and an attached memo from Richardson were about one man. Hugo Jardine, a European Member of Parliament, a City financier and businessman. Hugo Jardine was the man Hendersly claimed was the subject of a police investigation, was the reason for Chambers trawling the department's files, was the catalyst for all these extraordinary occurrences over the past few days.

The stakes were high, Richardson had been right. He felt his stomach churn. He wanted to panic. If he had known that Richardson lay dead, he would have. Later, Henry would be utterly confounded by his inability to have connected Richardson's disappearance with the turmoil of the security alert. His only concern now was for himself. He had to get out. Just then, the alarm bells cut off. With his ears still ringing, Henry spiralled down the stairs. The sound of his footsteps and breathing echoed in the stairwell, causing him to glance back several times under the misapprehension that somebody was following him. He reached the exit, panting and flushed. The light outside dazzled him. He squeezed his eyes together, blinked until the black flashes attacking his sight disappeared. Clutching Richardson's papers inside his coat pocket and checking he had his wallet, Henry dashed down the side of the building, out into the street and onto a passing Number 76 bus.

PART TWO

Chapter Nine

Alasdair Martin was a short man of sixty, plump but without any hint of excessive consumption. He had a professorial shock of grey hair, a goatee beard and pebble-dash glasses. Mr Martin, as he was known to everyone, including his wife, always wore checked carpet slippers, even to work. He surmised that since his feet spent most of their time behind the counter, it didn't matter what he had on his feet. Mr Martin worked in a cluttered little shop on the Strand selling First and Second World War memorabilia; guns, uniforms, medals, postcards and photographs. But his tour de force was stamps – he was the best known philatelic dealer of military stamps in the country and ran a thriving mail-order business. Such was the gloomy and run-down appearance of his shop that tourists rarely ventured from their trail to Trafalgar Square to fossick through his historical treasures.

It was getting dark and Mr Martin couldn't decide whether to put on the lights or to close for the day, when there was a dull banging on his door.

'Mr Jay,' he wheezed, clambering down from his high stool. 'Welcome, how welcome.'

Henry stood outside, his arms laden with four box files, unable to move.

'Sorry! Hang on a minute.' Mr Martin shuffled behind the counter and pressed a small button which released the lock on the door.

'Have to be careful, all these guns,' he said, helping Henry through the door. 'I've had a good day, Mr Jay, I can't tell you, one of the best this month and now you've come – I was just about to lock up.'

'I phoned –'

'You phoned – and here you are.'

'I've brought them with me, the lot.'

'To business then?'

'Might be a good idea, Mr Martin,' said Henry as he

removed his files and handed them to the dealer. 'I've got quite a lot on today.'

'I was thinking as you came in the door, Mr Jay, you look like a man who's been working mighty hard.' He inched himself onto a stool and with the delicate hands of an expert he examined several items from Henry's collection.

'Red Cross Prisoner of War postcard, Stalag Five.'

'Mmmm, I've got three without censor marks,' said Henry proudly pointing them out. 'I've separated the extremely rare stamps and POW cards, here . . . and I've categorised the others mainly under the different types of camp – Straflager, Sonderlager, Oflag's, Oflag Luft's – you see . . .'

But Mr Martin was busy holding a letter up to the light by the door. 'So,' he said replacing the rare card into Henry's painstakingly assembled file. 'We are talking of the entire collection, are we? You don't wish to divide it at all?'

'The entire set,' said Henry in a confident tone which belied his feelings. It would be a great loss, selling the collection. He loved it, had watched it grow, nurtured it. Whatever sum he was offered would be no compensation. But he urgently needed cash if he was to survive. He gazed nervously down at the collection.

He said, 'I know the collection of Thank You cards – the Kriegsgefangenenpost's in that folder won't fetch much and the . . .'

'It's all most interesting, fascinating,' Mr Martin interrupted. 'I have many collectors who would want *some* of the rarer POW material and perhaps I could find someone who has a, let's say, macabre, interest in some of these cards. But the entire collection – that's difficult.' He rubbed his chin, did a quick calculation of the collection's value. It was worth a handsome sum. He looked at Henry. Be able to knock him down a few pegs, Mr Martin thought to himself. Despite his scatty appearance, the man was a wily businessman.

'I have to know now,' said Henry.

'If you wanted the money now, would you expect to pay some sort of premium for the convenience of cash in hand?'

'That's right, as I explained on the phone to you. Cash.'

Mr Martin thumbed elaborately through one of his catalogues.

'Just checking one of the prices . . . hmmm.'

Henry began to hum nervously as he walked around the cluttered interior, careful not to knock over any of the stands.

Mr Martin straightened, adjusted his glasses and coughed. 'I'll take the lot for three thousand pounds.'

Henry paused, dug his hands into his pockets, pulled them out again. Then he said, 'Done.'

They shook hands.

Mr Martin disappeared to a small room somewhere in the back of his shop where he kept his safe. As soon as he'd gone, Henry reached over and grabbed the telephone, and dialled.

He spoke in a hoarse whisper, 'You suggested I ring back regarding your advertisement for a flat . . . oh, bedsit . . . yes. The name's Haig, that's H.A.I.G.,' he spelled it out, looking furtively to the back of the shop. 'One thing, it must have its own telephone – not an extension, or a coinbox. I see, well, thanks anyway.' He replaced the receiver on the hook and stuffed the torn square from the *New Standard* in his pocket.

About two minutes later, Mr Martin returned with a bag under his arm and two glasses and a bottle in his hands.

'I know it's bad for my liver,' he wheezed as he hobbled back along behind the counter. 'But for old customers like yourself, Mr Jay, I have an ancient Hungarian custom which I happen to have invented myself.'

The cork was wrenched from the bottle of cheap sherry with a swift popping sound. Mr Martin poured out the sherry, raised his glass.

'To the prince of hobbies and the hobby of princes.'

They drank.

'I was most surprised when you said you wanted to put your collection up for sale and deeply surprised when you came in – you house-hunting Mr Jay? New car, eh?' he quizzed.

'Neither. On behalf of a pal at the office,' replied Henry, downing his sherry in one gulp which made him blink. 'Won't keep you – I'll be in touch,' he said.

'Please, do. It's been a pleasure to do business with you again, Mr Jay,' Mr Martin smiled as he locked the door behind Henry. Three thousand pounds and not a murmur. The collection must be worth half as much again. Henry Jay must badly need the cash, he thought as he buttoned up his coat and pulled a hunting hat hard over his springy hair.

Twenty minutes and three vandalised phones later, Henry found a telephone that worked, in the entrance to Charing Cross Station. He had to shout to make himself heard above the noise. 'Does it have its own telephone . . . sorry, I didn't catch that . . . uh huh . . . it's not a party line or shared or anything? . . . Good, the flat sounds perfect. Can I come round now?' he asked. 'Right, I know where that is. See you in half an hour then.'

Henry decided to leave the car parked in Villiers Street by Charing Cross and take the tube to Euston. From the vivid wash of glossy yellows, greens and reds of Charing Cross Underground, he emerged into the gloomy surroundings of Euston Station. He headed for Drummond Street, to the block of flats owned and rented by Mr Patel. The street was still buzzing with activity – a van unloading a late delivery of towels to an Indian restaurant, one of several in the street. The fruit shop with its exotic root vegetables and fruits stacked neatly in rows outside was still open. But for all its activity, the street depressed Henry. He steeled himself and pressed the door bell.

An hour and minus two hundred pounds deposit on the flat later, Henry checked into the Charing Cross Hotel under his newly-acquired pseudonym, Brian Haig. He nervously checked the foyer to see if there was anyone following him and was gratified to spot only a group of American tourists. He went straight to his room. It was small with a single bed, a television in one corner and an exceedingly ugly dressing table in the other. But it was warm and clean. He took off his coat, jacket and shoes, stretched himself out on the bed and closed his eyes. Oh God! I haven't phoned Anne. He tried to sit up, his trunk and limbs seemed to weigh a tonne and he lay back, defeated. Eventually, he struggled into an upright position, straightened his glasses and dialled the switchboard. Could she connect him to a London number? A few minutes later the phone at his bedside rang.

'Anne?'

'Where are you? I've been sick with worry –'

'It's all right, I'm fine. I've been home and collected a few clothes and things.'

'I am aware of that – the bedroom was a wreck, I thought we'd been burgled at first, then I saw your note . . . Henry, do you know what you're doing?' her voice was shaking.

'Yes, everything will be fine. I'm going to keep my head low for a while. If anyone phones, tell them I'm still at home, just popped out and that I'll call them back. Even if it's Richardson.

'You mean you don't know?'

'Know what?'

'Richardson's dead – that was the reason for all that panic back at your office earlier today. No one seems certain how he died; two foreign-looking young men were seen darting from the building – the police are looking into that at the moment. I thought you knew, thought that was why you'd left in such a hurry. Then, as the hours slipped by and I hadn't heard . . . Henry . . . Henry? Are you still there?'

His mind was locked into her first two words, after that he'd ceased listening. Richardson dead, they'd got him. He felt extremely cold all of a sudden, goosepimples shivered up his arms and back and prickled over his scalp.

'They killed Richardson,' he mumbled, 'they'll try to kill me too, if they can. Now do you understand how dangerous this whole thing is?'

'Darling I do. That's why I think we should go to the caravan in Wales.'

'No! They'd follow me there, it's no good –'

'But at least tell me where you are –'

'I can't. This way, if anyone asks you won't know. I promise to phone you to let you know how I am and to see if you're all right.'

'Henry, I'm not one of them – I'm your *wife*,' her voice was a soft scream.

'I've got to go now. I'll phone you soon, look after yourself.'

'Don't go yet . . . Henry? Henry!' she cried, but he'd hung up.

She limply replaced the receiver and walked into the kitchen. She flicked off the switch to the oven – what was the point in cooking, she couldn't eat if she tried. She walked aimlessly about the house, turned television on, then off again. She tried listening to the radio but couldn't. She dragged herself upstairs and ran a bath. The warm water felt good around her tired body. For the first time in years she felt terribly alone, and lonely, and scared. Tears streamed down her face, her body shaking. She sat in the bath with her head bowed sobbing loudly. How was she going to cope? She'd only just managed to get through the trauma of being told her husband was, in their words, 'suffering from severe mental strain' and had two weeks' leave which she, they'd insisted, would share. She'd only just fought off panic when Henry was taken away into an office for further questioning, and was petrified when she realised he had gone missing. Anne couldn't remember the drive home, but somehow she'd made it. Now this! It was pointless contacting the police, she thought. They couldn't even protect their own. Sobbing quietly, she pulled out the plug with her toe and watched the water gurgle away. Then, trance-like she wrapped a bathrobe round herself and went to the drinks cabinet, poured a large bourbon and washed down a couple of Mogadon. Tonight, she didn't even want to dream.

All night the wind had blown, tearing along the granite wall of the hotel, slashing rain across his bedroom window. By morning, the air had cleansed itself of blackness.

'No! I can't,' Henry cried, tossing the bedclothes onto the floor. He startled from his sleep and swung his legs onto the floor. The light hurt his eyes and the suddenness of awaking from a night riddled with bad dreams made him dizzy. He seized his glasses from the bedside table and when he had got his bearings, crossed the room and stood by the window. He stared out to the street below, seeing nothing as he tried to shake off his nightmare. In it, he'd burnt all the files on Jardine, the scraps of paper from Richardson and Vacheron. He was in his office, it was late at night. He was trying to get at his report, to burn that too, to cleanse himself so that he could start again, pretend it hadn't happened. A torch flashed in his eyes, blinded him. Richardson – it was him. Richardson kept yelling at him, telling him it was too late, that he had gone too far, that they would try to kill him no matter what he did. He would have to go on. Henry started running, Richardson after him. They ran together. Hendersly appeared from a street alley. Then they were in a field, being chased by police, by Chambers, by Tomkins, everyone. The dream turned the location back to the City. They ran into a huge building. A suave-looking doorman held open the door. It was Hugo Jardine, MEP. The door slammed. And Henry had shuddered, sweating, back to reality.

He phoned for a mini-cab to take him to Green Park. It arrived half-an-hour later, a beat-up Audi.

'Won't be long – can you wait, please,' he asked the mini-cab driver as it pulled into the curb outside a row of shops. The cabbie shrugged and pulled a packet of cigarettes from his pocket. 'All right mate,' he replied lazily.

The shop was a huge expanse of cream-shag carpet stretching out to cream walls, against which were several white stands of varying heights. Each displayed a variety of computer equipment. He ambled slowly around the shop, the only customer in the vast West End showroom. He stopped frequently to run his fingers over a keyboard, or to examine one of the numerous computers on display.

'Can I help?' A voice came at him from nowhere. He looked around, startled. A young woman stood up and walked from behind her desk, she was attractive-looking, had a businesslike manner. Henry came straight to the point.

'I'm doing a lot more complex work from home, I need

a personal computer – I've used them before,' he added.

She nodded. 'Do you want to talk to the mainframe, collect and process information?'

'Yes, to both.'

'The Apple II would be the most suitable, I guess. It comes with its own interface card, has a 48K ram with main storage for 180 thousand characters.'

They walked across the room, feet sunk in carpet.

She continued her sales pitch. Henry knew most of it already, but for the sake of appearances nodded appreciatively, smiled every now and then.

'As far as display goes – you can have a video monitor, you could go for a printer, or use your television. If you're interested in a printer, may I suggest the Daisywheel — the quality of the print-out's good. We also stock the Dotmatrix.'

'How much?'

'Let's see,' she opened a glossy brochure, ran a long red fingernail down the price list. 'The Daisywheel is one thousand, nine hundred and ninety pounds; the Dotmatrix, five hundred. The price reflects the difference in quality.'

'I'll think about it,' Henry said, baulking at the near two thousand quid he'd have to fork out if he opted for the Daisywheel.

Off she went again on her spiel. 'Storage – you'll want two disks, of course; single-sided, single-density. Have you tried the floppies, they're extremely reliable?'

'Yes, of course,' said Henry patiently. 'Do you have the equipment in stock? I'll need an acoustic coupler as well.'

'Of course, sir.'

'How much for the lot.'

'You could be the owner of an Apple II for less than two thousand, three hundred pounds – cheaper than a photocopier, you know.'

'I'm sure. Fine, I'll take it, have it packed up quickly. I've got a car waiting.' He checked through the window as he said it.

'Thank you, sir,' she said holding open the door for Henry and a weedy assistant who struggled with a large cardboard box. There were three in all which Henry piled up on the back seat.

The car chugged to life.

'Present for the missus?' grinned the driver as he pulled away from the kerb.

Henry glared at him.

'Drummond Street – behind Euston,' he said tersely.

Bloody mini-cab drivers. Never knew where Euston was half the time.

The driver peered at Henry curiously. 'That's where you want to be dropped then?'

'Yes,' roared Henry.

It took most of the morning to install the computer. When he'd finished he slouched back into the only armchair in the squat living room and congratulated himself on acquiring so attractive a working companion. 'You're a real beauty,' he said grinning. 'I think I'll call you Seneca, only you'd better not get any smart ideas of your own and conk out on me.'

He slowly unbuttoned his soiled shirt, thinking how much more potent he now was with Seneca. With the computer he'd be able to run checks on anyone, everything, connected to Louis Vacheron and Hugo Jardine; he'd be able to monitor the Police Computer. Hell's teeth! That reminds me, I have to phone Anne! He snatched the phone. The car would have been towed away to the police pound by now, he figured, and he wanted to make sure she'd got the spare pair of keys and a credible story as to who left the car in Villiers Street and why.

Their conversation was brief and to the point. She seemed a lot calmer than last night and, if she was scared, she didn't let on, expressing keenness to play a part in whatever he was involved with. He told her her time would come, just talking to her helped a lot. Everything was going nicely, he thought as he hung up. Now, to work. The first step was to get hold of Sam Hinchcliffe, security adviser to the International Protective Trade Association, a commercial organisation which stored vast amounts of information on British citizens in its computers and had access to data within the EEC.

That wasn't as easy as he thought – Hinchcliffe's secretary was unmovable, wouldn't interrupt the meeting he'd attended and refused to even take a message. Eventually, he persuaded the switchboard operator it was a matter of life or death and was put through to him direct.

'Sorry to snatch you away . . . I was wondering, Sam, if I could pick your brains, it won't take long . . . thanks.' He nestled down into the chair, resting a pad on his knee, holding a pen at the ready. 'Remember when we met last and I was doing that report on computer and related frauds . . . yes, the one with the long title . . . well, you mentioned at the time if I ever wanted to do a test run on IPTA's security you'd help me out. I'm working on data protection and cryptography now and wondered if your offer was still open . . . terrific, sure I'll hang on.' What a coup, Hinchcliffe giving him the code and password to their computer. He hummed softly into the receiver, ' . . . sorry Sam, hadn't realised you were back,' he scrambled for the pen which had slipped down the side of the armchair. 'Right, what have you got?'

There was no doubt – IPTA had a complex entry system, which as he progressed through the security barriers to top secret information would undoubtedly make things tricky. But Seneca's first task was to extract Hannah Brent's address in Brussels. 'Child's play,' he said smugly as he peered at the information flashing green on his visual display screen. 'Keep this up and we'll get along just fine.'

Half-an-hour later Henry was hunched over the keyboard, stabbing at the 'continue' key. Row upon row of names floated up the screen, replaced by another list when he pressed another key. There must be an easier way than this, he sagged over the keyboard.

'Okay, take a break, Seneca. I'm popping across the road.'

He unplugged the Apple, holding his back as he creaked upright. Damp air, permeating through the rice-paper walls of the flat was probably the cause of his backache, he reckoned. But using the computer at the same time as the heater caused problems he hadn't envisaged. Never having rented a flat before, Henry hadn't encountered the method of feeding in endless sums of money to a meter to keep his lighting, heating and cooking on the go. And the Apple computer soaked up coins as though Henry owned the Mint.

It had begun to rain. Fat drops spattered onto the pavement and road. Henry pulled up his collar as high as it would reach and made a beeline for the fruiterer's. He noticed it stocked a line of groceries. Inside, he whipped off his glasses and wiped them on the lining of his coat. Then proceeded gingerly up one narrow aisle, turned into another as he picked out the essential ingredients for existence. Sausages, oven chips, bread rolls, cheese, chocolate digestive biscuits, baked beans, tinned lager and Tic-tacs. He reckoned that with that lot he wouldn't need to go out for days. Holed up in the sleazy side of town, it was very Cagneyesque, Henry mused.

He didn't feel quite so jaunty when he returned to his hide-out. The flocked wallpaper reverberated around the room with noisy clusters of red, green and brown. It clashed with the worn rose-patterned carpet and, in the kitchen, a stove, fridge and sink in the corner of the living room, the 'flocking' from the wallpaper had retreated behind huge globs of cooking fat. There was a red armchair by the window, a Formica table where Seneca lived and a settee which folded out into a bed. The bathroom was a dire affair – still, it was safe and the landlord didn't ask questions.

Chapter Ten

Detective Sergeant Vine read the departmental memo twice. Once standing over the drinks cabinet as he poured himself a generous measure of Scotch. Then again, submerged in a soft leather armchair where he became the subject of Trevor Chambers' dispassionate stare.

'Terrific read,' said Vine sarcastically. 'But I still think you're an incompetent bastard. You cocked it up totally, magnificently, monumentally, just like you did when you were in the Met. I mean, what loony would set up *two* divisions of the police force to put the frighteners on *one* rather weedy civil servant and *forget* to tell one of them what the other was doing. Jesus!'

Chambers leaned forward as if to ward off further attack. 'Purely precautionary – if you'd contacted me first you wouldn't have found yourself looking like the mug you did a couple of days ago with Henry Jay. Anyway, you were a little late with your entrance – it was designed to put the wind up Jay before, not after, his confrontation with me. It was meant to frighten him off taking the matter further. And you can see by that memo that "upstairs" is mighty sensitive about the whole issue.'

'Well, I can see that this Fraud Squad bloke, Richardson and Jay had this agreement whereby Richardson leaked him information the Department couldn't officially ask for, in return for getting info from here. But what was the leak that got Richardson killed?'

Chambers puffed out his cheeks and blew. 'If we knew that –'

'Come off it, Trev,' Vine leapt from his chair and grabbed Chambers by the arm, squeezing hard. 'Don't try that with me.'

Chambers winced. 'Let go and I'll tell you . . . OK,' he shook his arm free. 'There's a big fraud case about to break. And I mean BIG.'

'Keep talking.'

'I don't know the details, you'll have to check with Hendersly. I'll see if he's in his office.' He leaned over and made a phone call.

'Tony? Trevor. Would it be possible to see you for a few minutes, I've got a Detective Sergeant Vine from the Metropolitan Police here, to discuss Jay and the investigator . . . you'll come down? Thanks . . . see you, then.'

He looked up at Vine. 'Hendersly'll be down in a couple of minutes.'

'Time for a quick drink then,' said Vine. 'Can I get you one, from your stock of Stationery Office-supplied cabinet?' He grinned cheekily.

'No, thanks. Kind of you to offer though.' Chambers paused, said, 'I thought you'd dried out; rumour had it you'd knocked one back too many, were on your way out, so dried out.'

Vine finished topping up his glass with Scotch. 'Just goes to show; your contacts are still lousy,' he quipped.

'Did better out of the Met in the long run than you, though.' Chambers' words were seasoned with arrogance.

They sat, looking at each other, daggers drawn, until Hendersly arrived.

'Morning, Trevor. Super day, isn't it!' greeted Hendersly. 'Pleased to meet you, Detective Sergeant.'

He shook hands and they sat down.

Chambers got the ball rolling, asked Hendersly to fill them in. Hendersly began. 'The investigation is unusual on two counts. On the first, the size and scope of the suspected fraud and on the second, the political ramifications. I hinted as much to Jay when he came to me and Chambers, but I was wasting my time. By then, Richardson had got to him; seemed to have convinced him that Chambers and myself, indeed the entire department, were being used, albeit unwittingly, as a cover-up.'

Vine nodded, looked into his glass and asked. 'Wouldn't it have been better if you had taken Jay into your confidence from the outset? Then, perhaps, he mightn't have got so hot under the collar about his file being dry-cleaned.'

'True,' Hendersly admitted with a rueful smile. 'I concede that a few errors of judgement may have been made where Jay has been concerned . . . to err is human; it's only when one rises to Permanent Under-Secretary level that one ceases to be human,' he paused to smile at Chambers who flashed back a weak grin.

'But, Sergeant Vine,' Hendersly went on. 'You will appreciate that I have only been told a fragment of the full story on a need-to-know basis. I don't intend to make any more errors of judgement. From now on, Mr Chambers has my full support in setting aside all departmental duties to work alongside you. I shall give you access to Jay's personal records and I hope that you will not hesitate if any further assistance is required.'

'Thanks,' said Vine, quite bowled over by the offer.

'By the way,' said Hendersly. 'Who's the chap I should liaise with about this in the Metropolitan Police? Just to confirm –'

Vine noticed Chambers stiffen at the question. He put his whisky on the floor beside his chair and spoke. 'I'm a sort of supernumerary on this, Mr Hendersly. Not allocated to the murder team. I'm following my own lines of enquiry.'

'I see,' said Hendersly cautiously. 'You'll want to speak to Jay, of course.'

'If he was running with Richardson, he's clearly a target too.'

'You'll find his address in the files,' said Hendersly. He stopped talking as the tea lady entered, waited as she rattled around in search of an extra cup and saucer, then said. 'Locating Jay, however, may take longer than you think. I sent one of our men around with all his files from the office, to check he was all right. It seems he left home a few days ago in something of a panic.'

He met their glances with a shrug. 'Up to you, now.'

At that point he stood. 'Well, I'd better be getting back. Good luck,' he said and walked out.

'Phew!' said Chambers, his breathing easing a fraction. 'I thought for one moment you were going to admit to Hendersly you'd been pulled in to do a favour for an old chum.'

'Hardly – old chum.' He bit on the words.

Chambers cupped his hands round his pipe bowl and struck a match.

'I can see you're dying to crack this case,' he said smoke

billowing up towards the ceiling. 'We'll meet tonight at seven-thirty. I'll have Jay's file by then.'

'Not tonight. Gotta date elsewhere.'

'Pleasure before business now, is it?'

'A business date.'

'Okay. We'll have to wait till morning. Be here at nine on the dot.'

'Yes, Sirrrr!' Vine clicked his heels and stood to attention in mocking gesture.

'And stick your belly in, Vine. It's obscene.'

'Ah . . .' said Chambers appreciatively. He stepped back and surveyed the room with approval. The rich colours of the books lining the shelves, the solid wood-stained desk, the warm browns and golds of the furnishings. Everything in its place. 'So, this is Henry's study. You know, Mrs Jay, it's just as I imagined it to be.' Chambers turned to look at Anne. She was standing at the door, her arms crossed, her expression blank. Chambers moved back across the room and sat in Henry's broad armchair. Vine sat perched on the desk, his left leg maintaining contact with the floor.

'So, what's missing from here?' Chambers cast his eyes around the room once more.

'His collection . . . he collected stamps, specialised in Second World War issues, POW cards, postmarks, things like that,' she said darkly.

'Worth a few bob?' asked Vine.

'It's a very comprehensive collection. Whatever Henry does, he does thoroughly.'

'Indeed,' Chambers affirmed. 'Anything else missing?'

She shook her head. 'Not that I can see.'

'Anne,' said Chambers getting to his feet. 'I have to ask you a few awkward questions.'

She just looked at him with her wide eyes, her jaw clenched tight. Chambers stepped forward.

'He's never gone off before, has he? Absent without leave?'

'No.'

'Got any friends, anyone he trusts who would put him up

for a while and keep quiet.'

'I can't think of anyone off-hand. We have a few close friends. But no one who would fit the picture you're trying to make.'

'What about a flat? Has he got a little place in town somewhere? Where he might go occasionally if work keeps him late or maybe he's got . . .'

Anne exploded. 'If you're insinuating my husband has a *pied-à-terre* for some illicit purpose, you don't know him as much as you let on. He hasn't got a flat in town, never has, couldn't afford one. Not on the salary he gets. You must know that!'

'Sorry, sometimes my job involves asking sticky questions to extract the truth.'

'But not stupid ones,' Anne flashed back.

Chambers continued as though she had said nothing. 'But we're concerned about Henry. We'd like him back with us, with you too, as soon as possible.' He said, like a doctor soothing his patient. 'Why don't we go downstairs? More comfortable . . after you,' he gestured to Anne. Chambers stopped at the door, turned towards Vine and winked. Vine nodded and remained seated until they had reached the living room below. Then he tip-toed quietly downstairs to the hallway, to the telephone.

'How often does Henry contact you?' Chambers asked.

She didn't answer.

'Please, I have to know. It's for his good too, you know.'

Yes, you really expect me to believe that, don't you, thought Anne. After all the damage you have inflicted, you can sit back in our living room, reeking of sincerity and concern. Hypocritical wanker, I don't trust you as far as I could throw you.

'Henry left in a huff,' she said eventually. 'We had a row and he walked out; I said I never wanted to see him again, hear his boring voice again. So far, he hasn't written, or phoned. Knowing Henry, he'll take me at my word,' she lied.

'How did he leave, if you didn't drive him somewhere?'

'Took a train, I presume.'

'Rather difficult, wouldn't it, with all his baggage and stamp collection?'

'How do I know? I was out. I had the car. Maybe he got a taxi. Why don't you ask him when you find him? And what the hell does it matter?' she spoke acidly.

Chambers raised his hands. 'Fine. We'll leave the matter there.'

'Good. Now, would you mind leaving, both of you. Get your big friend and please leave. I've got a headache.'

'Of course. This must be an exceptionally trying time for you. Thanks for your help. We'll be on our way.' His voice rarely strayed from the deep, almost seductive tone of friendly chicanery.

'Ready to go then, Vine?'

'Yes, Mr Chambers,' said Vine leaning against the door frame. 'Thank you for taking the time to speak with us.'

Anne twisted her mouth in acknowledgement, shook hands with Vine and Chambers perfunctorily and showed them the door.

'Did you fix it?' asked Chambers as they drove off.

'No sweat. With that little bug nestled snugly inside the phone, we should be able to pick up every call. Clear as a bell. They'll never catch on.'

'Good,' said Chambers. 'Let's hope Jay phones soon – we need a few more leads.'

'Damned right we do,' said Vine. 'Tell me, are you enjoying this? Being back on the beat and all?'

'Like I'd never been away. Good to be working with you again, Eric.'

'Yeah?'

'A pleasure.'

Chambers had the right mentality for security work: laid-back and shrewd. He trusted no one, but people trusted him . . . usually. He covered his distrust as he always did with lavish servings of charm. He'd learnt that through spending years with the Met. In nearly twenty years he'd picked his way cautiously through even the trickiest moments. Until one day, he blew it. More to the point, Vine, his partner in crime, had blown it. Chambers resigned and soon after landed a job with the Department of Commercial Development. Nobody ever knew why Chambers had left so suddenly. Except for Vine. That well-kept secret kept them together, forever in each other's debt.

Vine had trudged all morning without success from one stamp dealer to another and now his stomach was crying out for replenishment. He crossed off a dealer in his notebook. There were only two more possibilities. He would check them out as soon as he had placated his rumbling belly.

Twenty-five minutes, a coffee and two Danish pastries later, he set off down the Strand, the sticky sweetness of the pastries branded on his lips. He pressed the buzzer of the shop's entrance and waited. It was a dowdy little place, tucked between a hamburger joint and a zappy boutique, a stubborn remnant of a time when the Strand was a more gentle place to amble down. An old man appeared from the shadows of the shop. The lock clicked back and Vine entered, pressing his hand across his scalp as he did to flatten the long wisps of hair slicked across a small balding patch.

'Mr Martin?' he enquired.

'That's what it says above the shop. That's right,' Mr Martin said. 'How can I help?'

'Routine police enquiry. We're trying to contact someone. I wonder if you've seen this man recently?'

Vine flipped open his book, extracted a photograph. Without hesitating, Mr Martin responded. 'Why, that's Mr Jay. A regular customer of mine.'

'Has he been in this week at all, Mr Martin?' asked Vine hastily. He had quickly learned that given half a chance stamp dealers would pour out a flood of recollections about stamp collectors who indulged in forgery to fund their hobby, convinced he would be interested.

Mr Martin paused and fondled his chin. 'Can't say I've seen him – no, I don't think he has.'

'Think a bit harder.'

'Hmm, difficult to say, really. Memory's not the same any more,' he smiled weakly.

Vine's eyes narrowed, he bent down over the counter until his face was close to the old man's. 'It's very important, vital, we contact Mr Jay,' he spoke as if confiding in him. 'He could be in trouble. If you know anything, tell me.'

By the time Chambers arrived, the stamp dealer had told Vine everything.

Said Vine: 'He gave him three grand in readies – sussed he was in some sort of trouble, needed the money quick –'

'Don't we all?' Chambers interjected.

'So he screwed him.'

Mr Martin shuffled uneasily behind the counter. 'I have explained everything to your colleague – that I haven't yet had time to attend to the VAT and income tax paperwork on the transaction.'

'No doubt you'll stay on late to catch up,' said Vine dourly.

'Jay is evidently using the name Haig to get a room – Mr Martin got whiff of a conversation while was was digging up a celebratory nip for the two of them.'

'Does that get us anywhere?'

'Could be. I'm working on something – could involve a few bob though.'

'What, exactly?'

'Tickle a mate who'll tickle a computer for us.'

Vine arrived at the Police National Computer Centre in Hendon via a liquid lunch with an old mate who ran a wine bar in Islington's Camden Passage, and who had more contacts with people from all strata of society than anyone Vine knew.

No harm in putting feelers out in all directions, he figured. He slammed the door of his car and without locking it walked into the PNC centre, straight to the operations room. Through the port-hole window of the door he spied Bill Dalgleish, a sinewy man with a flock of sandy-grey hair and a pallid skin. He tapped the glass – Dalgleish looked around and seeing Vine's face pressed up against the window, grinned broadly. He entered. Dalgleish greeted him.

'Still trying to kill time before retirement then, Eric?'

'Cheeky bugger,' said Vine.

They walked down the corridor to a small office and closed the door behind them.

'A black one? Whadaya mean?' Dalgleish looked puzzled.

'I want you to do a foreigner for me – control never need know.'

'I dunno, Eric. I dunno. It's getting tough around here – a couple of journalists are still sniffing around after that exposé last year. Things are much tighter now.'

'An' I was born yesterday – you're still slipping stuff to private detectives a tanner a go. I'll give you fifty for a complete run.'

'What's the enquiry?'

'Murder.'

'Gotta name?'

'Jay – Henry Victor, using the name Brian Haig to get himself digs.'

'Can't you put it through official?'

'Nope. There's leaks all over the place. We want to keep the ripples right out of this one. I'd like to know where he is. I want a trace on his car as stolen suspect, on him as a criminal name, as a missing person and check his credit-worthiness.'

'One hundred?'

Vine nodded.

'Don't expect miracles. We haven't got Maigret and Lord Peter Wimsey out there. Think of it as just a couple of million extra PC Plods walking up the street very slow and thinking even slower.'

'Missing nothing and getting an answer from you in ten seconds.'

'True – but I have to feed in a bit of corn.'

'We don't have much – we know he was insistent the room had its own phone – the Post Office Postcode Index could provide some help. But I don't know what that's worth to you.'

Dalgleish scratched his shoulder pensively.

'A direct telephone line eh? Interesting.'

'Yeah, fascinating,' said Vine facetiously.

It was a long shot, he knew, but there wasn't much else to go on and some extraordinary information ended up in the police computer, as *The Guardian* perennially loved to point out.

'This fella got any background in computers?' Dalgleish broke the silence.

'Only did a four-inch thick report on computer fraud for the Department of Commercial Development, didn't he?'

Dalgleish raised his eyebrows. 'I think you've got problems. You could grow old chasing him.'

Vine extracted a cigarette from a crumpled packet and tapped the end pensively on the edge of the table. 'You mean to say that if he had access to a computer he could plug into this lot?'

'He wouldn't need to, if he found a dick to get him the information but sounds as if he's lying real low; yeh, he could link in here – of course, it would take a bit of doing – he'd have to get through numerous security barriers and know the passwords, but it's technically feasible – even we have our weak links.'

Vine's face clouded over. 'So every time we get fed a bit of information that gets us nearer to him –'

'He's off in the other direction.'

If this was true and he could gain access to the police national computer – and it sounded far-fetched to him – using the force to track him down would be nigh on impossible. He put a match to his cigarette and blew smoke-rings up towards the ceiling. 'Has anyone ever tried this wheeze before?'

'A couple of times – all hushed-up. Don't want it known that the nation's suit of armour has too many chinks in it, we've already got enough problems on our hands.'

'How powerful would the computer have to be?'

Dalgleish shrugged. 'That doesn't really matter too much – anything over forty-eight K ram's.'

'Eh?'

'Could get away with it on a good portable,' said Dalgleish, smiling at the stupefied look on Vine's face.

'I'll give you the names of a handful of suppliers who'd be most likely to stock the software you're talking about. They might cough up with something or put you in touch with someone if they don't know. About those hundred readies . . .'

Vine stubbed his cigarette out under his shoe and shook his head. 'Fifty now, fifty later. It's pretty low when a copper has to start feeding another copper for small beer.'

'I hope whoever you're doing this for, Eric, won't see it like that,' Dalgleish said, stuffing the fifty pounds into his back pocket.

Henry placed the tinfoil containers in the oven, switched the temperature to three hundred and fifty degrees Fahrenheit and checked his watch. It would take around fifteen minutes, he estimated, to heat his chicken tikka and rice take-away.

Tonight was his first anniversary, he had been in the Drummond Street flat for exactly a week, during which time he had achieved quite a bit.

He had discovered some interesting points on Louis Vacheron and the Italbank fraud by trawling the police computer, though none of it was particularly useful for his research into the 'master' fraud. But by poring through *Who's Who* and numerous business directories, plus the micro fiche at Company's House, he had built up a comprehensive picture of Hugo Jardine. Jardine was an impressive character – chairman and main board director of several companies and a few small ones besides. He was a vociferous campaigner on energy and transport in the European Parliament. He was wealthy in his own right. At least, on paper. The Jardine fortune had been built on family money and wisely deployed; property in England and abroad, company acquisitions, large shareholdings in blue-chip companies. He was an astute businessman, an avowed wheeler-dealer. But nothing Henry saw smelled of illegality. On the surface, at least, Jardine was whiter than white. Still, he filed every snippet of information he had into the computer, however banal. One innocuous piece of information could, he hoped, provide the vital clue. Of course, things would have been different if Richardson had been alive. Together, they could have cracked the case in half the time. Henry despaired – how long could he keep this pace up? Time was not on his side. They'd murdered Richardson, they'd be working hard now to flush him out. And *they* had the advantage; they knew who he was, what he looked like. He had no idea who *they* were exactly. Only that there was no one he could trust.

He picked at his chicken. He had no appetite for it now. A walk would have been nice, he thought, only darkness had set in and his courage failed him. He hated going out at night, ventured outside only during the day, to buy food, collect information that was unobtainable over the telephone or via the computer. At night he kept the drab curtains closed. Henry rose and stood by the window, tweaked at the curtains and peered through a gap, scanned the street for anyone who lingered too long. Minutes passed by unnoticed. Nothing stirred below, only a waiter from the restaurant opposite who ran into the fruiterer's, presumably to buy something as inane as a lemon, Henry imagined. He dropped the curtain and returned to the couch. Plonked himself down. He didn't know why he bothered to keep vigil at the window. His daily monitoring of the police computer had thrown up no sign that anyone was onto him. And if somebody did come hot on his trail, he wasn't certain how he would react. A plan was needed, he figured.

Despair turned to boredom. He grabbed the jotter from the Formica table and locked himself in the bathroom. He did it because it was a change of scenery and because he didn't know what else to do. He sat on the toilet seat, balanced the jotter on his knees. Then plotted what he would do tomorrow. After that, he made a phone call before turning in for the night.

'Hello? Anne? It's me. Sorry I haven't called you before. Are you all right?'

'Fine. Except I can't sleep nights – I've been working in

the studio till all hours to kill time.' She sounded tired and depressed.

'Keep that up and you'll soon have enough to have your own one-woman show,' he said trying to sound cheerful.

She didn't respond.

'Any calls for me?' he asked.

'One or two, they didn't leave their names. And Mr Chambers and that detective, Viner or a name like that, paid a visit. They wanted to know what I knew. There wasn't much I could tell them since you won't tell me. They know about your stamps going missing.'

Henry groaned.

'How was I to know not to tell them about your collection – you didn't say anything,' she snapped. 'What have you done with it, anyway? You didn't sell it, did you?'

'I had to – I needed cash.'

'You're crazy! I never dreamed I'd hear you say that. Ever!'

'Enough of that,' he said wearily. 'Tell me what Chambers and Vine said. What else did they want?'

'They want to talk to you – they said your life was in danger. You know, stuff like that . . .'

'That all, nothing more?'

'Nothing more? That all?' she mimicked, her tone sharp. 'Isn't that enough?'

'Look, I won't be phoning for a few days,' he butted in. 'I've got to find somebody. I'll call you, maybe we could meet. I'll try to think of somewhere. Okay?'

'When?'

'I can't tell right now. Better hang up. Don't trust these GPO lines. Never know who might be tuning in.'

'Damn you, Henry! Why don't you say something real!' she slammed down the receiver, her body rigid with frustration, anger and fear.

Henry opened his mouth, but no words came. He felt totally deflated by Anne's irascible behaviour. He knew that he was to blame but could think of no way out. He put his head into his hands, sat, thinking about her, the two of them.

The persistent wail of a police siren floated up through the window. He shook himself back to reality. He began cleaning up the flat. When he had finished and the place was as spotless as its dinginess allowed, he packed his clothes into his suitcase, checked that his passport was in his coat pocket and that he had enough cash.

He was up before sunrise the next morning, fussing about the flat. By the time the first chink of light had broken through the dank morning mist and streamed into the kitchen area of the room, Henry had left. On his way out, he slipped an envelope beneath Mr Patel's door containing a week's rent, plus a handsome bonus which he hoped would keep his mouth shut, should anyone start to ask questions. His exit hadn't been quite as noiseless as he would have liked. 'Goddam bastard!' he had hissed at a mangy cat which darted in front of him, causing him to grip the banister to break his fall. With any luck, he hoped, the beast would be part of a Madras curry before he returned.

Chapter Eleven

The hall porter at the Hotel Amigo thought Henry was German and it was only when Henry protested in no uncertain terms in English (since that was the only language he spoke) that the porter apologised.

'I am sorry, sir,' he said in a raspy voice laced with a French accent. 'It was the way you organised yourself; you are so fussy and clean.'

Fussy and clean! Henry swung out of the door outraged by the mistake and made off down the street, clinging protectively to his small guide book, *Visiting Brussels*.

He had been in the Belgian city for a day-and-a-half and had passed the time wandering down its cobbled streets, salivating over the exquisite chocolates, visiting various tourist spots which interested him, such as the nuclear energy exhibition at the Atomium. It was fast approaching lunchtime as he scurried down Rue Royale. Soon, he was lost. He decided to do what he usually did when such chaos broke his routine. He took a taxi. Any taxi driver would know the words, European Commission, in Brussels he had figured.

He was dressed in precisely what he had described to Hannah Brent over the telephone. Green mackintosh, blue and gold floral tie, dark grey trousers. She said she had mousy brown hair, cut short and had a Nordic-looking face. She added she was rather dumpy. It was a sufficiently good description for him to spot her as she left the glass door entrance. As he approached her, Henry couldn't help thinking, however, that she had been less than kind to herself. She must have been in her mid-twenties, perhaps a little older. Her hair was brown, but shone in the sunlight. Her eyes were large and green, her complexion Scandinavian – as was her bone structure. There was nothing dumpy about her at all, except perhaps for her thighs which stretched tight the fabric of her pants.

'What do you want from me?' she asked unsmiling.

'As I explained to you over the phone this morning, my name is Henry Jay. I'm a Principal Scientific Officer in the Department of Commercial Development. I located you through the Commission's personnel records and as I explained, rather briefly, I'd like to talk to you about an English policeman, Chief Superintendent Richardson from the City of London Fraud Squad, who came to see you recently.'

She listened to him without any expression on her face and said:

'That's right. About Louis Vacheron. I lived with him.'

Henry nodded, relieved to find her willing to talk. They walked to the entrance of the Metro and stood there, eyeing each other up.

'Richardson has been killed, presumably by the same people who killed your boyfriend,' Henry said, watching her closely.

She looked at the ground and said nothing.

'Why don't you let me buy us a meal,' he offered. 'I gather Brussels is noted for office blocks and restaurants, and I've no wish to see the insides of more offices.'

It was the most opulent restaurant Henry had ever been in in his life. Rich red drapes hung hundreds of feet above him. The waiters moved swiftly and most cheerfully about the restaurant, like clones. There were flowers on the table, superb food and an exquisite wine list. But best of all, Hannah had managed to get a table by the open window from which hung a small balcony, which overlooked the most beautiful square in the City – Grand Place, with its exquisite Flemish architecture. When they had sat down and ordered aperitifs, Hannah pointed out a few famous residential homes in the square.

'They've tarted the Grand Place up beautifully, don't you think?'

He nodded and sipped his gin and tonic.

'They've added lots of gold paint,' she informed him, 'and there's a flower market; on Sundays they sell birds, mostly pigeons. It's very jolly. You should come and have a look.'

They talked for about half-an-hour about Brussels, where to go and what to see. A kind of ice-breaker chat before the main course. Then, he asked her about herself.

'I hated Brussels when I came to work in the Legal Department. Most of the girls hate it, despite the money. The new Europe – nine to five, it's the world's most boring town after Welshpool. And I was born and brought up in Welshpool, so I know,' she smiled lugubriously at him.

'So where did Louis come in?'

'He worked the bars, picking up bored secretaries like me. Only I didn't kick him out the next morning, or the one after that, and he stayed on,' she said. 'I knew he was . . .' she stopped as a waiter arrived with her main course: *Baron de lapereau mangetout* – rabbit cooked with spinach and turnips. Henry was always amazed at how such high-faluting names for dishes always seemed to breed such simple food. Hannah had chosen his dish on the grounds that he liked seafood but couldn't decipher the menu properly. It duly arrived. Salmon with vegetables – or, *Papillotes de saumon à l'étuvée de légumes*. Another waiter served the vegetables and another served the wine. When they had departed and Henry began eating, she resumed her conversation.

'I knew Louis was some sort of crook. It wasn't violence – I wouldn't, couldn't, have had his hands on me if it was. I assumed some sort of fraud when I thought about it at all. You know, cheque books, credit cards, currency . . . something like that,' she paused to bite into her rabbit. 'Mmmm, delicious – how's yours?'

'Delicious too,' he said, piling his fork high.

'Anyway, Louis'd be gone a few days, then he'd be back, we'd go to bed for two, three days at a time then . . .' she smiled, as if remembering, 'There was something good about Louis, no matter what he did for a living.' Henry bit into a carrot, waited for his mouth to empty.

'So Richardson thought.'

She said, 'He was scared a lot of the time, but it didn't show to anyone but me. That's why he boasted about his important connections – the list was as long as one of the Commission's briefing papers – the people he said would help him if he ever got arrested, or in trouble . . .'

'The Power?' asked Henry, claiming ignorance.

'Le Pouvoir? It only existed in his imagination.'

They fell into silence. She didn't seem to be hungry, only picking at her food. Unlike Henry, who had virtually wolfed his down and only courtesy prevented him from devouring hers as well.

'There's a European Member of Parliament and businessman called Hugo Jardine,' said Henry. 'Did Louis ever mention him to you?'

She shrugged. 'He mentioned so many, he could have. Mr Jay, Louis may have been a Euro-crook, but he was a very small-time one. He could never have been a threat to anyone important.'

'Yet he was killed – and so was Richardson. Soon after his return from Brussels.'

'As you walk about Brussels – take a look around you; bomb-proofed glass, security men, the ever-present eye. These are the eighties, Mr Jay. Death by violence counts as natural causes.'

'Doesn't seem to be here, does he?' Chambers stepped into the bedsitting room and abruptly turned on the lights. The first thing to catch his eye was Henry's computer. He let out a long, soft whistle. 'Take a look at this!'

But Vine was busy, fiddling with the broken lock on the door which he'd kicked in just a minute before. 'That'll teach the black bastard for playing dumb,' he cursed the landlord. He walked across the living room to where the worn carpet met the kitchen linoleum. He opened the refrigerator, peered inside and slammed the door, opened the cupboards above the sink and slammed those too.

'Well-organised blighter, isn't he?' Chambers looked up from the computer. 'Report in, shall I? Just to keep Hendersly happy?' He moved towards the phone.

'No.' Vine's tone was sharp. Chambers shrugged.

'Look, what's this crap about you being supernumerary on this case? You're either on the murder squad or you're not,' Vine said.

'There's a good chance that Richardson was killed by our team, not theirs. Every time the wind blows down from the Fraud Squad there's been a nasty smell of late. My reckoning is that whatever's going on is so big it involves enough money to buy up not just one-off coppers but entire departments.'

'What are you getting at – that they can fork out for political clout to protect themselves as well?'

'Something like that.' Vine cracked open a tin of cold lager from the fridge and sucked the foam oozing across the can. 'We'll give Jay twenty-four hours. If he's not back, we report to Hendersly then.'

'Not to your people?' Chambers looked at him surprised.

'I want to see how Hendersly jumps. How badly he wants Jay back. How badly the people Hendersly reports to want him back.'

He dropped into the armchair and put his feet on the table pulling back his lager. Chambers gazed down at him, his eyes sliding from Vine's feet to his paunch. 'Love a weekend away,' he said longingly. 'Somewhere it doesn't smell of coppers' feet.'

Vine poked a face at him. 'Brrrr . . . it's as cold as a witch's tit in this dump. Wonder where he's stashed the heater?' He got up and rummaged about in the cupboard.

'Just the job,' he said extracting a battered single bar heater with a frayed cord. He plugged it in and returned to his seat. The silence between them lengthened. Chambers pulled out his pipe and began an elaborate cleaning and refilling process. Vine put his feet back on the table, tucked his hands behind his head and closed his eyes. Chambers puffed contentedly on his pipe. They settled into a routine of blissful somnolence. Vine's leg twitched involuntarily. He opened one eye and grinned at Chambers. 'Old war wound playing up again.'

Chambers grunted and continued to suck pensively on his now extinguished pipe.

'Only twenty-three more hours to go,' he said flatly.

'Mmmmm, I have to confess – I've got a bad dose of the munchies, but I don't share the same taste buds as Henry Jay.'

'Pity, because the Indian takeaways have shut up shop for the night,' replied Chambers glancing at his watch. It was nearly midnight.

'Yeah, but there must be plenty of greasy spoons around here; fancy a bite?'

'You make it sound bloody tantalising but I don't fancy either of us sitting here alone with that door swinging to and fro.'

'You have gone soft since you left the Met, Eric . . . All right. Tell you what we'll do. You get the nosh, I'll stay on guard here.'

'I shouldn't need to knock – you'll smell me coming.'

'Get outa here,' said Vine.

Vine gazed up at the ceiling. Somebody was coming up the

stairs. He lifted his bulky weight onto his feet without a sound and positioned himself behind the door, heard 'Meals on wheels!'

He relaxed and shoved aside the chair propped up under the door handle.

By the time Chambers and Vine had finished eating it was approaching one o'clock. Tiredness crept into their conversation and eventually they petered out. Vine got up to look for another drink, but there wasn't any lager left. He turned his attentions to the cupboards. Nothing drinkable anyway. He gave up the hunt and watched Chambers watching something through a crack in the curtains. 'See anything?'

'Just a couple of drunken coons.' Chambers jerked his head round. 'One of us should try to get some sleep – toss you.'

'Heads.'

'Tails,' said Chambers.

'I'll wake you in an hour,' said Vine, not entirely convinced with the verdict.

'Two.'

Chambers crashed out on the couch, falling asleep almost immediately. Two hours later, Vine shook him. 'Come on, you lazy bastard, on your feet.'

Mechanically he obeyed.

They took it in turns until the room was grey with dawn and the street noises made further sleep quite impossible. Chambers disappeared to the street below, returned with a great heap of newspapers. He read them all from cover to cover, indifferent to their contents. He spent a good deal of time walking up and down Henry's living room, running his hand through his hair and getting on Vine's nerves. Breakfast-time turned to lunch-time turned to supper-time. Eating was their only release from the interminable monotony.

'He's not going to show up.'

'Who?'

'Who! Henry Jay, our *raison d'être*,' spluttered Chambers.

Vine yawned and shoved the telephone at him. 'Right then. Let's take a chance on Hendersly.'

'Are you sure?' Chambers hesitated.

'No. But even I'm getting jumpy waiting for that door to open.'

Hendersly did not arrive until after nine o'clock; two hours after Chambers had phoned. They heard him clump up the stairs, two at a time. Chambers opened the door as soon as he knocked and felt Hendersly's disapproving eye scan his somewhat dishevelled appearance. He nodded acknowledgement at Vine and raised his eyebrows when he saw Henry's computer.

'We know where he is,' he said throwing the words at them with such rapidity that Chambers and Vine did not at first catch them. 'Henry, we've found Henry,' said Hendersly mistaking their blank faces for stupidity.

'Don't tell me – he's been in the staff canteen all this time and nobody thought to look.'

'He's in Brussels,' retorted Hendersly, humourlessly.

'I've been to Brussels,' said Vine reaching for his coat. 'They pull a good pint of Guinness in Brussels.'

'What are you doing?' said Hendersly, his voice a mixture of superiority and dislike.

'We'll be off then, now that it's known where he is.'

'I'm not a policeman and I can't give you orders, Mr Vine. But I think it might be wisest to assume that knowing where my Principal Scientific Officer is and laying hands on him may be two different things.'

'He's not been picked up?'

'There's a chance they'll get him on Sunday, but in the meantime he may well get back into this country and find his way here,' replied Hendersly smoothly.

Vine threw his coat over the chair and sat down.

'I think he should stay on with us, if only to represent the Departmental interest,' Hendersly said.

Chambers stared disconsolately, pulling at his ear.

'I'd forgotten how hard it was to kill time on this sort of job.'

Hendersly turned his head slowly and caught Chambers' eye.

'"There will be time, there will be time to prepare a face to meet the faces that you meet: There will be time to murder and create" – T. S. Eliot.'

He cocked his head at Chambers, smiled a superior smile, and left.

They waited until his footsteps had faded out before moving.

Chambers spoke.

'Anyone of the rank of Principal is a prat – T. A. Chambers . . . Did you cop that, representing Departmental interest? Crikey! You know what it's all about, don't you? It's to pay me back for ballsing it up over Henry.'

'And you thought we'd been so fucking smart when we tracked down Jay's hideaway address from that mini-cab driver. Now we're stuck with it.'

Vine gazed out the window.

'Does Hendersly's rank normally pull an official car and driver?'

'No, he's a tube and taxi wallah like the rest of us. Why do you ask?'

'Take a load of this –'

Chambers peered over Vine's shoulder and watched a black Vauxhall pull away from the kerb, Hendersly sitting in the back.

'Hell's teeth and buggy wheels,' said Chambers under his breath.

Vine sucked his lips, looked pensive. 'I think I know who's giving him his orders. I reckon I know who's pulling all our strings.'

Chapter Twelve

They ambled up Place Schumen, bundled up against the cold morning Brussels air. The street was deserted, the cafés closed and the offices unlit. It was Sunday. Henry and Hannah Brent walked side by side along the narrow pavement, staring ahead.

'Could you perhaps have discovered something, through your work in the Legal Department? Something that Louis could have blackmailed Jardine with?' Henry asked.

She gave him a withering look. He didn't notice.

'I'm a secretary,' she said as if that in itself was a sufficient explanation. Then added, 'I handle routine, boring paperwork – and I never talk about it after hours.'

Henry ploughed on. 'We know the system is riddled with fraud. In agriculture, dairy produce, in wine, in oil and so on. Inevitable, I suppose, where there are artificial price barriers and a corruptible non-accountable bureaucracy there will be fraud . . .'

'Fraud is often only a different way of interpreting regulations. But as I told you, Louis could have learned nothing from me to blackmail Jardine into helping him. I know absolutely nothing about Jardine.'

'You're not alone. There's not a lot on him on file. I borrowed – stole – some computer time from a commercial intelligence organisation. It came up with very little on him, apart from what's generally available, that is.'

'Perhaps Jardine is the wrong direction to look in,' suggested Hannah.

'And perhaps there are very good reasons why he should want the details kept as far as possible in that increasingly rare condition called private.'

They relapsed into silence again. It was nice being with her, Henry thought. She made him feel good, made it easy for him to talk to her. She wasn't strikingly pretty, but she pulled him to her with her saucer eyes. She was also extremely bright, had a good education built on street-cunning, it seemed to him. No wonder Louis Vacheron was so attracted to her. She was the first woman Henry had felt any tingle of excitement about, apart from Anne – and that was different. He wanted to reach down and kiss her but couldn't bring himself to. As if she'd perceived his thoughts, Hannah tucked her arm in his. He glimpsed her face. There was a hint of a smile forming on her lips. He tucked his elbow into his side, squeezing her arm. They walked on. Everything was relaxed and easy. Henry couldn't remember when he had felt so happy and carefree in somebody's company. Even though he thumped his questions out interminably, it was as if he was operating in an isolated pocket where reality did not exist and so it followed that danger didn't either.

They stopped for a beer, walked, cut through the centre of the city, passed the Palais Royale, stopped again for a meal. By then both had had enough. It was getting late.

'I don't know about you,' sighed Hannah, 'but I couldn't walk another centimetre.'

'I'll see you home,' said Henry.

She flagged down a taxi, and clambered in. Henry followed. 'Schaerbeek – Rue Albert de Latar,' she instructed the driver.

'You sure you won't come up?' she looked at him with her watery eyes. They were outside her flat, a low-rise block. She stood on the step, he was on the pavement, they stared at each other eye-to-eye, their warm breath visibly mingling in the early evening air. Henry swallowed.

'I have so enjoyed today, but no, thank you.' Now he couldn't take his eyes off her. He stared so hard without blinking the cold stung his eyes.

'I'll see what I come up with on this list of questions.'

'That would be very kind.'

'Anything to help you find out who killed Louis,' she said her gaze fixed on him. 'I enjoyed the day too, Henry . . . are you sure?' She invited him again.

He struggled with the temptation of such an offer, his expression confused with lust and embarrassment.

'You don't know what an extraordinary change the past few weeks, especially these past couple of days, have been in the pattern of my life. Perhaps I would find something further surprising about myself if I accepted the invitation.' He had thrown out a challenge – he wanted to go up to her flat, yet he didn't. He wanted her to accept on his behalf.

'It seems you will never know,' she whispered.

The moment was over. In a way, he was relieved.

'Tomorrow, then. Outside my office,' she said.

'Till then.'

She fumbled in her shoulder bag for her keys. 'Damn, I must have left them on the hall table,' she cursed. 'Will you hang on till the caretaker lets me in?' she asked, pressing the button to summon the caretaker.

'Of course,' he said. He cupped his hand around her neck, drew her to him and kissed her. Her lips were full and warm and moved against his passionately. He felt incredibly turned on and broke away. 'Oh dear,' he groaned with pleasure.

'Night, Henry. Sweet dreams.' The door buzzed, the lock clicked open and she went inside.

It took ages for him to find a taxi. He asked the driver to drop him off a couple of streets away from the hotel. He wanted to savour the night air and, more important, wanted to think about Hannah with a clear head. He was a quarter of a mile away from Hotel Amigo when a Honda sped up behind him and screeched to a halt. He turned swiftly. It was the night porter, the one he had paid off on his first night to let him know if anyone asked any questions, acted suspiciously. He walked back and got into the passenger seat.

'A raid,' said the night porter, who sported a thick handlebar moustache which twitched rabbit-like as he spoke. He reached into the back seat of the Honda and grabbed a brief-case. Yanked it into the front between them. Henry recognised it immediately. It was his.

'Thank you so much for this, for all your trouble.'

'Don't mention it.'

'How many police arrived?'

The porter seemed very certain. 'Five. They were a little special, these police. Very polite. Very discreet.'

'You got the case out before they arrived?'

'Yes.' The reception asked me because they couldn't find your key. I went straight to your room and got it then.' His voice was slurred with a French accent.

'Thanks.' Henry dipped into his pocket, shelled out a wad of rather crinkly Belgian francs which the man pocketed.

'You wish for an address?'

'No thanks,' said Henry. 'I should not like to put you in the embarrassing position of being asked if you would like to make two very large tips in one evening.'

His sarcasm escaped the night porter. He got out of the car and patted the rooftop. The Honda pulled away at speed. Henry turned and walked back the way he had just come. He felt shaken by what the porter had told him. Somebody had blown his cover. But who?

Outside the Hotel Amigo, a plainclothes policeman got into the back of the dark saloon, one of three cars parked in the forecourt. He crossed his arms and looked at the driver.

'Nothing. Not a trace of anything in his room,' he said in Flemish. Then in English he turned to his back-seat companion.

'Are you sure he didn't have a suitcase, or something when he was with you?'

Hannah Brent shook her head. 'Positive.'

'Then he's got a friend. The receptionist and the lift boy swear he hadn't been back since he went out with you.'

She shook her head again. The car purred slowly out into the street, passed the night porter driving towards the hotel.

Henry arrived breathless and sweaty. Hannah had arrived before him and sat, drinking a fruit cocktail through a long straw at the airport bar. She looked calm and businesslike in her dark red suit. Henry caught his breath and gushed.

'I'm sorry I'm late, the queues at the check-out were so long. I gave up in the end.' He pointed to his suitcase and briefcase by his side. 'And thanks for coming to the airport,' he added.

'I wanted to. By the way, it'll take some days to get the records of Jardine's expenses claims. His off-shore business interests and connections will take longer.'

'I really can't stay,' Henry said, popping a peanut from a small bowl on the bar into his mouth.

She put down her drink and rested her hand on his. She said, 'Not even for a few days?'

He looked at her miserably and shook his head.

'I did enjoy our walk yesterday, and the meal,' Hannah said.

'So did I. It will be strange going back. I suppose I will miss you . . . you may have my address in London, provided you're not taping everything we say.'

'Hannah shifted her hand, slipped it inside his coat, around his waist. 'I wanted a record of our meetings. In case anything happens to you.'

He nodded and gazed at her.

'There were police in my hotel room last night, after I met you,' Henry spoke evenly.

'You've obviously upset some important people . . .'

The rest of her conversation was drowned out by the high-pitched monologue over the intercom, announcing his London flight.

'I have to go,' he said and stood.

She walked beside him towards the departure lounge, her arm linked in his. He would miss her, in a few short days he felt as if he had grown quite close to her. They stopped at the bookstall and faced each other. She laughed and said, 'Come on you old duffer, don't look so mopey!'

'Tell me, is my French up to Commission staff standards if I want a job here, when all this blows over?'

She looked at him mockingly. 'You've hardly used any. The Englishman abroad, convinced that all foreign languages are indecent, or even worse, silly.'

He jutted out his chin and began reciting.

'Hibou et minou allèrent à la mer dans une barque peinte en jaune-canari. Ils prirent du miel roux et beacoup de sous . . .'

'*The Owl and the Pussycat!*' she trilled.

'Yes, do you know it?'

'Not in French. But it's very charming.'

Her words came at him like a massive body blow. His mouth hung open, his eyes fixed like rivets on her.

'Oh, my God. You should know if you're who you claim to be. It was the code which would tell Louis' girlfriend who it was safe to talk to.'

Her face gave her away, but he was no longer conscious of her expression. With a sharp push he knocked her against a revolving book stand and ran off, his suitcase colliding with a trolley as he made for the exit. He scoured the line of waiting cars. He spotted the silver Honda and ran. The night porter saw him. By the time Henry had flopped into the passenger seat and before he could even close the door, the car was speeding along the road. The porter looked at him and frowned. 'Whatever line you're in, sir, dirty books, smuggling or diplomacy, may I suggest you take a course of exercise before you come abroad again.'

'I've seen enough of abroad, thank you very much,' said Henry breathlessly. 'Have you got a cigarette?'

The hotel porter tossed him a packet of Gauloise and a box of matches. Henry held the cigarette in his pursed lips, tried to light it with a shaking hand. It was his first cigarette for over twenty years. He sucked deeply and coughed.

'You can't trust anyone at home, but at least you can buy a decent cigarette.' The porter smirked.

'Why you? It's hardly your style,' said Anne, contemptuously. I would have thought you'd prefer to rustle up a couple of plainclothes policemen to give me a hard time.'

Hendersly had arrived at Anne's house late that evening, just as she was about to spend the evening kneading some clay. Since Henry had left sleep had eluded her and she found pottery a soothing, if not a mindless occupation to distil her fears. He wanted to know if Henry had phoned, seemed mollified when she jumped down his throat, accusing him of already knowing the answer since the phone was probably tapped. He insisted that he stayed – the night, longer if necessary – until Henry contacted her. He felt that perhaps his presence would be of comfort to her. He said he understood what it must be like, to be alone in a house at night, wondering if Henry was all right and fearing for her own safety. She told him not to be patronising, that she had coped perfectly well up until now and would continue to do so, however long that might be. He made her feel uncomfortable; after all, Hendersly was her husband's boss. But he was insistent. He said he had no way of getting back to town at that hour of night and that if he didn't wait, somebody else would be sent, he was no more a free agent in this affair than any of his colleagues since Henry had set more more wheels in motion that he ever dreamed of.

'It's settled then?'

'I suppose I shall have to grin and bear it,' she said reluctantly.

'I'll get you a couple of blankets from upstairs; you can sleep on the couch – at least you'll be able to hear the phone ring, perhaps you could even answer it, save waking me up . . .' She stormed out of the living room before he had a chance to retort. When she returned with the blankets and a pillow he leapt to his feet and tried to take them from her.

'Allow me –'

'I'm perfectly capable of handling them myself. I have carried heavier things than woolly blankets in my time, Mr Hendersly.'

'Can't we at least talk pleasantly to each other for the duration? I'm sure we must have many things in common – Henry, for starters.'

She stared at him coldly, wishing the blankets back upstairs and Hendersly out of the house.

'I don't think we need speak to each other at all. I shall be working at the back of the house, when I've completed that I shall take a bath and then I shall go to bed. I would not wish you to talk to me in any one of those locations, with respect.'

'I see.' Hendersly bit his lip. They stood facing each other awkwardly. 'Tell me one thing – do you understand fully what Henry is involved with, what he's doing?'

'I do not wish to understand, I don't know where he is. I just know that I want him back safely here and for us to get on with our lives, unimpeded by the police or your Department, not threatened with violence.'

'Believe me when I tell you, Mrs Jay, that that is exactly what we are working towards.'

Anne snorted disbelievingly. 'If you'll excuse me – I've got some clay laid out, I don't want it to dry up.'

She worked until the early hours of the morning, kneading and cutting the clay and placing the fist-sized balls into moist plastic bags. Her hands were coated with a thick film of clay which had dried and cracked. Her hair was matted where she had brushed it away from her eyes with the back of her hand. Her eyes stung from the strain of working under the dull yellow light which cast long shadows across the marble bench. She washed her hands under the kitchen tap, dried them on a tea towel and crept through the darkened hallway.

'Mr Hendersly.' she whispered through the door. She heard his soft breathing. 'Are you asleep?' No answer. It must be one of the stupidest questions I've ever asked, she thought as she ascended the stairs.

A hot, sudsy bath and two sleeping tablets later Anne lay wide-eyed in bed. A host of questions flooded her mind for which she could find no satisfactory answers. Why Hendersly should take on the task of waiting for Henry to phone her puzzled and concerned her. Surely it was too demeaning a role for someone of his seniority? Who had issued the instructions? Someone in Whitehall? If that was the case – how high up the hierarchical ladder did the interest in Henry Jay extend? One thing was certain. They knew where Henry was and expected him to return, soon. They were determined not to let him slip through their fingers this time. And there was no way she could warn him. She was totally dependent on him phoning her; by then, it might be too late. If Richardson's killers didn't get him, the Department would.

But why were they so keen, taking such inordinate steps to return him to the fold? At first, she'd contemplated Henry's predicament, her own even, with utter disbelief. Then, as it sank in, a calm despair had taken over. But whatever he was doing now, wherever he was, Anne knew that they couldn't destroy the qualities inbred in him; for all his faults Henry was courageous, honest . . . and loyal. And knowing that kept her sane when all else failed.

'He phoned.'

'Mmmm?' Hendersly rubbed the sleep from his eyes.

'He wants you to meet him. Not because he trusts you. Because if anyone's to be shot alongside him he wants it to be you – who got him into this trouble.' Her voice was bitter. She looked down at him, at his face creased with the texture of the couch, his lank blond hair, usually greased back, hung around his ears. She disliked his face – his eyes were too close together for a start. She'd been warned once never to trust men with light blue eyes rimmed by dark blue; Hendersly had eyes like that.

'Did he say where?'

'Of course. You'll find the instructions on a pad by the phone in the hall – on your way out.'

'Thank you, Mrs Jay,' said Hendersly civilly as she swung around and walked out. He tried standing, his leg gave way. Damn! That's what comes from curling up on a couch in Westcombe Park in October, he berated himself. He wrapped the blanket round his waist and tried again. That was when he noticed it. A large, ugly man with pig-eyes and a sardonic smile with over-size ears. It was Anne's caricature drawing of him.

Chapter Thirteen

Henry Jay slouched in the vinyl chair in the barren waiting room of the Department of Commercial Development's administration block and said in a tired voice, 'Mr Hendersly, don't you think this is all a bit futile when I've already been interrogated by Special Branch?'

'They've interrogated you; we'll be debriefing you.'

'I fail to see the difference.' He got up and stood by the window. He could see the Founder's Arms where once – a lifetime ago – he and Richardson had exchanged information over a pint of beer. He spied a helicopter lying idle like a dozing dragonfly on the heliport barge and remembered the day when Richardson stood him up and he'd returned to find him waiting in the office, with Tomkins. Poor Richardson. Dear old Tomkins, no doubt thriving like a hot-house plant.

'Well, might as well feed myself to the lions now as any other time.' His voice was empty. He seemed incapable of projecting any unqualified emotion. He walked down the corridor to the Principal Establishment Officer's door and knocked. He looked back and saw Hendersly's eyes still fixed upon him.

He entered.

The room was dark, except for a cone of light which streamed from a slide projector at the far end of the room. When his eyes adjusted to the dark he noticed someone beckoning him to sit down beside him at the back of the room. The carousel on the projector whined, jerkily dropping a slide into the path of the light.

'What on –'

'Shhh,' said the man, the Principal Establishment Officer, Mr Bridgnorth, Henry presumed. They sat in adjacent chairs, one on each side of the projector, in silence and stared ahead at the screen. Black and white scenes of bloodied corpses, bombed buildings, close-ups of grotesque murders. Henry recognised some of the victims – Italian politicians.

Eventually, a thick, North-country voice cut across the incessant hum of the projector.

'All very well these political chaps getting together to lower the barriers, Henry, but apart from those horrible bloody French apples, there's one or two exports we British could do without . . . the German sense of the ridiculous, the Irish gift for mechanical engineering and the quiet pace of public life in Italy. There's no one these people can't get to – former Prime Ministers, Heads of Prison Security, the police, the army, business and the civil service. I take a special interest in Italian intelligence, see. And together with their better wines, they're now exporting this.' A thick black silhouette of a finger appeared on the screen like a giant mortar shell. The carousel moved on. Henry's jaw dropped when he saw the blow-up shot on the screen – of himself with Hannah Brent in Brussels.

'You lot were tagging me there?'

'Looks like it, doesn't it.'

'She's one of your team, isn't she? I thought so, but couldn't be sure.'

'Why didn't you drop Louis Vacheron's rhyme and check her out straight away?'

'I suppose I was afraid she'd fail it. Sounds stupid now, but then I was hoping against hope to find some way out of the maze – I had to play along, to pick up any lead.' Henry paused. 'How did you know I was going to approach her?'

'Simple. You tripped a wire on computer security when you tried to get her records.'

Through the murky light Henry saw his face. He was ageless, looking to Henry, like a large blancmange, studded with a confectionary of closely-set features set off by thick, dark eyebrows. Bridgnorth looked impassively ahead. 'You'll want to know what this is all about – I don't blame you. I think I can give you a pretty clear picture.'

Henry didn't reply – it had just dawned on him they knew all along he had a computer; Hannah Brent was one of his first enquiries. How many more security wires had he 'tripped' he wondered. He would ask about that later. Right now there were other, more important issues to delve into.

'Where is the real Hannah Brent, since the woman taunting me on the screen is patently a fake?'

'In the foundation of a Brussels office block, most likely,' Bridgnorth answered coolly.

'Since you were so hot off the mark, why didn't you grab me earlier. Why play it so delicately?'

The fluorescent lighting above cracked and flickered.

'Why don't you let me answer that, Mr Bridgnorth?' It was a woman's voice. Henry blinked in the full light. It was Hannah Brent, or the woman purporting to be her.

'You!' Henry stammered.

'Yes. Me,' she smiled pertly. 'We played it delicately, to use your word, to find out how much you knew. And because the Belgians tend to be touchier than most about foreign nationals committing official mayhem on the streets.'

'Lots of history in Belgium. Lots of war graves,' said Bridgnorth darkly.

Henry and the girl contemplated each other for several minutes, without speaking, while Bridgnorth fiddled about with the projector. Their expressions were immobile but it was clear that both of them were casting their minds back to their days together in Brussels. Bridgnorth looked around and smiled, almost benignly. 'Come on, let's go into the next room for some tea.'

As the astonishing evidence unrolled itself, Henry could barely believe Bridgnorth was being so candid with him.

'We have to assume that the real Hannah Brent found something on Jardine in the Legal Department files of the Commission. The Italbank fraud – which her boyfriend was arrested for – had nothing to do with Jardine, but Vacheron boasted that once he got to Italy the Power would get him off. He was ecstatic when he heard he was going to be tried in Turin and not here and small wonder. The Power, he assumed, would use his blackmail of Jardine.'

Bridgnorth paused to sip his tea.

Henry jumped in.

'Then the Power really does exist? Who did it use to kill Vacheron and Richardson?'

'Does that matter, Henry?'

'In that it may try to kill me too, yes. Very much.'

'The Power,' said Bridgnorth sounding as if he were launching into a political lecture, 'is more a loose federation of people who temporarily find it an advantage to work with each other, repay each other for favours past or future, than a solid structure –'

'I gathered as much from Richardson. That's what makes it so dangerous.'

Bridgnorth set down his cup and looked patiently at Henry. 'I'm not sure I can explain . . . there's a grey area in this sort of business,' he began. 'Terrorism shades into organised crime, into police undercover operations, into how the state security apparatus responds to the havoc that small, mobile, internationally-minded crooks and politicos have been creating since the sixties – especially here in Europe.' He stopped to catch his breath. 'Asking questions of anyone is unlikely to produce an answer – many of them aren't in a position to know. Even those who did the killing might be unaware which favour they were repaying to whom.'

Henry's face crinkled into a baffled frown. 'You're saying that on the one hand Richardson and Vacheron may have been killed by ordinary, decent criminals? Or on the other, they were killed – and my life is threatened – by people in the police or security services?'

'It's a grey area, as I say,' said Bridgnorth flatly. His reluctance to be drawn was apparent, but Henry badly wanted him to answer one more question. He asked.

'Give me one grey hint, then. What's Jardine involved with?'

'Security – he's working with us,' said Bridgnorth looking at the girl Henry only knew as Hannah. 'And you and Richardson the past couple of weeks have been trying damned hard to get his cover exposed and get him killed.'

The tightly-sprung coils in Henry's chest played havoc with his breathing. He felt such a fool for having been so easily duped by this woman, for having allowed himself to fall for her charms. It was a cruel deception, one which made him feel especially vulnerable as he sat uncomfortably in the room. Having been tricked once, he was uncertain now how to react to the welter of information being passed to him by Bridgnorth.

Like a conjurer bringing on his next act, Bridgnorth wheeled a movie projector in front of Henry who had to tuck his legs beneath the seat to avoid being crushed asunder. Bridgnorth tinkered about with the ancient equipment, pushed knobs, flicked switches, huffed and puffed until, at last, he raised his head and gave a nod. The room plunged into darkness, the film began its countdown, then suddenly the screen was a wash of colour; surging rioters, masked police, water cannon, rubber bullets, flying bottles and stones. The film cut abruptly to another scene, to a man being gunned down in a hail of bullets. The camera closed in on the man's face, he was still alive, pleading. The film rolled on. One violent scene stacked on another, made all the more hypnotic for the lack of sound, save for the clack-clack of the projector – and Bridgnorth's voice.

'What are we seeing – isolated violence, or the destabilisation of an entire continent?' Bridgnorth addressed his small audience. 'I'm not one of the college of cardinals upstairs, thank God; I don't have to bother my head with theory and counter-theory. I'm just a desk man with a case load, and responsibility for Jardine's cover.'

Somebody grunted in the dark. Bridgnorth was, in fact, quite senior in the Department, he reported directly to the Permanent Secretary, liaised with every security man known in Whitehall, and a few outside who weren't. His North-country gruffness masked a complex, talented man, with a mind racier than his speech – and he capitalised on his deceptive appearance.

The screen flickered on to another grotesque murder – a political assassination in Italy. Bridgnorth continued with his commentary.

'The tactical bases are outside Italy, so are the strategic

and propaganda people, for the most part. Not West Germany, mainly because our black leather-jacketed friends have locked it up tight after Baader Meinhof. Libya, perhaps. But more likely only as an arms dump and training facility. Belgium – too small. Holland – too boring, and France – who'd trust the French? So it has to be here. This is where they run the show from.'

The film spluttered to an end and flapped noisily in the darkness. A chair crashed to the floor as someone moved. 'Shit,' said Hannah as she fumbled for the light switch.

Henry rose to stretch his legs. The darkness had made him forget it was still day. He stood, leaning up against a desk and observed Hannah's face. He wondered what her real name was and why they hadn't told him when they had been so frank about other issues. She looked hard in the artificial light, her broad jaw gave her a common look, her lips were pursed. She must have felt his eyes on her because she looked up at him. He turned his glance quickly towards Hendersly who had begun to speak.

'. . . and the department, at very senior level, agreed to provide Jardine with cover,' he said in his clipped business voice. 'That meant he had to compromise himself in order to attract attention from these people, who would find his ease of travel across Europe and entrée to industry and politics invaluable. Vacherон's girlfriend obviously learnt some details of the paper frauds Jardine was implicated in.'

Bridgnorth stared up at Hendersly, irritated. 'Come on, man. They weren't *all* paper frauds. Level with the man, for Christ's sake.'

Hendersly coughed into his hand. 'No, they weren't. Some were very irregular arrangements made with the Fraud Squad. Well, you could appreciate the Department's embarrassment, to say the least, if any of this became public.'

Bridgnorth took up the story. 'That's why we took such pains to sanitise the files, Henry. No one guessed – or I wasn't informed if they did – that you would get your teeth into the rug, despite being told to let go.' His eyes never once left Hendersly's face, although it was to Henry he spoke.

'Well, it was my file that was tampered with . . .'

'Henry, let's not go into all that again, please,' said Hendersly with a hint of exasperation in his voice.

They didn't get back from lunch until after three o'clock. The woman thinly-disguised as Hannah Brent went off to 'powder her nose'. Henry followed Bridgnorth and Hendersly down the corridor, past the office Bridgnorth had used as the projection room and into a cluttered office. It was ten feet by fifteen feet but looked much smaller – books were stacked everywhere; on shelves which teetered against all four walls. There were huge, grey filing cabinets with documents piled three feet high, a desk coated with papers, reference books, paper clips and school photographs of two scruffy boys. Henry guessed they belonged to Bridgnorth.

'Take a seat,' said Bridgnorth waving his arm airily about the room. Henry looked at the mountain of papers on the two 'spare' chairs, bent over and carefully scooped the pile into his arms. He looked desperately for a place to drop them. Bridgnorth was engrossed in a search of his own, ruffling through his desk in search of something or another. Surreptitiously, Henry sandwiched his load between the chair and a filing cabinet and sat down. Hendersly followed suit, reluctantly.

'Ah ha!' Bridgnorth pounced on his catch, a large brown envelope, as if there was a chance it would attempt an escape.

'Take a look at these photographs, Henry, they might interest you.'

What he saw made his mind flip. Richardson's corpse laid out in the mortuary. He turned his head away and nodded unhappily.

'He was killed by the Italian security services, wasn't he? Or by someone acting for them?'

Bridgnorth tossed the photographs on his desk and shrugged.

'You'll never get an answer to that. Nor would I, if I asked. I'm just thankful someone's determined enough to save Jardine's neck and cover.'

'I'm afraid I can't share that feeling – if only because, briefly, I knew Richardson and I've never met Jardine.' He gazed stoically ahead. Seeing Richardson's dead body had upset him more than he dared show.

'Am I still in danger, by the way?'

'No.'

'You sound very positive.'

'I am.'

'How can you be?'

'With any luck, Henry, you'll subside to your normal state of happy anonymity. Another grey face on the eight-fifteen or whatever to Blackfriars.' Bridgnorth smiled. 'And wouldn't you prefer it?'

'All I want to do, Mr Bridgnorth, is get back to my desk after my special leave and try to recover my lost ground. I've probably already lost out to Harry Tomkins in the promotions stakes. This sort of life just isn't for me; living out of suitcases, having to hide from people . . .'

'Speaking of Tomkins,' Hendersly interjected. 'I had him check the office to see if Richardson brought anything for you that day.'

'What should he bring me?'

'Perhaps a file?'

'No file,' said Henry. He had an inherent dislike of Hendersly and it hadn't been lessened by the way he'd suddenly taken him into his confidence. Bridgnorth sensed the animosity between them and stepped in.

'Henry, you mentioned some clippings in Brussels – containing references to Hugo Jardine's business interests.'

'Oh, those. Yes, there was an envelope of odds and ends in my out-tray.'

He could see Hendersly's jaw grinding and realised how easily he was irritated.

'Richardson died delivering those odds and ends,' Hendersly said in a caustic tone.

'I destroyed them. I panicked in Brussels – tore them up and scattered them. Of course, I'm sure a newspaper office or an agency would have them on file if–'

'It's all right. We just wanted to account for the file you had,' said Hendersly catching Bridgnorth's eye.

'I see,' Henry sighed. 'I suppose it was a sort of gesture for Richardson, the way I got rid of them.'

'What do you mean?'

'Richardson had been to Brussels too, hadn't he? Before he came to my office where he was hunted down. He'd gone to see Hannah Brent too.' Bridgnorth dived for the phone. 'Get up here – right away, will you?'

The meeting was almost at an end. Henry couldn't bear listening to her any longer.

'You all killed Richardson – you in particular,' he stabbed his finger at the girl. 'You let him get back from Brussels to be hunted down. So that you could find out what other contacts he'd made. Even if you knew the Italians were going to kill him you wouldn't have interfered . . .'

Bridgnorth's face turned to granite. 'Take your clerk home, Hendersly.'

But Henry was nearly hysterical with rage and would not budge. 'You listened to what Richardson asked you in Brussels, you told him a pack of lies, you didn't tell him he was compromising a security operation.'

His voice had reached such a crescendo it was almost inaudible. His cheeks and neck were flushed, his hands clenched angrily by his side. The girl backed away toward Bridgnorth, gazing uncertainly at Henry.

'Get him out of here!' yelled Bridgnorth. 'If we were, *perhaps*, responsible for Richardson meeting his maker, *you* could have sunk Jardine – and with him a four-year-old operation that too many people have risked their lives setting up. Get out of here, civilian,' he spat the words out contemptuously. 'Just get out. This is where the dirty work gets done – dirty work that means people like you can safely get the eight-fifteen every morning and lead boring little lives. Be thankful for your fucking eight-fifteen. Be grateful for your boring little life. And for the fact we let you go back to it, in one piece, or at all.' His eyes were fixed and blazing. The look had a threatening air.

'All the same . . . you could have saved him.' Henry's voice was pitted with anguish.

Chapter Fourteen

They drove straight to Westcombe Park, staring solemnly ahead all the way. Anne was waiting for him on the porch as the car pulled in. 'Welcome home, darling,' she said, almost shyly. They hugged, their bodies pressed close to each other. He felt her warmth, smelled the soft mixture of perfume and oil paint. He noticed the sleekness of her long brown hair, the creaminess of her skin. Each one of his senses was perceived in a single moment; overwhelming him with their intensity. He desired her so much. Smiling at him she pulled back.

'Come inside, Henry – before you change your mind.' They grinned happily at each other. She looked sideways, said, 'And perhaps I should say welcome back to you too, Mr Hendersly.'

Henry picked up his suitcase and led the way into the kitchen.

'Tea, or coffee, anyone?' Anne asked.

'Tea sounds wonderful,' said Hendersly, gratefully.

'Me too, love," said Henry, hanging his coat in the cupboard under the stairs.

'I didn't expect you back so early, the central heating hasn't quite taken the chill out of the front room yet. Do you mind having tea in the studio – it's the only warm room in the house?'

The two men nodded. They stood watching her rummage through the cupboards, fill the tray with the best china cups and saucers, milk jug, tea-pot and spoons. It was her way of avoiding a conversation for as long as possible, until she and Henry were alone.

'Never thought you'd be so pleased to see home eh, Henry?'

The question, a genuine attempt by Hendersly to be cheerful, met with a silent nod from Henry and a cup of tea from Anne.

'Nice painting, Mrs Jay,' said Hendersly bending over a canvas propped against the easel in the studio. 'English landscape?'

'Seascape, actually.'

'Oh. Very good it is too.'

They sipped their tea.

Nobody said anything much. Anne and Henry exchanged fond glances. Hendersly's eyes swept round the room, not knowing where to rest. Then, without any warning, Henry stood up and grabbed the cup from Hendersly's hand. 'Will you get out of my house? Now . . . Please?'

There was an awkward silence. Hendersly stifled an indignant protestation and looked, interrogatively first at Henry, then at Anne. She nodded, indicating he should leave.

'Well, I suppose I'd better be making tracks, leave you two to catch up on all the news,' he said as though he was the originator of his departure.

'Thank you for bringing Henry home,' said Anne walking towards the door. Hendersly smiled thinly and turned to shake hands with Henry. He could not catch his eye. Muffling the rebuff by slipping his hands into his pockets he left the room.

'Thank you again, Mr Hendersly,' she said without feeling and closed the door behind him.

'I understand totally, Henry,' said Anne clasping her arms around his large frame. 'I don't take to your Mr Hendersly much myself.'

They stood for ages, intertwined. Minutes passed. Henry felt the sensation of his finger-tips as he moved his hands under her jumper up her back. He sighed deeply and kissed her passionately on the lips.

'Oh, Henry, it's so good to have you back,' she said. 'For all I know, you're probably a great hero and I'll be complaining next week about polishing all your medals . . . or maybe you've just been my same old Henry, plodding along, following your nose, anxious about your files. Either way – you're back and we can start all over again.'

Henry didn't answer. He took her hands and squeezed them gently. It was true, he was still one of life's plodders. But instead of going about his life mindlessly, his thoughts and actions pressed into a mould which turned out habits, he discovered that by not doing what was expected of him he had created a new awareness within himself; he didn't quite know how. It was as if someone had lifted a hood from his face, gloves from his hands and he could touch, see, hear, taste and think more acutely than ever. He had changed. It excited him, invigorated him, sometimes terrified him.

'Henry, what is it? What are you thinking?'

'I don't really know how to say it, except that even though I love you and want to be back, I can't. Not yet, anyway.'

She yanked her hands free of his. 'Why ever not?'

'Because they're still lying to me.'

'What difference does that make?' Her stare was fierce and direct, a mask which covered her confusion and alarm.

'This could be the time when you stop believing me, Anne. When your patience and maybe your love for me run out.'

Her voice softened. 'Let's talk about it. Over a sherry?'

He nodded. She disappeared into the living room. He heard the clink of glasses, the decanter top roll in circles on the side-board and noted the generous serving of sherry when she handed him his glass.

He waited until she sat down beside him at the kitchen table. Then he spoke. 'They figured out everything they thought I knew – pooled all the odds and ends and bits of pieces and came up with a story – I can't give you all the details but it involves one of the many branches of security and intelligence claiming Jardine for their own.'

'And they're lying?'

'Yes.'

'Is that all they've lied to you about?'

'I can't tell for certain; it's the only thing I'm pretty certain about.'

'Well, maybe they had good reason to hide the truth from you, national security at stake and all that.'

'I don't know the reason for them lying – perhaps it could be that Jardine's fraud is so big that part of security is bound up in it. But I've got to clear that file.'

'For God's sake!' she hissed. 'Get things into perspective. If they lied to you – and you don't have documentary proof of that – perhaps it was to allow you to come home; they could just as easily get rid of you like they got rid of Richardson.'

He looked at her thoughtfully. 'They won't do that. Not yet. They know Richardson got an envelope to me, implicating Jardine. They suspect I might not have destroyed it – I told them I had. I also said they were only news clippings which isn't entirely true, and I don't think they bought that either.'

'Have you destroyed the envelope and its contents?'

She watched him go to the pile of mail by the telephone in the hallway and sort through it. He returned with a large envelope with Belgian stamps. 'In the age of electronic surveillance, the postal package can be under-valued as a communication tool. My report on computer fraud.' He leaned over and kissed her on the forehead.

'Give me an hour or two clear. This time, it's open season on me. And anyone who has anything to do with me.'

He lowered his eyes to meet the desperation on her face.

'You've only just got here,' she said. 'You can't leave just yet. At least stay the night can't you?'

He eyed her gravely. 'That would give them a real head-start. No, I've got to go now.'

'But why? Why even go at all?'

'I can't tell you why, I can't explain. Not even to myself most of the time. People spend years with shrinks trying to understand *why* they do things and rarely come up with an answer. I just know that while my life is in danger I'm living now as I've never done before. You've always gone on about me being a plodder, being boring old Henry. I've seen myself in a way I've never seen before. It's a very powerful feeling Anne. Like I have a total grip on things. Do you understand what I mean?'

She smiled at him sadly. 'I don't want you to leave, I'm tired and I'm frightened and I miss you desperately. But I can't stop you, so I'll back you all the way.'

He felt moved, close to tears.

'Darling, I can't tell you how much that means to me. Thank you.' He kissed her passionately, tasting the lingering sweetness of sherry on her tongue.

He stood over her for a moment. He didn't move, or speak. She looked into his fatigue-stained eyes. He squeezed her shoulder fondly, smiled, then sat back on his chair.

'Will you do me a favour?' he said.

'What?'

'I need all the cash we have, our credit and banking cards.'

'No way. I'm not going to sit round here starving while you're gallivanting off somewhere with all our money.'

'Please! Keep one back for your own use. But I need the rest.' His voice was grim.

She sighed. 'Talk about wading straight in. You're incorrigible.'

Tony Chambers glanced up at the windows and grimaced. He was heartily sick of the place, he hated Drummond Street, he despised the small bedsit with an unprecedented loathing and Vine was getting on his nerves. Today, to relieve the boredom of Kentucky Fried Chicken, hamburgers and Indian curries, he'd splashed out on a Chinese takeaway; spring rolls, chop suey, beef with ginger, crab and spring onions, fried rice, the works. This'll keep Vine's jaws moving and his vocal chords silent long enough to give me peace and quiet, he mused as he turned the key to the main door. He trudged up the stairs, casting his hand through his trouser pocket for the key to the bedsit. He found it tangled up with a cash receipt. He opened the door (thanks to Vine a new lock had been fitted the day after they arrived which eased his nerves considerably). He placed the paper bag with the food on the table beside Henry's computer and stared down at the receipt. 'Here's something useful next time you're going through someone's pockets or handbag, Eric. I never noticed before – this has got the time and date on it –'

He jerked his head round to see Vine spread out on the couch, his head slumped over the edge. There was a lot of blood round his neck. Vine was dead. Chambers felt his stomach contract, the saliva withdraw from his mouth. He retched. He couldn't move, his feet wouldn't take him forward to Vine's body.

'Don't turn round, just move a little to your left Mr Jay.'

The voice behind him was slow, monotone and Italian.

Chambers had no time to protest, not even to step sideways. With a single bullet squeezed through the gun's silencer, Chambers fell, his head crashing across the computer keyboard.

With a sharp 'click' the video screen lit up. 'Enter password.'

Bridgnorth could hear his own heart pumping a heavy beat. He had come as soon as he could – when Chambers hadn't phoned in as usual after lunch he began thinking perhaps something had gone wrong. He tried phoning, but there was no answer. So he came straight over . . . to find this. Bridgnorth took a couple of steps towards Chambers. There was no movement, not even the rise and fall of breathing. It had been a comparatively clean kill; he comforted himself that Chambers would have felt nothing. He turned to Vine. The assassin had not found him so easy a target. There were two bullet holes, one in Vine's neck, the other through his head. A small calibre weapon had drained the lives of both men and the killer had walked quietly away. His hand trembled involuntarily as he lifted the telephone receiver. He cleared his throat and took several deep breaths as he dialled.

' . . . Purley please . . . Removals and renovations.'

Tomkins glanced up at the clock on the wall. Nine forty-five. He chewed his bottom lip and brushed his hand over his shiny dome. Tomkins was trying to pluck up the courage to see Hendersly in his office; so far he'd wasted thirty-five minutes nervously standing up, sitting down, fiddling with the stapler, walking around the office. Before his nerve failed him he jumped up and marched across the corridor, his chest pounding. He knocked and entered. But Hendersly wasn't at his desk. Deflated, he ambled back to his room kicking his briefcase out of the way.

Bridgnorth walked up the corridor briskly and popped his head around the corner. Tomkins met his glance.

'Fetch us a mug of tea will you – there's a good lad,' said Bridgnorth jovially. He walked straight to Hendersly's door and entered without knocking. Tomkins sat fuming. He wagged his head and mimicked 'there's a good lad,' as he sloped off to the drink machine on the next floor. Bridgnorth was a chameleon character – jolly, when it suited him, sour, gruff, conniving, pleasant, witty, foul-mouthed, you could never tell from one day to the next what mood he'd be in, Tomkins grumbled. Fortunately, he had only ever met him twice before in his life – on both occasions Bridgnorth had assumed a paternalistic role.

Hendersly tweaked his tie nervously. His eyes swam about the room, resting finally on Bridgnorth who stood, leaning over his desk.

'. . . the wise man operates on the assumption that all you can expect is the unpredictable. Therefore there's no way I could have planned for this, but I'm sorry to make cryptic early morning phone calls all the same. I like a quiet life myself,' he said looking eye-ball to eye-ball at Hendersly. 'No questions. I have things to attend to in my section; you must see that Chambers is booked out for two weeks' special leave starting this morning. Make sure that's done. If the police at local level start asking where Vine is, tell them it's a top security matter and refer them to me. I'll arrange other cover. Got it? Excellent. We understand each other well . . .'

'Cover for what?' asked Hendersly curtly.

'Didn't I tell you on the phone? Could have sworn I did . . . Vine and Chambers have been shot, dead. While they were waiting for Henry Jay in the bedsit. Foreigners? You can't trust them.'

Hendersly's face drained to an unhealthy shade of white, his eyes blinked rapidly. 'Your procedures in your division may well be designed to cover this sort of thing –'

'Yes, you wouldn't believe the paperwork, just to tidy up a rented room –'

'– but mine aren't,' continued Hendersly fiercely. 'I have to take this higher. I have to get authority.'

'*I* am giving you the authority. It's *you* this thing is being handled through in the Department, Hendersly. You're line management on this.'

'Not even my superiors can be told, on the need-to-know basis?'

'Precisely. Now where's that boy with the tea?'

Hendersly stretched his arms behind his head and sat back. 'I have broken just about every rule of Civil Service and departmental security in this affair, *Charlie*. I have compromised my career to help you and the Security service protect Hugo Jardine, whom you advise me is risking his life in a drawn-out and elaborate intelligence operation. On the need-to-know basis, I have only had contact with yourself, *Charlie*.'

He paused to allow the last point to take effect. 'As this operation staggers from one blunder to the next, from the death of Richardson and the hounding of Jay, to the murder of yet another policeman and my Departmental security adviser I have kept my head down, convinced that you know what you are doing. Now I'm not so sure. And even more serious. I question just who it is I'm ultimately working for, and to where your loyalties truly lie.' His voice was even and calculated but his eyes blazed in anger. He felt the muscles at the side of his mouth twitch. Bridgnorth shook his head sadly and straightened his back.

'You're doing exactly what your PSO Jay did, do you

know that? Lifting your head off the desk, worrying over what's not your concern. I'm surprised at you. You know better than anyone the poundage per square inch pressure that was put on Jay when he did that.'

There was a knock at the door. Bridgnorth pivoted around to see Tomkins standing there with a mug of tea in his hands. Hendersly gave him a strange look. Tomkins rolled his eyes in embarrassment. He set the tea down on the desk and hovered.

'You look a worrier, son. Worriers don't get on. It's them that causes the worry that gets on,' said Bridgnorth playing up his North-country accent.

Tomkins ignored the remark. 'Did Mr Jay leave a forwarding address?' he asked Hendersly softly. 'I called him this morning, to see how he was, to tell him I had some stamp club stuff for him. Has he gone off on holiday, or something?'

Bridgnorth looked warily at Hendersly and set down his tea. 'I won't be stopping. You have the cuppa. I'll be in touch,' he nodded and walked out.

'I'll see Henry gets his stamp club material, Tomkins. Thank you.'

'There's something else I have to see you about Mr Hendersly –'

'Later.'

'It won't take very long.'

'No! Later! I have to arrange special leave for Mr Chambers. He won't be in for a week or two either.' He said it as though it was Tomkins' fault that Chambers wouldn't be in. And then he stormed out of the office. What on earth's bitten him this morning? Tomkins wondered.

PART THREE

Chapter Fifteen

'Journalists . . . all the same. Work harder than any other lazy person in the world,' muttered Henry. The morning was passing quickly into lunchtime. He bent his left knee, straightened it, bent the right knee. He passed his weight from foot to foot, bending and straightening.

Where was she? Out on a story, he supposed. He began to feel irritated. I can't stand here all day – what happens if I'm recognised? he worried. Irritation turned to discomfort. He sank his hands into his pockets and looked at his feet, wishing himself invisible. He needn't have worried. In the late morning whirl of London EC4 it was obvious the thoughts and concerns of passers-by lay somewhere straight ahead. Tight-faced businessmen hurled past, clutching briefcases and ink-smudged copies of the *Financial Times*. Pudgy secretaries walked in bunches carrying white paper-bags full of carbohydrates from the corner patisserie.

He peeked at himself in the copper-coloured glass of an adjacent building. He looked dreadful, unrecognisable. That at least had its advantages, he supposed. He'd meant to go back to his bedsit last night after he'd left Anne, but his nerve failed him at the last minute; instead he put his suitcase in a locker and slept in a seedy hotel by King's Cross. And he'd gone there only after hours of plodding the nearly empty streets and drinking voluminous cups of coffee. It was no wonder he looked a fright. What had once passed as a suit of wearable proportions now corrugated itself up around his calves, between his thighs and around his arm-pits. His jacket pocket bulged with yesterday's tie, leaving an open shirt with a black tide-mark on the inside of the collar. His face had become reluctant host to the first prickle of a beard. He wanted to turn and walk away from the entrance to her office, ashamed and disgusted with himself. But he knew she could help. Rochelle had promised, admittedly six months had passed since he'd met her at a press briefing. She said she worked as a freelance journalist for *International Business Weekly* and seemed genuinely interested when he talked about his interest in high technology. She was sharp that way. And she had a reputation for a few more things besides, he'd heard.

Henry returned to swapping the weight from one leg to another, back and forth, left, right. I could do with a leak, he thought, looking desperately about for sign of a public convenience. Nothing. He tried a short walk to take his mind of his biological dilemma. And decided that standing still worked better.

She's gone away, abroad. Could be away for months. The thought lodged. He couldn't bear that. For all his tenacity and grit, the tensions which he thought he'd dissolved now began pressing down on him. If Rochelle didn't show up that would be the last straw. He tried not to think the worst. His eyes skied up and down Chancery Lane, cast right to El Vino's, the last bastion of the Englishman's right to drink at a public bar without the hindrance of women, and inched their way down a fragment of Fleet Street. Clogged with traffic, as usual, he noticed. A car pulled up in front of him, alongside a parking space made out of bounds by two 'no parking' cones. A woman got out – Henry noticed he wasn't the only person noticing her. Without a glance left or right, she snatched up the plastic pyramids and flung them into the back seat of her car and lurched into the empty space. Henry stood in silent admiration, then, as she approached the main door to the building, stepped forward to intercept her.

'Excuse me . . .'

'Penny for the Guy – bit early though, aren't you?' she exhaled trying to walk round him.

'I need your help. You said I should get in touch if anything came up – I've got information I think will interest you,' Henry entreated.

'Didn't you used to be Henry Jay?' she peered quizzically at him. 'To be frank I wasn't expecting you to contact me after all this time – and certainly not dressed like that. Come on, let's get you out of sight.'

For over two hours they talked; she made him repeat his story, slanting her questions differently each time, extracting new slivers of information. She taped the entire conversation and took copious notes. When they had finished she cooked lunch – soup and toast. She told him to clean himself up, make himself at home in her apartment-cum-office, then she left.

Henry sank into a large, bumpy, leather couch and unravelled his tired frame. He was exhausted. He lay there gulping in air through his mouth, his stomach rising and falling like bellows. He remained there for half-an-hour, breathing deeply, so tired now he could barely think. Then he swivelled himself into an upright position and made to stand up. He heaved but couldn't find the strength. He tried again – and this time rose in a wobbly fashion and sauntered across the room in his socks to a bright red coffee machine in the corner. There was a grinder next to it and he carefully poured some beans into the neck and flicked the switch. He yelped as the beans shot up into the air, scattering themselves about the room.

'Damn!' He really needed that cup of coffee to jolt him awake. It struck him that a far easier way of getting a cup of coffee would be to go to the patisserie up the road. Crushing beans underfoot, he tried the door. It wouldn't budge. He found his shoes, put them on and tried again, rattling the locks, tugging angrily at the handle. But it was no use. He wandered through the rest of the apartment, hoping to find another exit; but even the fire-escape door was clammed tight. Well, if he had to be a prisoner anywhere, Henry thought, he couldn't think of a better place than here. Rochelle's office was quite the most salubrious he had ever laid eyes on. Rich cream carpet set off the chunky leather furniture – all black – at one end of the room. Huge ferns towered self-consciously on each side of the couch. A black glass coffee table with aluminium legs squatted in front. At the other end of the room – the back of the apartment – was an aluminium-piped desk, coated with a flock of press releases, note-pads, periodicals, newspaper clippings and an empty 'out' tray. Next to it, running along the wall, was another desk with an electric typewriter and telephone answering machine. Aluminium book-shelves were full of reference books, books with titles such as *Manias, Panics and Crashes, a History of Financial Crises* and *How to Double Your Profits Within the Year*. They were nearly all financial or economic. The rest were either on micro-electronics or Select Committee Reports, courtesy of HMSO.

Set back in another corner was a small video screen, a computer and a television. He reached out and pulled a knob. Nothing happened. Disgusted, he returned to his horizontal position on the couch. There was obviously a central control panel for all her contraptions, he figured. He hated being solitary now. If only Rochelle would return. Up until now he'd borne the responsibility for his task alone, something he'd never done before, he contemplated. There was always a rank in the Civil Service above him onto whom he could shovel his problems; nothing burdensome about the civil service – rank upon rank of hierarchy – conscious drones, each tinkering with the nuts and bolts of Whitehall, never embracing the entire machine. Nothing flummoxed him in his job – Governments would come and go with the passing of an election. They never tinkered with the machine, even the Tories hadn't changed the production line. These turgid thoughts almost had him asleep when the door clicked. He startled upright. It was Rochelle. He sank back into the couch. She strode across the room, and tossed the keys to his bedsit on his lap. 'Thanks. Didn't need them.'

He stared dumbly at them, waiting for her to say more. But she walked back across the room and pressed something on the side of her desk. Instantly the coffee machine lit up and began to gurgle. She stood there with her back to him, watching the coffee heat up. Then she spoke.

'I drove straight to your bedsit – Christ! You really went for Grotsville, didn't you?' She didn't say any more until the coffee was ready and she was sitting down beside him, hunched forward in easy reach of the ash-tray.

'I waited for ages, so depressing . . . anyway I was just

about to drive off when these two little men dressed in khaki whatsits come limping out under a huge packing case. They dump it into the back of their khaki van and disappear back through the front door. A few minutes later, back they come, hunched up under another gigantic tea chest. Only this one's got some gadget perched on top.'

Henry raised his eyebrows and opened his mouth as if to say something.

'No love – a vacuum-cleaner,' said Rochelle squashing his question before he had a chance to formulate it in words.

'I watched them drive away in their Matchbox van and as I was getting out of the car, this pinstripe job walks out the door – a dignified heavy, you know the type. He doesn't even see me, not so much as a glance.' She tossed her head back in mock exasperation. If there was one thing Rochelle liked, it was to be noticed. Admiration from any quarter, however anonymous, was always appreciated, though rarely acknowledged.

'He obviously had something to do with the khaki duo. Kept looking up and down the street and checking his watch. By the time he'd left and I'd got up to your room, I was convinced they were as thick as thieves. Funny thing though – they didn't nick your Apple II – another thing, I noticed blood, just a bit, on your keyboard. Did you, by any chance cut yourself?'

'No, I didn't,' said Henry pensively.

'Probably one of the removal men rubbing himself up against the tea chest,' grinned Rochelle. 'Here, take a look at this while I check my mail.'

Rochelle tapped adeptly at her computer keyboard. In ten seconds she had the information she wanted. 'There you are, Henry. Take it from there.'

He blinked, disbelievingly. For there, flashing up on the VDU was a potted history of his professional career and observations.

'Henry Jay, Principal Scientific Officer, Department of Commercial Development, Mercury House, Queen Victoria Street, Tel. 248 1111. Speciality: Computer and related fraud, articles published *Business Weekly* (Issues 1,953/5/9). Offered to collaborate on research for future projects. First impression: Jay would be out of depth in a car park puddle. Nevertheless, a noted expert on his subject. Recently completed "Fraud and Related Security Risks in the Age of Advanced Computer Intelligence and Electronic Accounting." Copy unavailable for general circ. Possible to gain access via Jay. Has strong sense of moral propriety. Cash offer therefore be rejected. Shouldn't come expensive.'

Henry looked at Rochelle, his lips pursed with indignation. She was still head down with her mail, attacking each envelope savagely with an ornately-carved letter opener. It was a daily ritual she clearly enjoyed. Without looking up she sensed his mood.

'You can see from that I'd have been in touch with you again, even if you didn't contact me.'

'Hmmmm.' He didn't feel exactly placated by her words.

'Coffee, Henry?'

'Please, thank you, that would be wonderful.'

'It's only coffee, don't get too excited. Black, with sugar, isn't it?'

'No, it's white without, actually.'

'I didn't ask you last time did I? Sorry. You should have said.'

'That's all right,' said Henry. 'I didn't really notice.'

In fact, every sip had been a struggle to get down. He just couldn't bring himself to tell her, that was all.

Henry riveted his eyes on her as she returned to her desk. She was most attractive he decided. Then changed his mind and concluded she was more sexy than beautiful. She dressed exquisitely. She was wearing a calf-length skirt in soft brown leather with boots to match, and the upper part of her body was covered with a moss-coloured rib sweater which obediently followed the curves of her breasts. Henry couldn't help noticing they were on the large side. And her jewellery, that was nice too – jade and cornelian. Henry had only just managed to raise his eyes to her chin when she looked up. He smiled sheepishly at her. She smiled back, seemingly unaware of his embarrassment.

'I think I'll feed what I've got on this case so far into the system.' Rochelle began dictating into a microphone at the end of which, beneath a stack of annual reports and a great wodge of press releases, presumably was a tape recorder.

'Jay makes contact on the twentieth – says he needs help, looks it and offers information. Pours out same garbled story. Involves a murdered Fraud Squad Super who passes him a file. In it, a key name, suggestions of massive fraud running into billions. Jay claims continued harassment by Department security and others and reckons his bed-sit bolt-hole is too hot. Now landed up here.' Henry listened to her with his eyes closed, his mouth set into a waxen pout. He hated being talked about, especially when it was within his earshot.

'Checked out his Drummond Street nest. Place cleaned out – except for Jay's Apple II computer and the bits and pieces with it. Van leaves, presumably containing tea-chests and cases. Defies reason. Back-up from creepy little landlord - needed a fiver before his mouth would work. Said there'd been a lot of activity, described two men in particular; early to mid-forties, one distinguished-looking the other a bit of a slob. Thought they were cops. Van reg. number DLT 953T. To trace through Swansea using usual source. That's about it for now. Ends here.' She got up and poured herself more coffee. 'By the way, the tape wipes automatically after twelve hours if I don't voice activate it.'

'Great!' said Henry blandly. 'What's that supposed to mean?'

'Nothing, I thought you'd be interested. OK?'

'Are you interested in helping me?'

'Not really. Not on the strength of what I saw this morning. An empty flat, two removal men, a pinstripe. So what?'

'But the tape you've just made – you mentioned chasing up leads . . .'

'Like I said, it wipes automatically. Henry, it just doesn't add up to much, not for me, anyway.'

'Well, thanks for the coffee.' He grabbed the file and stood to leave, trying to look as unperturbed and dignified as he could. It was a hopeless effort, he felt too despondent and looked too unkempt to create any illusion.

'By the way, I couldn't open the door before – when you were speeding *fruitlessly* to my bed-sitting room,' he added sarcastically.

'Probably – I'm a gadget freak,' she ignored his snipe. 'There's a remote lock behind the security desk downstairs in the main entrance I press on my way out. I've always been of the belief that it's as important to lock people in the office sometimes as it is to keep them out,' she grinned cheekily. 'Oh, for God's sake, Henry, sit down. Let me have a look at the file this poor chap Richardson passed to you.'

'But you said you weren't interested.'

'Stringing you along a bit, I'm afraid. I've been working on a project long-term, collecting snippets as they come my way. In return for taking a look at your file, you might be interested in seeing what I've come up with.'

She pressed three digits on the computer keyboard. Then typed an instruction. The screen flickered and in a flash, Hugo Jardine's name appeared. Henry's mind did a fifty-yard dash – what did she have on Jardine, how much did she know already?

'Just press "continue" when you want to go on – the digital read-out just here tells you how many pages left and when you've run out,' she pointed.

They sat, back to back, engrossed in each other's files, for a good hour.

'Your friend, Richardson, was a good copper,' said Rochelle as she returned the last piece of paper to the folder and turned her head. 'From what I know of the enormity of this story I can only begin to guess some of the risks he took.'

Henry was still peering at the monitor.

'Yes, I did like him,' he said without looking up. 'I'd like to tell you I was doing this for his memory – but I can't pretend I've arrived where I am any way but a little reluctantly.'

'Well, I'd like to tell you, Mr Jay, that you're not going to just dump all this in my lap and waddle off into the sunset. I know that's what you're used to. But if we do it together, we could blow the lid off this fraud, slip it to one of the nationals. It'd have them running for their cheque-books to say nothing of the kudos for me – and you, of course,' she added rapidly.

'I think it would work better if you did the work and I acted as advisor, a researcher, if you like,' he said hesitantly.

'Listen Henry. I owe you nothing. I don't have to get involved and I don't need somebody tagging *behind* me. We work together.' She punched out her words.

'You've already been working on the story for some time – and I've done you a huge favour –'

'Stop whining! This story is mammoth, you should know that better than anyone. Just because you think you've got my interest doesn't mean you can now take a back seat. It's going to be a hard slog to button down all the details – even then it might still be too hot to print. Another thing, Henry – I like my job, I've worked hard and it's paid off and the last thing I want is to collect the Investigative Journalist of the Year Award looking like a stitch-pattern sheet.' She fixed Henry with a firm glint in her eye.

'So what do you want me to do?' he asked, his voice little more than a whisper.

'Let's start by getting you a decent suit and shirt. I'm taking you West, young man, for a high-class afternoon.'

He followed her down into the street, protesting. 'Where are we going – what's happening?'

'Shut up and hang onto these.' Two parking cones came flying towards him. 'When I pull out, stick them in the parking space . . . Okay?' she shouted. She slammed the door and revved the engine.

Chapter Sixteen

Henry tugged at the collar of his new, blue shirt. It was too tight. Within the hour his sensitive skin would be up in a rash, a thin red line around his neck.

'Stop fussing about, Henry, and get in there.' Rochelle smacked his hand in fond rebuke. 'I'm surprised at you – thought your first port of call on the Jardine trail would have been this cosy little escort agency. Still, better late than never. Now come on, get a wriggle on – and don't forget what you've gone there for . . . And give me a buzz as soon as you're done. Here's the number.' She tossed a piece of paper at him and watched impatiently as he fiddled with the door handle. 'Good luck!' she shouted as she roared off, leaving a trail of blue smoke in her wake.

He tugged at his collar again, more from apprehension, and entered through the glass door beneath the discreet neon sign: 'Julia Bradwell-Scott's Escort Agency'.

There was nobody at reception. Henry stood there, wondering what to do next. He'd never been to an escort agency before, though he'd seen them advertised in the personal columns of newspapers. It was, he supposed, much like being at the dentist; you waited until some person, presumably a woman, came from behind the screen and attended to you. He was about to pour himself uneasily into one of the low, chunky armchairs in the waiting room when he spied a woman between a crack in the screen and the doorway. She was bent over a large potted fern and appeared to be talking to it. Her appearance puzzled him. He had imagined that anyone who worked in a joint like this wore slinky black or frilly red. But this woman, he presumed it was Julia, wore a camel coat, rather like one Anne might wear. Only this one, as far as he could make out, was expensive. He thought it strange too, that she should even wear a coat; it wasn't cold and it wasn't closing time, if escort agencies had closing times.

He coughed. She didn't hear him. He tapped his knuckles tunefully on the reception desk and coughed again. This time she looked up and through the same crack in the screen, caught his eye. She straightened and came towards him. She spoke.

'Half-day closing. Death in the family. Called out of town on urgent business. Closed, I'm sorry.' Her voice was throaty, her speech deliberately slow. She looked at him angrily.

'I'm looking for Julia.'

'Kidnapped. Left home. Never heard of her.'

'Please, don't mock. I phoned through. Perhaps you didn't get the message.'

'We're personal contact only. And it's *you* not getting the message, friend.' Her voice was more biting now.

Henry remained unperturbed. He stood his ground, hands firmly entrenched in the pockets of his new jacket, his fingers played with the spare buttons in a plastic bag, courtesy of the manufacturer.

She sensed his intransigence and looked him up and down, unimpressed. She yelled. 'Ernie! Here a minute, love!' She turned back to Henry, savage-eyed. 'Scramble, friend. There's plenty about town what you're after.' Her classless accent slipped just a fraction to reveal a sliver of Cockney in her voice.

'How do you know what I want?'

She stared at his clothes again, lip curled. 'Photographic model, an escort, somebody's shoulder to cry on?'

He shook his head. 'Not quite. A high-class whore, as discreetly supplied to Very Important People, such as politicians,' he said evenly, his eyes fixed on her doll-like face. She didn't flinch. Her waxen-hard complexion was blank, her deep violet eyes bereft of feeling. Her mask was back in place. Her peach gloss lips parted. 'Ernie!' she cried out again.

'Come off it, will you – there's nobody there,' Henry remonstrated. 'I've been watching for a good hour and I've only seen you.'

He hoped he was right. The last thing he wanted was a thick-set Ernie to lurch from the back room and to catapult him from the premises. 'By the way, my personal contact is Hugo Jardine.'

The mask cracked. Her eyes squinted. 'You'd better leave right away, fat boy. I don't know who you are. I don't want to, frankly. But I think you'd better be back in Burton's window before they shut shop.'

Henry despised her for that remark. But kept his cool.

'People like you and Jardine should never underestimate what we ordinary people can do, when we're pushed to it,' he said drily.

'Is that my fault?' she replied eyebrows raised.

Henry pushed out his bottom lip by way of an answer. 'By the way, Henry Jay's my name. And you are Julia, aren't you?'

She studied his hand, extended towards her, with an icy glare. Her hands remained fixed by her side. Then, without apparent reason her expression changed. Her shoulders dropped a fraction and without answering him directly she said. 'I'm an ordinary person myself, Henry. I'm one of you – not one of the others.' Then, she took his hand in hers and shook it, her grip firm.

'Come, let's go into my office. We can lay a few cards on the table there.' She smiled.

Julia was on the wrong side of forty. But her body, Henry couldn't help noticing, was exquisite. The dress beneath her coat was a film of delicate fabric, probably silk, of black and bronze, which clung to her, accentuated her breasts. She had style; didn't wear too many rings on her fingers (none on her marriage finger at all, he noticed), didn't have her hair candy-flossed into a tall creation as many women of her age and sophistication did; it flowed shining and natural blonde down her back, curled about her neck. Even the few lines radiating from her mouth and around her eyes added to, rather than detracted from her appearance, in Henry's view. Made her less of a Sindy Doll than she would have been without them.

Gracefully, she sank into her chair and signalled to him with her hands to sit down. She took a black Sobranie cigarette from an intricately-carved box on her desk and lit up.

'I'm taking six weeks owing me in St Kitts early this year because of what's happening in Jardine's world, *their* world.' She pulled in smoke from her cigarette, exhaled through her nose and mouth and watched Henry's reaction. A mixture of relief and undisguised pleasure once she had opened up to him. Just as she expected. Julia continued. 'I don't frighten easily, not after all these years in the game. But I'm telling you, I'm scared now. I've known Jardine for more years than I care to recount – so take a working girl's advice and get out, love.'

'Jardine and the people working for him won't let me,' said Henry.

She smiled at him, a sad sort of smile. 'Hugo has some very odd business partners. There's a couple of them over here at the moment. From the Italian end. Met them yet?'

Henry shook his head.

'I sent them a couple of girls last night,' she went on. 'My best girls.'

'I'd like to talk to them, if I can.'

'Bit late for that, I'm afraid. They'll be touching down in Tenerife about now. Flew out first thing – that's how scared they were of those two. I put them on the first flight I could get. I look after all my girls, take care of everything for them.'

Henry nodded respectfully. There was no answer to that and it wasn't the time to start asking about the escort business. 'Did your girls find out what business Jardine has in mind for those two Italians?' He stumbled over the word, 'girls'. They were hardly Girl Guides after all.

She shook her head. 'It certainly wasn't deep-fish pizza franchises.'

'Mind if I use the phone?'

'Police?' she asked, her voice laced with irony.

'If only you knew.'

'All right, sunshine. There it is.'

'I'd prefer to use the one at reception, actually, if that's possible, I mean,' he fumbled his request.

'Why not be really secretive and leave here and use the phone at the tube station?' She poked absently at her burning cigarette in the ashtray, her head down. 'Frankly, I don't give a toss.'

Henry sighed and picked up the telephone receiver on her desk, stabbed at the digits. Rochelle answered almost immediately. He explained as briefly and concisely as he could what Julia had told him so far.

'Got it, Henry,' said Rochelle. 'So don't buy an ice-cream off anyone with a curly moustache. Listen, Tiger, the conversation moves sort of sideways whenever Jardine's mentioned in the City. The Old Boy network is really out in force and I've yet to pluck a straggler from the pack . . . So get the nice lady to tell you all she knows about Jardine. I'm sure you'll manage just fine.' She growled tiger-like into the receiver. 'While you're getting your rocks off down there, I will walk the Corridors of Power. How'd your ex-boss Hendersly like a visit from a crusading journalist?'

Henry chuckled.

'Just as I thought. Like bird-shit on his bowler.'

Julia had plugged in a small tape-recorder half-way through his conversation. When he set the receiver on the hook he looked at her enquiringly.

'No, love. Not your voice. Mine. I've got to do a bit of dictation, messages for the head girl who's staying behind to mind the shop . . . Who's your friend?' Julia pointed to the telephone.

'Collaborator.'

'Handy,' she said, then began speaking into the microphone. 'Angie and Lois to Cannes, to be met at the airport. One week on yacht, same clients as last time. Lots of evening gear. White underwear only, remember.' She switched off the mike and looked at his wide-eyed expression. 'Puritanical streak lurks below the surface of this shipping magnate. Good payer and gives the girls a good time.'

Henry nodded. He asked her how she knew Jardine.

'I did a bit of business with Hugo years back. We were mates long before that. I was modelling, he took me out. Then, when my face began to obey gravity he suggested I go into this line of work. He promised to push custom my way. Nothing happened for a few years.' She switched the mike back on. 'Get Barbie off the hotel circuit. She's working one with the Maltesers.'

'Was he involved in politics then?' Henry asked. She switched the mike off again. 'He was into money. Nothing but money. And big stuff, too. Must admit, I raised the plucked eyebrow when I read he'd become a Euro MP. It's not being a *proper* MP, I know, and half of them are journalists. But . . .' she cut off and resumed her dictation. 'No more blacks for his Lordship. He's getting funny with them.'

Henry blanched.

'And keep an eye on Billy when she's working the airport hotels. There's things sticking to her fingers.'

She was enjoying this. She turned to him. 'Credit cards, mainly. Been sold up West for a C before the mugs missed it. I believe that what goes on for the price goes on, but I won't have anyone being funny with any of my girls. Same goes for my girls. Play the rules or they're out.'

Henry nodded. 'But how'd you get to meet Jardine?'

She laughed, sourly, Henry thought.

'Knew him before Mrs Jardine came along, didn't I. We were lovers for five years,' she said not answering, just reiterating. 'Then he went abroad for a while. When he came back, I was down on my luck, spitting feathers. So I went to see him, talk about old times, sniff the wind, see what the pickings were – out he comes with an offer. Always a fast worker, except when it comes to business with the girls,' she chortled, her throaty laugh degenerating into a cough. She drew a handkerchief from her coat pocket and put it to her mouth, a redundant gesture.

'He pays a lot of favours off through me, does Hugo. To business people. Diplomats. Politicians.'

'But it doesn't stop at favours, does it?' Henry put on his

best interrogating voice. 'It involves getting information, blackmail.'

'Murder? Perhaps,' she said levelly.

'But why? What's it all for?'

Her voice grated. 'I don't know because I don't ask because I don't want to know. But whatever, it's very big – it's mega-bucks – and it's all about to happen. That's why I'm clearing the fall-out zone till it's over. That's why you should make a deal with him.'

'The deal he wanted to make with me involved me stopping breathing, thanks very much.'

She lit a Sobranie cigarette, exhaling as she spoke.

'You've got him worried. He wouldn't have risked bringing over the Italians otherwise.'

Henry bolted upright. His voice exploded. '*He's* worried about *me*? I'm the one who's been living like a tramp for days. I'm the one who had to sell his prized philatelic collection to stay alive and keep one step ahead.'

'If the roof falls in on Hugo, a lot of people, including me, are going to be knee-deep in rubble.' Julia stood up and walked about the room, pointing her cigarette in the air to emphasise her words. 'Get in there, Henry. Why be a minor irritation when you can be a bloody great nuisance, and get paid off in fifty pound notes?'

'Forgetting the moral side of it . . .'

'Like anybody with any sense . . .' she raised her eyebrows at him.

Of course she was right. He knew that. If, as she said, the big deal was about to happen, they'd really be closing in on him. He might as well make a colossal nuisance of himself, hit them where it hurt most – get Jardine. He didn't look at her, said, 'That's all well and good. But there's the practical side. How do I know where Jardine is at any given moment?'

'Funny you should mention that, Henry,' she said. She reached into her drawer, pulled out two A4 sheets of typed paper, stapled together. 'You've just beaten this to the shredder.'

He took the paper from her desk and read. An official VIP

list for the current month of arrivals, departures, who was meeting who. One name stood out above all the others. Hugo Jardine. European Member of Parliament, Dorset. Meetings with the British Minister of Transport and his French counterpart, the chairman and secretary of the Select Committee on Transport and the Under-Secretary from the Ministry of Environment. His arrival was only a few days away. Henry puffed out his cheeks and gave a silent whistle. He couldn't believe his luck. 'Thanks, this is exactly what I've been looking for,' he said to Julia.

'Who knows, next time I might produce much more for you,' she said eyeing him playfully.

Henry fought off embarrassment by cleaning his glasses on his new tie. 'Well, better be on my way, I suppose. Leave you to sort things out here.'

They both stood at the same time, shook hands. Julia gave him a peck on the cheek. 'Good luck, love,' she said.

'Same to you. And have a nice holiday.'

Hard as nails, tough as an old boot, was Julia. Yet beneath that exterior a good sort; well-meaning and kind. A bit like an avocado pear in character, she was. Tough on the outside, soft and mushy inside, but still had that hard core in the centre. He felt much more positive as he walked away.

For Julia it was different. When the door was bolted, she went into the office rest-room and lay down on the couch, just as she was, with her coat on. She stared at the ceiling. Thin red strain lines marked her forehead. After years in the business it had come to this – a messy tangled demise. Thirty-six hours to put her de luxe girls – the dozen or so who exclusively catered to the needs of British aristocrats, politicians and businessmen – into hibernation. The foreign circuit and the shop-window agency girls would go on much as before. But it was all over for her for good – death threats and blackmail and no safety-net. Time to get out.

Chapter Seventeen

At four o'clock, Rochelle Halliday walked slowly into Hendersly's office, closed the door behind her, approached the desk, sat in the chair in front of the desk and stared. It was an audacious entrance, planned to take Hendersly completely by surprise. She sat there waiting, completely at ease. She heard him approach, heard Tomkins scrape back his chair and scurry across the corridor – that was the advantage of cheap partitioning, she mused, you could hear most things. Hendersly entered, flushed from alcohol and a brisk walk back to the office.

'Forgive me, I was under the impression that this was *my* office,' he bellowed.

Tomkins sprang from behind. 'Miss Halliday is a journalist. She said the Press Office had arranged an interview with you, Mr Hendersly. It wasn't in your diary.'

What a prick, thought Rochelle. She watched Hendersly remove his coat, hang it in the cupboard by the door. Just as she had expected, her appearance rattled him.

'Hello,' she said, 'I'm from *International Business Weekly*. Do you know the magazine?'

'Certainly. I know your editor and several of your colleagues . . . and not one of them has had the temerity to turn up in my office without first receiving clearance from the Press Office – which I assume you haven't. I am sure you are well aware of the procedure, that a Press Officer accompanies a journalist at all interviews in Government departments, and I suggest, Miss Halliday, that before I consider uttering one word, either on the record, or off the record, on whatever subject you think I am capable of expounding, you contact the Press Office and arrange an appointment. Tomkins, see her out of the building, will you. Goodbye, Miss Halliday.'

It was a miracle Hendersly managed to complete the speech at all, for he had long run out of breath. His face was even more flushed now than when he arrived, almost purple in fact. He was unused to dealing with the press and after a morning such as the one he had gone through with Bridgnorth, the last person he wished to see ensconced in his office was a journalist.

'Mr Hendersly, I know the procedure, probably better than you do,' Rochelle purred. 'But I came to you directly to discuss an investigation being carried out by the Fraud Squad which involves this department. Am I right, or am I right?'

Hendersly sighed. 'It's all right, Tomkins. I understand what it's all about now.' He turned to Rochelle when Tomkins had gone. 'I've no idea what you're talking about.'

'Then why didn't you get rid of me while you had the chance? I think you do know, and a lot more besides.'

'And I think you should leave,' he said aggressively. 'Listen. Classified information, some of it with top security rating, has been passed on to me. I'm sure you'd be interested at the very least in putting the record straight and confirm that such an investigation does involve the Department of Commercial Development.'

'I will do no such thing.' Hendersly's brain was working overtime. Who had fed her the information? How much did she really know? And, if she knew, how many others knew?

'Mr Hendersly,' she pulled him away from his thoughts, 'I tried to get hold of your internal security officer when I couldn't find you an hour ago.' The remark was aimed straight at Hendersly's late return from lunch. 'It seems he's packed up and gone on Special Leave.'

'Yes, family problems,' said Hendersly.

'And while I was chatting to your clerk out there . . .'

'What clerk?'

'The little balding outfit sitting twiddling his thumbs across the corridor.'

'That's Tomkins. He's a Principal Scientific Officer, a rank highly respected within this Department and by Whitehall generally,' he replied testily.

'All right, all right. Principal Scientific Officer Tomkins out there mentioned he had a colleague who had also been granted special leave.'

'So what?'

'Well, there seems to be a proliferation of staff taking special leave all of a sudden, don't you agree?'

'No.'

'Oh come on! Why has Tomkins' colleague taken his break now?'

Health reasons. Work in the Department can be quite stressful, though *you* might not believe that,' said Hendersly. He was beginning to lose his temper.

'Oh, I *do*, Mr Hendersly,' she said fervently. Her voice was soft, yet sharp. 'I also believe that working here can be injurious to health. Even to outsiders – like the City of London Fraud Squad Officer who puffed his last within these four walls.'

'There is nothing I have to say on any of the matters you have raised. But may I advise you to check very thoroughly the accusations passed on to you by your "mole". I suspect there may be more of a grudge than truth behind his claims.'

'Who said it was a man? And, as the Duke of Wellington replied when someone asked, "Mr Jones, I believe?" – "If you believe that, you'll believe anything".'

Hendersly swung into his chair, clasped his hand to his forehead. Then he leaned forward, his eyes blazing. 'Jay sent you, didn't he? He's your contact, isn't he?'

'What makes you think that?'

'He isn't well. You shouldn't allow yourself to become involved in Jay's private fantasies about the wrongdoings of this department.'

'Now it's my turn to say, "I don't know what you're talking about".'

'And now, I think you had better leave,' said Hendersly rising. 'I have a busy day ahead of me. Please contact the Press Office. I'm sure they'll be only too happy to arrange something. Give my regards to your editor.'

She nodded walked towards the door, opened it. 'By the way, there's a rumour about someone in your department involved in some shady political and business deal; with a man called Jardine. Heard of him?'

'No.'

'Well, if you do come across the name, perhaps you could call me?' She looked almost helpless as she said it, as she gave him her card. About as helpless and trustworthy as a rattlesnake, thought Hendersly as he watched her walk down the corridor to the lift. But a damned sight more sexy.

The phone burred. He jumped and answered it before it could ring a second time. '. . . Bridgnorth . . . Where are you? . . . I see . . . Yes. I thought I'd make a long weekend of it, I'll be incommunicado. Speak to you when I get back then? Good. The other point. I've just had a journalist onto me. Rochelle Halliday. *International Business Weekly*. My bet is, Jay's been blubbing to the press. I think we should act swiftly on this . . . yes, yes . . . Fine. See you next week then.'

He shuffled through a pile of notes on his otherwise spotless desk, filled his briefcase with one or two files, eased into his coat and left the office.

Tomkins pounced. 'Can I have a quick word with you, Mr Hendersly?'

'Not now, Tomkins. I'm not feeling well. You'll have to wait.'

'This is the second time I've tried to talk to you today. It can't wait.'

'Then get on with it, man. What is it?'

'It's about Henry . . .'

'And . . .?'

'About his files.' Tomkins fixed a determined eye on his boss. He took a deep breath. 'I've photocopied Henry Jay's files.'

The news seemed to stun Hendersly. He didn't move for a second. 'You've what? What on earth for?' he said, slicing his words.

Tomkins shuffled uneasily. 'People will do all sorts of things to clinch promotion. I'm sure you know that Henry was prepared to swap leak for leak with the Fraud Squad and Inland Revenue Special Investigations. I didn't have those kind of contacts. But I didn't want to be left behind.' He stared at the ground, at his feet.

'So you photocopied Henry Jay's files,' said Hendersly softly.

'How long has this been going on?'

'You mean, have I got a copy of Henry's computer fraud file . . . the one you had Mr Chambers destroy?'

'How did you know?'

'Henry let it slip, I think.'

'Well, man. Have you?'

'Yes, I've got it,' said Tomkins miserably. 'And to be frank, I'm scared shitless. I feel I ought to put the file through the shredder, forget it all. Just hope that Henry comes out of the whole thing in one piece.'

'What do you know about Henry?'

'Nothing really. He just seemed very twitchy and put out about his report, complained that it had been tampered with by Chambers – then he went off on special leave and now I can't contact him.'

'Well I can tell you this much. There's a helluva lot more at stake than your promotion, Tomkins,' he said gravely. 'I really don't know if I can advise you . . .'

'But you're my boss. The decision has to be yours. Whatever it is, I'll go along with – I trust you implicitly.'

'Henry Jay used to trust me too. Then he lost that trust – and he was right to,' his voice trailed off and for just a second he seemed genuinely upset. 'Tomkins, I don't think I should handle these files,' he said more positively, 'but I will turn a blind eye if you delivered them to Jay.'

Tomkins nodded.

'That's settled then? Take them this evening – that's a good chap. Have a good weekend.'

'You too, sir.'

Tomkins had never been to Henry Jay's house, never spoken to Anne, his wife, although he'd seen her the day Henry walked out of the office on special leave. Whatever Henry was up to had something to do with his computer fraud report – he would need a copy. And for once, Tomkins was more than glad to help.

Bridgnorth cupped his hand over the telephone receiver and hissed. 'Hold it lads. I can't hear myself think.'

The 'lads' were men in their forties, dressed in khaki overcoats. They continued to quietly dismantle the living room, they wrenched the drawers from the sideboard and tossed the contents on the floor. Books, plates, cutlery, records, were scattered over the floor. The rest of the house was in the same shambled state.

Bridgnorth put the receiver back to his ear and lit a cigarette.

'Sorry about the background noise, Hendersly . . . Yes, I'm at the house now. Trying to dig up a clue as to where our Henry's hopped to this time. We haven't dug up any files he might have left in the happy home . . . What? Didn't catch that.' He listened. 'Right, we'll have to get onto that immediately.'

The conversation came to an end and he slammed down the phone and dipped his cigarette into the vase of flowers on the side table. It fizzed. He paused and chucked the soggy filter in.

'Come on lads. Let's get out of here.'

They left, trampling all over their chaos.

Anne had sat in the corner armchair throughout, numb, speechless with dismay. She couldn't even watch them go.

She sat, not moving. She blinked her eyes, held her fingers over the lids. Tears squeezed from the corners of her eyes, flooded down her cheeks, the salty mixture dropped into her mouth. It triggered something inside her. She burst out crying, uncontrollably, gasping for breath between sobs.

'Hel-lo? Anybody here?'

Anne smudged the wetness from her face with the back of her hand, and again with the hem of her dress. She stood to face a young woman. It was Rochelle.

'Oh, my God! What have they done?' She stooped and picked up a few objects in her path. She put them on the sideboard, looked at Anne's swollen eyes. 'The bastards.'

Anne looked at her with a numbed expression. 'I'm sorry, I don't seem to know who you are.'

'My apologies. I've been working on a story your husband's helping me with. My name's Rochelle Halliday. He asked me to stop by; as you know, he can't move for fear of being tracked down. Seems we're dealing with a right pack of hooligans . . . any idea who they might be?'

Anne nodded. 'They had to be Civil Service – one of those supposedly soft-shoe shuffle departments you rarely get to hear about and never in a million light years expect to see.'

'You sure about that?'

'Oh, yes. I've worked in the service since I left university. I married someone who started at the ground floor and worked his way up. I know the way they go about things.'

'Who could have sent them?'

'Don't know.'

'Could Hendersly?'

'I doubt it. But he definitely knew they were here. The plump one in a suit phoned him.'

'In front of you?'

'They don't give a damn. They know what power they wield. The terrifying thing is though, the casual way in which they put it to use.'

The phone let out a sharp ring. Anne jumped. 'I can't answer it, I just can't. Please, could you . . .'

Rochelle grabbed the telephone.

'Henry? . . .Yes, she's here. She's fine, absolutely fine. Hang on. I'll pass you over to her.'

As she reached across to Anne with the receiver she put her finger to her lips and shook her head. She figured the one thing these bully boys would love would be for Henry to crawl out of the woodwork to comfort his wife, set his house in order, display his loyalty and indignation.

Anne chatted lightly to Henry, reassured him things were as they should be, only she missed him terribly. Then, Rochelle took the phone. She listened carefully. 'Say that again, Henry.'

He spoke breathlessly. 'The hall porter – he was nowhere to be seen. His tea was on his desk, warm and not a drop taken. I figured that was pretty unusual, what with you setting such store by the physical security of your office. So, I set that remote lock of yours behind the front desk and made for the nearest phone box. Just to be sure.'

'Don't you think you're being a bit dramatic about all this Henry?'

'Look, I know there's nothing concrete to go on, but I don't think I'm being dramatic. Just careful. That's all.'

'Let's hope the lapse is nothing more than the hall porter taking a piss. Don't panic, okay? There's a steamy little coffee bar up the road. Go there and stay there and I'll be there as soon as I can.' She gazed sympathetically at Anne who had begun to gather up the household belongings – she knew and understood the awfulness, the emptiness, the suffering Anne was going through and wished she could do more to help.

'I have to go,' she said. 'Nothing to worry about. Just Henry being over-cautious.'

'Always been one of his faults. Ever since I've known him.' She stood and walked with Rochelle to the door. 'By the way, this might be useful for you to know – Hendersly phoned earlier; said he wanted Henry to know that he'd done what he could. Now that he'd finally woken up to what was going on. He said that what he'd arranged to do for Henry wasn't much – but it was all in his power to do . . .'

'Anne . . .'

'He didn't pretend, oddly enough, that his motives were anything other than cowardice. Unusual, most out of character from what I've seen and heard. He intimated he was hedging his bets, if Henry should achieve the impossible and . . .'

'Anne!' Rochelle said sharply cutting her off. 'What, exactly did Hendersly say he was going to do for Henry?'

Anne looked limp, exhausted, confused. 'He said he was sending Tomkins, that's Henry's colleague, around here tonight with copies of some files. Including, let me think . . . yes, that fraud file. The one they had destroyed to protect some Euro MP. That was when Henry got all het up and got into all this trouble . . .' her voice faded.

'Anne, that's marvellous news. Henry will be over the moon. Will you be here tonight?'

'I will. But what do I do with the file? How can I get it to Henry?'

'Here's my address and telephone number. Contact me in the morning, maybe in a couple of days' time if you feel uneasy about somebody watching the place. Make sure it's well hidden so these bastards can't get their sticky fingers on it. Okay? Take care, now.'

Chapter Eighteen

The café in Chancery Lane was nearly empty. Henry sat, elbows perched on the Formica table, sipping coffee from a fat white cup. It was his eighth. The anorexic waitress had stopped chatting to him after his third cup and had ceased even looking at him after his fifth. This, in Henry's view, was a great blessing.

In the corner, a man in a brown suit and checked-tie sat, cross-legged, slowly turning the pages of the *Daily Star*. One of Fleet Street's printers, he mused. They usually dressed more smartly than the journalists who worked on floors above the machine room.

Henry took another gulp of the thick, bitter mixture. Rochelle would soon arrive. He hoped so. An overwhelming sensation gripped him – he was fast becoming water-logged and there wasn't a sign or arrow indicating a public convenience in sight. If only he too had a newspaper in which to bury his thoughts. Instead, he fished into his jacket pocket and glanced absently down the list of names printed neatly on the headed notepaper given to him by Julia. He couldn't concentrate. He gently folded the paper and slipped it back into his pocket, wondering how he could spin out the time until she came. A piece of cheesecake, perhaps?

The table wobbled. A man, solidly-built squeezed into a space beside Henry, who raised his cup and lowered it, deliberately ignoring the stranger's existence. They sat, side by side, in silence.

'They say that stuff gives you cancer of the pancreas.' Henry nodded. The last thing he wanted was to engage in some spurious debate on the pros and cons of caffeine – cancer, sterility, anxiety, ulcers, whatever. Not with this garrulous man, whose voice was tinged with an Antipodean accent.

Henry signalled the waitress for another cup of coffee; it was an act of defiance and he slurped his 'poison' loudly.

'Ah, come on Henry. It's high time you left that ferret's piss alone.'

Henry turned sharply. The man's face was brown, his eyes flecked green-blue and he had a warm smile, belying the tone in his voice. He was obviously not a stray Australian or New Zealander who'd lost his way or had become bored with the sights.

'One thing's for certain, Henry, these things don't half give you a bad head.'

In the palm of his hand was cradled a lead-tipped sap.

'I hope you're not one of these blighters who's gonna take a stubborn line. Come on, get a wriggle on, Henry. You and me got an appointment.'

Henry stood, shakily, stuffed two pound notes under the sugar bowl and turned to leave. As he did, he dropped the folded paper to the ground.

'Dropping litter can get you into hot water, Jaybird. And you need trouble like Labour needs that Tony Benn.'

The man chuckled at his joke. Henry stared back, his face a blank. Inside, his pulse thumped, he could feel it jar through his fingers, his arms, his chest, inside his ears. The noise grew louder as they walked out into the street, louder and louder as they turned into the block of flats where Rochelle lived. He stopped. Glared.

'You're on their side! You and Rochelle. With Jardine. You double-crossing, conniving, low down pack of . . .'

'Dunno what the fuck you're talking about,' the man said, greatly amused by Henry's outburst. 'Who's Jardine, for Chrissake?'

They were still arguing as they reached Rochelle's door. She was standing there watching them. 'Don't tell him a thing, Henry. And as for you, Lanch, you greasy bugger, what the hell do you think you're up to?'

'Get off the grass, Ro. You know bloody well nobody goes more hairy-arsed after a story than me. Gotta keep up the good old image of Aussie journalist.'

'You! E. B. Lanchbury! That's a laugh. Stick around Mother England, sweetheart, and we'll have you done over under the Trade Descriptions Act. Journalist, my arse. You couldn't fold a paper hat. You, with your pockets stuffed with cheques. Still dishing them out to the needy – the mad axeman's wife, the pop star's pregnant girlfriend, the vicar's spurned wife. I'll say one thing for you, Lanch. You're better off doing that. So leave the real investigations to me, huh?'

Lanchbury grinned, his mouth stretched across his face.

'Hey, Henry. You must have some pretty hot grub for old Ro here. Never seen her cheeks so red since I gave her her first good one.'

Henry cleared his throat. 'Excuse me. I think I'll leave you two to fight this one out.' He scuttled past them and locked himself in the bathroom.

'Poor old Henry,' said Lanchbury as he poured himself a Scotch from Rochelle's drinks cabinet. 'Thought I was one of the other team, come to ream him. I tell you, Ro, he was whiter than a shark's dingaling at six foot off.'

'As if you'd know,' she snorted. 'And while you're draining my Scotch, how about pouring me a small drink. Mine's with soda. Economy measure.'

'Sure thing, chick.'

'Cut the chick bit, will you?' she said taking her drink.

'Well. Bottoms up.' He tossed back his Scotch, swallowing the contents in two audible gulps.

'Missed me?' he asked. 'You have to admit. I do a great horizontal rumba, don't I?'

'When I'm down on my luck, want a cheap thrill, sure, I might give you a ring to find out.' She sipped her drink, lit a cigarette. The smoke curled from her lips, thinned out into nothingness. She watched him pour himself another Scotch, unable to decide whether she loathed him or simply had a grudging admiration for his cheek. Either way, she hated the power he had over her, made her think about him often, blow hot and cold.

Henry awoke to darkness. For a while, he lay there, feeling the strange sensation in his head. It was as though his brain was encased in a box of cotton wool, everything about him seemed once-removed, foggy. He stretched out his arm, fumbling for the bedside lamp. He flicked the switch and lay back, reassured. He wondered what Rochelle was doing now and if Lanchbury was still around. Slowly he rose and hobbled painfully towards the office, his legs under attack by a battalion of pins and needles.

Rochelle was alone, rumbling through the carousel which stored the computer disks. She was still wearing the flowing robe she had worn when she greeted him earlier at the door. The desk clock told him he had been sleeping for three and a quarter hours. It seemed longer. She began talking, her back towards him.

'One hears about a softly-softly campaign to buy up warehousing estates south of the river; once purchased, the entire contents are chucked. The place remains empty. One picks up a sliver of information about a European Member of Parliament who suddenly seems to be behind enough dough to snap up a couple of private steel companies and an industrial ventilating firm, among many others. A mishmash of information without rhyme or reason. A few years ago I'd have stacked each little deal away in my files to gather dust. Now abracadabra! Into the machine it all goes and out pop connections I'd never dreamed of. I reckon we've cracked it, Henry. What do you say?'

'Sure,' said Henry without any spark to his voice. He was still trying to get his head together.

'Yes, I reckon that in a couple of days, maybe less, if you

and I go into a huddle and break it down to bite-size chunks, we'll have a story we may be able to place with one of the Sundays.'

Henry's mind raced into action.

'Maybe? What do you mean? If you can prove that Jardine's mixed up in all this and can show the extent to which people have gone to protect him . . .'

'Henry. The fraud is real and it's huge. But Jardine's clean – technically-speaking. He's keeping within the letter of the law, if not, then the spirit of it. We could get our fingers badly burned if we rushed it.'

'Why the cover-up then? Why all the murdering? Why go through all the palaver of sweeping me under the carpet?'

'If I'm right about Jardine and this file of yours backs me up – we have a story. So, keep your hat on and don't panic. But Jardine wouldn't spend more than half-an-hour in the dock, the exposé wouldn't wipe out his career – he'd hibernate for a while and bounce back with a vengeance. It would, though, bring dozens of others down, like a pack of cards.'

'Couldn't the Power save them all?' said Henry, confused by her equivocation.

'Le Pouvoir,' he went on, ominously. 'Where politicians and businessmen gather together with organised crime. I don't know if there's one man controlling the organisation – some say no – but whatever, it's real enough.'

'I don't think even Le Pouvoir could save them,' Rochelle said, shaking her head. 'Nothing will save them, once this gets out – unless I'm very much mistaken.'

Everything was closing in on him now, crowding him. He leaned against her desk, his thoughts were miles away.

'Are you listening to me?' she said, her voice was harsh. 'I'll have to confront Jardine before writing up the piece. Do you know where he's going to be?'

'He flies back from a parliamentary visit to Greece next week. Stop-overs at Frankfurt and Brussels.'

'You're certain of that?'

She pierced him with her eyes.

'Of course. I have a list of MEP's, officials, their comings and goings. I've checked it against the lists published by the European Parliament press and information office in London. And Julia gave me the real seed corn – a list which helps her girls co-ordinate their schedules.'

'Clever, clever Julia.'

'She doesn't altogether trust Jardine. Known him for years, but doesn't trust him – she gave me that impression, anyway.'

'Julia obviously wants you on her side – just as Hendersly does if you pull this off.'

Henry gave her a sideways glance, frowned.

'Hendersly?'

'Yeh, didn't I tell you? He's sending Tomkins round to your place this evening with the photocopies of your file. It seems that Tomkins was busy on early shift keeping copies of all your work. He was a devout copier, I understand. Promotion – what crimes are committed in thy name?'

They exchanged smiles. They were conspirators. Their bond was one, not of physical attraction, but something far outside their own perimeter of existence. For one of them, the relationship provided the ultimate masturbation exercise in journalism, a scoop. For the other, the relationship would hopefully clinch a return to normality where the only glossy coating on an otherwise mundane existence was a night out at the theatre or, perhaps, a mention in the local 'beano'.

Rochelle stared silently at the flickering screen. She pressed a key, more names bubbled onto the computer's monitor. She said, 'Henry, the people Jardine's scheduled on Friday – they're big-wigs. Here, take a look at these . . .'

He bent down, leaned over her shoulder.

She pointed at the monitor. 'This one's a senior official at the Bank of England. This guy's a leading economist with one of the clearing banks. This one, very big in the insurance world, this one's in the ECGD. Then there are a few small-fry. I can't trace the others on the computer.'

She got up, pulled her gown around her and said, 'Think I'll take a long, hot bath. Have a closer look, if you like.'

She disappeared into the bathroom.

He took her seat, ogled the monitor. She was very thorough, he thought as he pressed a key, flashed up another page. The phone rang. He let it ring a few times. Rochelle came tearing from the bathroom, foam splodged down her arms and legs. She was wrapped in the biggest towel he had ever laid eyes on. She picked up the receiver. It was Lanchbury. Rochelle hardly spoke, nodded a lot, then she hung up.

'Lanchbury has arranged for us to use an office as a safe house for us both to work from. Safer than here for you and we'll be able to plough through the work there, unimpeded, in no time. Great, eh?'

He smiled up at her, was pleased to have her as his ally.

'Get your glad rags on, Henry,' she said, shivering slightly. 'We'll go out to celebrate.'

Then she turned with an exaggerated sweep of her arms and went back into the bathroom. He could hear her humming, something from Bizet's *Carmen*, he thought.

Nowhere in London was night and day so neatly clipped in two as Soho. When it was light, the sidewalks were packed with tight-bottomed young men with their giant black design folders, students striding with faces buried in fresh steaming croissants from the Italian coffee shop into the National Broadcasting School in Greek Street, and tourists with flared check trousers and two cameras slung over their shoulders. Now it was night, and as Rochelle and Henry stepped drowsily from L'Escargot into the crisp air there was only the scantiest of activity along the street. Small groups, mostly men, had coagulated on the pavement outside neon-lit establishments which could no longer legally display their wares. The record shop, which provided a feast of megadecibels during the day, was locked and barred. Directly opposite, behind a bold window, a lone broadcasting student hunched with muffed ears, his hands sweeping wild over a control panel, mouthed into a microphone a message to millions in his fantasy. On the floor above, his sole listener, a cleaning lady, whisked speedily over surfaces with her duster.

Arm in arm, Henry and Rochelle made their way towards

Soho Square, where tramps had settled down for the night on the hard wood-slatted benches and where, incredibly, Rochelle had eased her car between a Post Office van and a Volvo.

'Do we have to go back to your office? Couldn't we just pick up the file from Anne straight away and then go to this safe house Lanchbury has lined up?'

Henry whined, partly because the alcohol he had consumed had insulated him from the complications of life and shuttle-cocking back and forth across London seemed an odious complication. And partly because he felt utterly exhausted and the sooner he could crawl into a bed the better off he'd be. Soho's contrived decadence had enthralled him. So too had the trendiness of the restaurant. Where everyone seemed to know someone and numerous kisses were exchanged in the upstairs room. He had never before experienced anything like it. He had felt awkward at first. His shoes didn't seem to fit. His trousers bagged ostentatiously at the crotch and his jacket hunched high at the back and drooped low at the front. But nobody had stared at him for more than a second, their expressions remarkable for their blandness once they had eyed him over. It only occurred to him later that Rochelle had hogged all the limelight. Her, with her black dress, black rose, her whippet figure as she walked confidently to their table, bending to whisper something into the ear of a good-looking man with glasses en route. It was the only time Henry had ever seen National Health glasses look fashionable.

He should have known that while she listened attentively to his complaints she had no intention of heeding his whims. They screeched from street to street, Rochelle rarely changing gear and driving at break-neck speed. They pulled up outside her office. Henry vaguely noticed Lanchbury, grinning at them like a Cheshire cat.

'Park here, Ro. Plenniaroom.'

'I always park here,' she said almost primly. 'Move the parking cones will you – if it won't bring on your hernia, that is.'

He stood in the gutter, hands tucked stubbornly into his belt. They glared at each other, like two tom cats on a bad night out. Henry decided to leave them to it, again. 'Shall I phone Anne? Tell her we're on our way?'

Rochelle threw him the keys without looking. She continued in her attempt to outstare Lanchbury into submission. 'Tell Anne twenty minutes. Tell her to be ready to come with us!' Rochelle shouted after Henry.

'Ro, I think Henry was onto something about there being somebody in the office,' Lanchbury said. 'I can't be sure, but I gotta hunch somebody was there. You're really up against the pros. I'd get out of this as soon as I could – if I was you.'

For once, there wasn't a hint of facetiousness in his voice as he spoke.

He stooped, knees creaking, to lift the cones.

He had only a second. A splinter of time, to gaze bewildered at the small, brown paper package on the ground beneath the cone. Rochelle saw it too. Her mouth dropped. She tried to cry out. But there was no time. A flash. The parcel exploded. Flames cut through the air, through the smoke engulfing the night. In that blinding moment, Lanchbury felt nothing. Like a movie in slow motion, he could feel his entire body disintegrate – but it was as if he was watching it happen to somebody else. There was no sound. Then, there was nothing. His cloth-doll body catapulted into the dark, above the smoke and fire, and landed twenty yards down the road. Somewhere, in the blazing inferno which now licked up the parked car lay the body of Rochelle.

The blast had been ferocious and Henry had been blown into the foyer door. Glass and wood fragments spattered everywhere. His glasses had shot from his nose. Dazed, he fingered through the rubble for them. Crawling on all fours he turned unbelieving to squint hazily at the holocaust beyond. Then he edged toward the security desk, still kneeling, to the phone. She had to be warned.

'Anne! Anne! It's me. Get out. Now. Don't ask – just run.'

Tomkins knew it was late. The Camera Club meeting had gone on far longer than usual and the voting for new officers had produced a vociferous debate. So tiresome, tiring, he thought as he quietly closed the gate behind him. He began the short walk to the Jays' front door, noticed there were no lights on. He hoped she was still awake. Still, if she'd gone to bed, he could always hide the briefcase somewhere at the back of the house and telephone her in the morning. It was the first time he had seen their home. Even at night he could tell that it was nothing out of the ordinary: Victorian detached, immaculately kept. The grass was shaved to the right height above the paving stones, roses clipped according to the latest gardening guide, steps painted white, door-knocker in gleaming brass. All maintained with almost obsessional neatness. Tomkins gently placed the briefcase at his feet and reached for the door-knocker. No, he thought, she might not hear that. His gloved hand made for the door buzzer on the side. Inside, he could hear the telephone ring, unattended. It was the last sound he ever heard. Just as his hand made contact with the buzzer, the door flew at him with an almighty force. Dust and flames everywhere, the porch demolished, the windows smashed, the rose bushes buried beneath the debris. Just as Tomkins' body was. He was already dead by the time the neighbours rushed, screaming in their dressing gowns, into the street to stand like frightened but curious animals, keeping their distance. Everyone, that was, except for Anne. She had rushed from the neighbours, where she had finally retreated for comfort, thinking that Tomkins would not arrive. She stood among them briefly, spied a body crushed beneath glass, wood and metal. Her stomach lurched. For one awful moment she thought it might be Henry. She rushed up the path, crunching glass beneath her feet. Saw Tomkins' disfigured face, saw the briefcase. She grabbed it and ran, up the road, around the corner, where there was no sound, no horrible burning smell. She vomited, her stomach continued to retch, she ached. She felt like dying.

The car outside the block of flats had vanished behind a shroud of grumous smoke. Henry could neither taste nor smell the acrid burning of upholstery, paint, petrol and flesh. He was a voyeur, witness to the event by proxy. Behind him, the telephone receiver dangled in the air, revolved one way, paused to gather momentum, then twirled around in the opposite direction. The tone still pleaded for someone to answer. Quietly, he reached down, replaced the receiver on the hook. She couldn't be at home, she must be out, he thought, prayed. But how could he know what had happened to her? He found it hard to catch his breath and shivered uncontrollably. His eyes were frightened and angry as he looked at the hall porter, a wizened man with padded shoulders who had appeared, jack-in-a-box-style from behind the desk, quivering with fright.

'You set her up. You set her up.' Henry's voice was the modicum of control. His tone was flat, emotionless.

The old man stared with fear-crazed eyes. 'I just told them how she parked,' he whispered hoarsely. 'They asked. And I told them . . . all I told them was where she parked and the bit about those cones. That's all.'

'You set her up. You know that, don't you? Don't you? You bastard.' Henry grabbed the porter by the lapels and shook him. From low monotone, his voice reached a crescendo. He let the porter go, his arms hung by his side. Henry turned, looked again at the grotesque sight beyond the front door, and cried.

PART FOUR

Chapter Nineteen

Anthony Hendersly stepped warily out of the lift into darkness. He edged down the corridor gripping a suitcase in one hand, guiding his hand along the wall with the other. The lonely clatter of his footsteps drowned the night-hum of the air-conditioning, and grated on the raw edges of his nerves. He had always found it an eery experience, being alone in a vast building at night. Tonight he felt even more jumpy than usual. He reached his office door and lowered his hand until it touched the handle. He turned it and entered.

'My God!' he gasped. 'You!'

His desk lamp was on casting its light across the sagged and puffy face of Bridgnorth.

'Application form for urgent special leave? Certainly, Mr Hendersly.'

His voice oiled with irony, he reached into the top drawer, already opened, and calmly withdrew a form. Hendersly's eyes froze on Bridgnorth's face and for several seconds neither of them moved. Then, without warning, the door behind Hendersly slammed. He twisted around and in the half-light saw the outline of two men, stocky and carrying small calibre weapons. He whirled back round, his mouth gaping, his eyes wide. Bridgnorth looked quite different in the harsh yellow light. There was a look of bitterness about him, a discernible animosity on his face.

'No sign of Jay. Jardine getting fretful. People clearing off all over the place. Heard you paid a visit to the travel agents this afternoon, Hendersly – got one of the boys to check your destination. And I thought. Why not wait for Hendersly to come back and file his holiday address like Staff Code says he should? Habit. It can be a killer.'

One of the men guarding the door flexed his arm, causing his stiff leather jacket to creak. Hendersly didn't dare turn round, his stomach was bound in knots, his mouth dry and his forehead damp with baubles of sweat. His lips cracked apart to speak but before he could utter a word, Bridgnorth nodded to one of the men.

'Dino, get his passport, tickets and take those ridiculous labels off his case, will you?' Without prompting, Hendersly slipped his hand into his breast pocket to get his passport.

'Ah ah – not so fast, Mr Hendersly,' said Dino, his voice thickly-coated with an Italian accent. He gripped Hendersly's wrist tightly, wrenched the documents from the top pocket and threw them down in front of Bridgnorth. Then, he turned and brushed roughly past Hendersly, who was made aware of the man's broad shoulders and sturdy belly. He also noticed that despite this his face was exceptionally lean, with skin stretched like parchment tightly across his face and crinkled around his black eyes. His hair was greasy and black. Hendersly didn't dare turn to glimpse at the other man.

'Well, Hendersly. Since we've deprived you of one trip, we thought we'd take you on another of our own.' Bridgnorth levered himself up, stuffed the tickets and passport in his pocket and moved round to the front of the desk. He looked at Hendersly from top to toe and smiled approvingly on detecting the fear in his face.

Bridgnorth led the way down the corridor. Hendersly followed the sound of his steps, shoved from behind by two strong-men. The lift doors opened and they got in, the two men talking in rapid Italian.

The one called Dino laughed coarsely.

'What did they say?' asked Hendersly.

Bridgnorth listened.

'They're talking about the lift.'

Hendersly looked at the Italians disparagingly. Of course! 'These two killed Richardson here, didn't they? Who the hell are you working for, Bridgnorth? And who have you had *me* working for?'

'I'm building us all a better future,' he said without smiling. Then, more harshly. 'And if you don't do as you're told and watch your mouth, you're not going to be part of anything but the very dead past.'

Hendersly looked at the ground. The lift jerked to a halt. They were in the underground car park.

'Am I to be killed too?' Hendersly dropped the question so casually he could easily have been asking for a light.

'There's arguments in favour. You're now the only one who knows the lengths I've had to go to to protect Jardine. On the other hand, the disappearance of three of the Department's officials in such a short time might raise eyebrows even in these cynical days . . . don't worry. No one's going to touch a hair on the head of Mrs Hendersly's little boy. Not until I'm sure I know why he decided to cut and run so suddenly.'

Bridgnorth opened his fist, revealing the labels from Hendersly's suitcase. His voice was cutting, his mouth turned downwards in a scowl.

'Who's your mate?' Hendersly pointed gingerly at the Italian guarding him.

'That's Mario, Dino's sidekick.'

'Doesn't say very much.'

'Can't speaka the Eengleesh . . . Oh, here's Dino with the car. Get in.'

With a screech of tyres, Dino steered the black Rover to within inches of where they stood.

'Where are we going?'

'Heathrow. These two are flying back to Rome straightaway.'

Dino cut in. 'No way are we flying out.'

'That was the arrangement.'

'Arrangements change,' said Dino. 'Rome's not happy about your handling of this so far. *We* have been instructed to look after Jardine's arrival ourselves.'

Bridgnorth looked as if he was about to explode. The colour in his face rose, bringing out a pulsating vein on his temple. But instead of a torrent of outrage, Bridgnorth exhaled noisily and stretched out his hand, palm upwards.

'If that's the case you'd better give me the keys and find your own way out. Hendersly, you can drive.' He threw the suitcase into the boot and climbed into the passenger seat.

'Mind the muggers,' he smirked as they drove past the Italians.

'Excitable, open and outgoing? I don't even have a phone number for them. If Rome wants quality control, they can have it. Let's check up the sharp end ourselves.'

It was late morning and they were tired of each other's company. But Bridgnorth had no intention of letting loose his grip on Hendersly. Wearily, they sat in armchairs on opposite sides of the room. It was Hugo Jardine's office, his consulting engineers firm. The room was capacious, neat and had the kind of smell that offices do when they are rarely used. There was a massive desk in solid wood in one corner by the window and along the full stretch of the inside wall was an intricate scale model of a bridge, tunnel and several buildings. An hour before, Bridgnorth had been totally mesmerised by the model, but after fingering and probing it, he had returned to his corner of the room. Hendersly refused thereafter to show any interest in the model at all, on principle. He sat with his feet stretched out in front of him, his shoe-tips pointing to the ceiling, his arms were crossed resolutely over his chest.

'What are we doing here?' he said sullenly.

'Waiting,' came the reply.

'That's bloody obvious. Why *here* of all places?' Hendersly shot him an exasperated look.

'Waiting, for someone,' said Bridgnorth lazily.

'Jardine? Thought as much. Is he coming to London today?'

'Yep.'

Bridgnorth stood up and hitched his trousers up round his waist and began pacing the floor like an angry child locked up in a playpen. It was just as tedious for him to be locked up with Hendersly as Hendersly patently believed it was to be with Bridgnorth. He went to the liquor cabinet, a walnut and mirrors outfit – probably a gift from a grateful client – Bridgnorth mused and poured two glasses of Scotch. He handed one to Hendersly without a word and returned to his seat. It had been a reflex action to fill the vacuum of words rather than any signal of camaraderie.

Bridgnorth didn't like Hendersly much. They were poles apart on any level he wished to enumerate. Bridgnorth saw himself as the bright-eyed boy from a small village in the North who had won a scholarship to Cambridge and never looked back since. He had manoeuvred himself into political circles, landed a good job – and a wife who possessed the same fiery ambitions for him as he had for himself. He worked hard at establishing contact with the right people. Now he had the ear of the Permanent Secretary and was himself the ear for many people down the chain of command in various Government departments. He'd been a shrewd adviser and was respected as such. Gradually, however, he realised that despite his tenacity, his intelligence, his charm and a host of other qualities, he would never rise much beyond his present post. He blamed it on the prejudice of the class structure, his North-country accent and on the fact the country was going to the dogs and couldn't, in any case, use his expertise. Hendersly on the other hand was, in Bridgnorth's view, neither bright nor talented and was thus probably just the man to be promoted up through the hierarchy. He'd been born with a silver spoon in his mouth and had progressed to manhood over a rich carpet of family, friends and favours owed. His job in the Department of Commercial Development owed more to his wife, Valerie's liaisons with Cabinet ministers than to Hendersly's proficiency. Hendersly was arrogant and priggish and occasionally got under people's skins, Bridgnorth noted. But that wouldn't stop him from promotion to Permanent Under Secretary level. He swilled the remaining whisky in his glass down his throat and noisily exhaled the thick fumes through his mouth. Glaring at Hendersly he spoke.

'What was Tomkins doing at Jay's house last night?'

The question caught Hendersly off-guard.

'Tomkins?'

'Your *other* PSO,' said Bridgnorth sarcastically. 'The sweaty little man who sat at the desk opposite Jay's. What was he doing knocking on Jay's front door at five past ten last night?'

'How do you know he was?' Hendersly found himself unable to look Bridgnorth in the eye. Instead he focussed on the bridge of his nose – a device someone had once passed on when he confessed that under duress he couldn't look anyone in the eye. It was a useful tip – it gave the impression of steadfast attentiveness, of not being daunted.

'Word came through when we were at the Reform Club last night – that was the time he was blown up instead of Jay's wife at Westcombe Park.'

Hendersly gave him a look that should have split a rock in two.

'Tomkins . . . blown up?' He repeated the phrase, his jaw hanging in unconcealed horror. 'You didn't have the guts to tell me till now –'

'Nothing to do with guts, Tony . . . And for God's sake, sit down. You're not going anywhere – there's nowhere for you to go.'

Hendersly complied. His body sagged back into his chair. Of course it would be futile to make a run for it. He felt a fool for having so unthinkingly bolted across the room. Bridgnorth was right. Where could he go. Valerie thought he was in Strasbourg, thanks to a telephone call Bridgnorth insisted he made last night. By now, the office would think likewise and Bridgnorth, no doubt would have slickly arranged for a hotel in Strasbourg to take messages for a Mr Hendersly. He was well and truly taped. He would have to swim with the tide, play the game, do what Bridgnorth and his cohorts demanded, if he was to save his own neck. They wouldn't give him another chance, not after last time. It had come as a great shock, to discover Bridgnorth had sold his mind, contacts and colleagues to an omnipotent organisation; that he espoused some great new cause.

And he had helped him. One thing had led to another. Now, whether he liked it or not – and he most positively did not – he had to go along with his scheme. He had tried to make a run for it, and failed. Hendersly figured they wouldn't try to kill him. Not yet. A Hendersly alive was more use to them than a Hendersly dead. And anyway, too many disappearances in the Department of Commercial Development within such a short time would have even the sleepiest journalist asking questions. It would be bound to get out. His head flopped onto his chest and startled him from his doze. He shook his head and cocked a bleary eye in Bridgnorth's direction. He was standing over him, his hands in the pockets of his baggy trousers. Bridgnorth did not blink, he stared at Hendersly, gimlet-eyed.

'Was Tomkins having it off with Jay's missis? Or was he delivering something? What was in the briefcase?' Bridgnorth batted the questions with an even tone, without pause. 'Best available witness says Tomkins had a briefcase at the front gate. It wasn't there by the time the police got there to pick up the bits. Eye-witness says Jay's wife picked it up. Why was Tomkins calling round last night?' He repeated.

'I don't know.'

'You bloody do. The Italians would gut it from you in five minutes flat. They're not available right now so I'll show you the stake we're playing for. Being a high-flyer you'll then tell me of your own accord – because you'll see there's no way you can hold out.'

Hendersly grunted. He was acutely aware of Bridgnorth's vituperative tone, of the way he spat out 'high-flyer'. Bridgnorth was jealous of his family political links and had never tired of rubbing Hendersly's nose in great dollops of paranoid vitriol – nepotism, wife screwing her way to the top. None of it was true – but that didn't stop Bridgnorth. Hendersly's appointment had been made over his head and Bridgnorth was in no hurry to forget it. Over the years he had gone out of his way to prove to his peers their folly.

He followed him across the room, still silent.

The transformation on Bridgnorth's face was staggering. He swapped his deep-set vicious look for a totally besotted one. He rested his hand on part of the giant model and, for a minute, gazed silently.

'Do you know what this beauty is?' he asked softly.

Hendersly shook his head, intrigued by Bridgnorth's fervour.

'Five thousand million pounds worth of steel and concrete and rock fill and armour and ventilating plant and cable. Work for one hundred and twenty thousand people in engineering and construction. Fifty, sixty thousand new service and retail jobs. Only Jardine had the political will and the financial clout to stitch the deal together. Road and rail links, side by side, the Rolls-Royce solution to the channel link, not the cheap 'mousehole' job that the Government came up with only to lose the nerve half-a-mile out. The final round of meetings starts this afternoon. After Jardine and the British and French have signed on the dotted line, nobody can stop this getting built. Just think. A channel tunnel!'

'Should anyone want to stop a Channel link between England and France?'

'There's been somebody around for over a hundred and fifty years putting the kibosh on the project – ever since Napoleon first dreamed up the idea. There's always been a reason. Now the argument is that this Rolls-Royce solution will monopolise the crossing. Not only driving out the business of air-freight because it's cheaper to travel by the Chunnel, but also the ports and ferries. It'll also make an easy mark for military terrorist or industrial action. Five years after this uncorks, squeeze the tunnel here at the French end or somewhere in the middle and a lot of people start to choke.'

'Why not blow up Piccadilly Circus – there would be a lot more victims?'

'Politically, it'd be much more of a hot potato to cut off the Channel Tunnel – affect businesses on both sides of the water.'

'You think they'll say yes, despite that?'

'The Elysée says yes, thinking of a market of fifty-five-and-a-half million two hours' drive away. Brussels says yes, on loftier grounds of Eurocant. Whitehall and Westminster will say yes, seeing those jobs, the likely spin-offs from a moon-size project like this. Particularly at a time when unemployment's denting their popularity and there's an election just round the corner. They'll also say yes because they don't have to pay a penny for it. Over a third of the money is EEC cash. The rest comes from French national banks and the City banks and institutions – thanks to Jardine who has a stake in just about every company that'll cut a metre of that, or lay a cable in it.'

If that is the case, thought Hendersly, then where did Jardine raise his money? Certainly not on the open market and certainly not in his own name. The Government would never allow one man to have such an influence over a project as politically sensitive as this.

Bridgnorth sniffed out his thoughts and pre-empted the question. 'Not even Jardine could set this up on his own, even with his knowledge of how to rig the EEC one-arm bandit. He took a little deal to this multi-national which has roots in Italy. Soon it became a bigger deal. In the finish, he found they really do operate an aggressive acquisition policy, these people.'

'Who are they – what's the multi-national Jardine used?'

'You won't find it in the Business Registry, nor in the book of associations. It's much more loosely constructed, yet more powerful than anything you could imagine. And it doesn't really have a name, not a name you could identify with, anyway.'

'Who's behind the organisation?'

'Different people controlling different strands of business.'

'Political affiliation?'

'Chameleon – wherever the money is; whoever's willing to buy or sell. Keeps it simple, non-partisan.' Bridgnorth walked contemplatively round the model. 'It'll be magnificent,' he smiled at Hendersly, the first time he had acknowledged his existence in any way other than hostile since he'd been 'captured'.

'Yes, it won't stop at turning this into one of the biggest model train-sets in the world,' said Bridgnorth.

Hendersly understood 'it' to mean the organisation, unnamed and mysterious.

'Just think, Hendersly. While everybody else is worrying about re-nationalisation, tail-spin recession, these people are looking forward to better business, mega growth.'

'You mean operate a massive black economy?'

Bridgnorth ignored the remark. 'One. Monopolise the Channel route – buy out the competition –'

'If they don't want to sell?'

'They will, soon enough,' Bridgnorth grinned sadistically. 'Two. Pick off the transport companies. Teamsters-style, one by one. By hiking the tariff, blacking their drivers, losing their wagons. The Tunnel Commission won't interfere, it'll have been bought off, Euro-style.'

'And what about British Airways and other airlines doing European routes and the ferry companies? They can't be bought off – not for all the money in the world.'

'You'd be surprised what can and will be achieved in the next decade or two . . . Point three,' he continued: 'Having bought out or bankrupted the truckers, go for the companies who import or export through them. Three beginners' steps and inside a decade a take from every firm using the link. That means every firm who buys or sells through Europe being part of Great Britain Limited. Road, rail, food, drink, goods out, goods in, we have the say, we take a cut. Governments will stop us? I doubt it.'

Hendersly noticed the word 'we' had crept surreptitiously in though he didn't say anything. He stared attentively between Bridgnorth's eyes.

'So you see, Tony, how high the stakes are, what's at risk. Now, what was Tomkins delivering chez Jay last night?'

Hendersly decided now was as good a time as any to cough up with the information. 'Photostats of Jay's files. Including the appendix and references which linked Jardine with Louis Vacheron of the Italbank fraud.'

'No wonder you wanted a fast plane out.'

'Well, since I'm still here I might be of some use to you now. Do you know what happened to Jay's wife?'

'Not yet.'

'She probably took the files to the weekend retreat – Henry and Anne bought a caravan about five years ago in the foothills somewhere in South Wales. That's where she'd go.'

Chapter Twenty

He leaned up against the highly-polished Daimler and glimpsed with almost childish glee at his new persona in the side mirror. The dark chauffeur's uniform, the black, stiff-peaked cap which, to his mind, made him taller, more svelte. The disguise was set off with a pair of dark glasses and a bristly moustache which he had painstakingly attached to his top lip before setting off to collect the car from the hire firm early that morning. Everything was going according to plan. And so smoothly it almost frightened him. The Government car pool had accepted the cancellation of a car for Hugo Jardine with a minimum of questioning. The uniform had been a doddle to come by, thanks to the hall porter in Rochelle's block of flats. Clearly, the old man had been deeply affected by the brutal murders right on his doorstep. So he should. The bastard had as good as killed Rochelle and Lanchbury when he told the killers about Rochelle's eccentric parking habit. And now, they'd murdered Anne. Two radio stations had reported an explosion at a house in Westcombe Park, resulting in a death. The cause was unknown, police suspected a gas leak. They named the street, wouldn't release the name of the victim until relatives had been notified.

Henry had spent the previous night pacing the box-size room in the porter's flat. Everything was moving so quickly, so horrifyingly, like an unwieldy hurdy-gurdy machine, out of control. He cried. But rage soon dried his tears. He'd see that Hugo Jardine rotted in hell for these murders. More than anything else, Henry wanted Jardine to suffer, slowly, painfully for the lives he had destroyed. Thinking about Anne made him go numb; he almost gave up that night. But revenge drove him on. The events of the past few weeks *had* changed him. He was still in the game, still determined to win; yet with Anne's death he had lost much of his capacity to enjoy it. His appetite was blunted. He was being swept along by feelings he could not properly control. Revenge was his most powerful weapon yet. He wondered if he would ever change again once he'd broken Jardine. Now, he understood what power could do to a man. It was in his grasp, a drug which he had yet to become addicted to though he revelled in its might.

He checked his watch, eleven forty-six. Hugo Jardine was late. He squinted into the distance, there was no sign yet of the helicopter beetling its way over the Thames to the helipad on the river directly before him. He kicked the gravel with the points of his shoes, built a small mound and squashed it underfoot. Compulsively, he looked at his watch again Barely two minutes had passed. Nonchalantly, he slid into the driver's seat. Outside the car, the world hummed contentedly. A river boat bearing ogle-eyed tourists chugged by on its way to Greenwich. A train rattled over Blackfriars Bridge. And there, across the river, was the Founder's Arms, where he and Richardson had met to chew the fat, down a pint and had exchanged information. Those days were gone forever. He broke out in a cold sweat of apprehension. The shock of death, his decisive actions had sublimated most of his fears and anxieties. He fought to block them out of his mind and turned his thoughts to Jardine, to revenge, to the unbridled hatred he had for a man he had never met.

In a few minutes from now, Jardine would step off that barge and into his car. Like a fly unwittingly crawling into a Venus Flytrap. While the rest of London's inhabitants went about their routine tasks, Henry would be launching his most daring act yet. Alone. His stomach lurched and his hands stuck clammily to the steering wheel. The buzz of a helicopter came closer and closer, the noise grew to a roar as it hovered only fifty yards away from him above the barge, flicking back the water and sending the wind-sock crazy. Then, silence. Henry prayed. He wasn't the least bit religious, but now more than ever he wanted somebody to root for him and figured that God was his only chance.

'God, make this work. Make me live long enough to seek my justice with this man . . . just this once . . .'

He stepped nimbly from the car and stood by the back door as Jardine disembarked, shaking hands warmly with the pilot. His pulse reverberated around his ears as the symbol of his hatred approached. Jardine was shorter than he'd imagined at around five foot seven and his hair was greyer round the temples. He was tanned and good-looking for a man of fifty-seven, though slightly raffish. He possessed the kind of charisma invariably found in men of wealth and intelligence. In a way it was almost disappointing to see him in the flesh after living with him through the eyes of the press and computer print-outs. He seemed so ordinary. Henry nodded stiffly as Jardine bent over to climb into the car. He received in return a politician's smile. Henry eased himself behind the steering wheel, adjusted the rear-vision mirror so he could watch Jardine without having to crane his neck.

The car pulled up at an intersection, stopped by traffic lights. Henry had a chilling feeling that somebody was watching him. He checked the rear-vision mirror. Jardine licked his thumb and turned a page of his *Financial Times*, unaware of Henry's scrutiny. He looked nervously at the vehicle behind the Daimler – a beat-up Deux Chevaux with a young couple, unlikely candidates for giving chase. Another car drew level with his – a glistening blue Jaguar XJ6. At the wheel was a swarthy young man in his thirties with jet black hair and tightly-stretched skin. Henry noticed he was wearing hole-punched driving gloves. Next to him was a man who could have been a twin – the same southern European complexion, dark hair, tightly stretched skin around his unsmiling mouth and small, piggy eyes. He fixed his gaze on Henry in such a way that the small hairs on the back of his neck stood erect. Henry had never seen them in his life before but he was sure they were onto him. He would soon find out. The lights changed and the two cars leapt forward. Henry accelerated. So did the Jaguar. Henry changed gear and sped up. The Jaguar nipped in front of the Deux Chevaux and slowed down. He changed gear again and put his foot on the brake pedal, swerved into the fast lane and spun the car into a screaming U-turn.

Jardine's body was flung against the door, his briefcase tumbled to the floor and the newspaper fell apart across his lap.

'What the hell are you doing man?'

Henry looked into the side mirror and then into the rear vision mirror. 'Sorry, sir. Spot of bother with a Jaguar. That bootlegger turn seems to have fixed them.'

Jardine grunted and pressed his *Financial Times* into readable shape. Henry swivelled his eyes between the road ahead and the rear mirrors. Perhaps he'd been mistaken, he thought. Later he would learn just who the two men were and be glad he had looked at them so scrupulously.

The car veered left. Bracken House loomed – the widget factory of the press world where a daily digest of financial and economic information was churned out under the banner of *The Financial Times*. Ahead of them was the Bank of America and as Henry turned the corner and came to a halt at another set of lights, the exquisite whiteness of the Credit Lyonnais building.

'Driver – didn't you receive directions before you picked me up? I have to be at Westminster by eleven fifteen. This is *completely* wrong.'

Henry smiled to himself. 'Yes, Mr Jardine. I know.'He leaned forward and pressed a knob on the panel between the front seats. Instantly, all the doors locked. Jardine heard the soft click and leaned forward.

'I say, what is all this? What *are* you doing?'

Henry turned into a small cobblestoned street he knew well from his lunchtime sojourns in the City and stopped the car. He drew a small calibre handgun from his breast pocket and turned to Jardine.

'Just sit tight. Nothing will happen to you, so long as you sit tight and do as you're told. I promise you, I won't hesitate to use this if I have to.'

Jardine slumped back and closed his eyes. 'Where are you taking me?'

'You'll see soon enough.'

'Who are you – what do you want?'

'You'll find that out soon enough, too, Mr Jardine,' said Henry spitting out his words.

'Look, I have a series of meetings to attend. There will be people looking for me.'

Henry didn't answer. The car twisted through small streets, back-tracking several times to make absolutely certain no one was following them. He steered with his left hand; in his right he clutched the loaded gun, pointed at Jardine's balls.

Jardine showed no sign of being afraid. He sat in the back of the car and looked calmly out of the window. He could well have been going to a board meeting, such was his demeanour. Casually, Jardine lit a fat cigar and drew the thick smoke to his lungs. He flicked the ash onto the floor, as one who no longer cares what people think of him. His ease made Henry feel uncomfortable, small and vulnerable. He had come prepared to do battle. But the man he so reviled was quite unperturbed by his kidnap – at least he seemed that way. It would not last, thought Henry, smugly.

It took almost an hour to reach the tiny dirt road leading to the warehouse. Nobody came there any more, except for a few wild cats which had made this isolated part of Woolwich their home and for a few teenagers who were too old for school, couldn't find work and who came up here occasionally to kill time. It was a discarded memento of the Great British Empire, when sea trade to the colonies from London boomed. The old warehouse had once stored diesel tractor engines. Outside, it was battered and unwelcoming. The weatherboard sign above the great wooden doors had flaked and warped, the company's name long obliterated. Inside, it smelled damp and bitter. Henry knew because he had been here only a few days before, to prepare for this moment.

His nerves jangled, yet he felt in control. He abandoned the car on the dirt track and pushed Jardine in front of him, twisting the gun in the small of his back.

Jardine stopped, said calmly, 'There's no need. I won't run, I give you my word.'

'Move it,' Henry snarled.

They stepped uneasily across the wasteland to the warehouse. Henry unlocked the great door, nudged Jardine inside. They stood for a moment, until their eyes became adjusted to the gloom.

They clattered across the bumpy wooden tiles, every sound they made seemed wired to a loud-speaker system, echoed across the empty floor in the dim light. He sensed Jardine's growing unease and felt comforted by that. He gestured with the gun.

'Up there, the steps on the left – and no funny business.'

It sounded so corny, but he didn't know how else to say it. He had never held a gun before, apart from his childhood days. In fact, the situation was so abnormal, so extraordinary, that he found himself acting with exceptional cool.

They reached a small office at the top. It was windowless, except for the partition which overlooked the main floor. Henry lit a gas lamp. It cast its jaundiced light over the grimy, painted walls and passed over Jardine's face. His jawline was set in a challenging pose, his eyes gleamed in the dim light. Jardine loosened his tie and sat down on a wooden crate in the centre of the room, stared across at Henry and said, 'How did you know about the car pool arrangements?'

Of all the questions Henry had expected him to ask, this was the least likely. But he replied, 'I spent a very dull three months on attached duty there a few years ago for Organisation and Methods. I got to understand their little ways. All very boring. About the only bright spot was the defensive driving course.'

Jardine sucked his lips thoughtfully, nodded. 'I see.' He stared down at his hands, thought again and said eventually. 'Let me give you a telephone number in Rome. My contacts can be here inside a matter of hours.'

'Your contacts!' Henry spat out the words with hate. 'Your contacts killed my wife. I'd rather deal with a mamba.'

Jardine gazed at him. 'I'm sorry to hear about your wife.'

'My wife's dead and you're sorry! Haven't you even got the guts to accept the responsibility? I suppose you'll tell me now that you had nothing to do with it. You're all the same, you lot. Keep your hands clean and get the boys below to carry out your dirty work.'

'I honestly had nothing whatsoever to do with your wife's death. That's not my side of things.'

'Not your side of things, I'm sure. You murdered Louis Vacheron – you knew about *him* didn't you?' You murdered Richardson, the Fraud Squad superintendent, you murdered four, maybe five more people – including my wife – Anne Jay. *My wife!* Did you get that? My name is Henry Jay. Does that mean anything to you?'

Henry towered above him, his eyes bulging with rage.

Jardine shrugged. 'I'm sorry, now. Names. Faces. I see so many. Don't you understand, I have people to handle these things for me. I have people imposed on me. I have no say in their methods. I am sorry about what happened to your wife, and to those others. But you and I, as man to man, have no argument with each other. Why don't we phone Rome and have someone work things out with you?'

Henry stared disbelieving. This man's composure was unfathomable. How could he really be so untouched by what he had heard, even if he hadn't actually pulled a trigger, set off explosives? He paused. Looked at Jardine, decided.

'What's the number?' he asked almost reluctantly.

'Four, seven, five, four, five, double two . . . I think the Rome prefix is zero, one zero, thirty-nine, six. You can check.'

'And what makes you think they haven't wiped their hands of you? Won't shaft me? Why should I trust you or them after what they've done, you've done?'

'I'm needed in one piece. They need you to lead them to me. After that, it's up to you. You'll just have to trust me. But you're a shrewd man, you could handle it, I'm sure. After all, you kidnapped me with amazing ease.' He grinned, with strain, not pleasure.

'Forget the flattery, will you? I don't like you, don't trust you. Just lie down on that rug . . . There! Face down!'

Henry tied him up, not minding that he hurt his captive.

Jardine's hands were clammy and cold as he grabbed them. Just the right texture for a crooked European Member of Parliament and City big-wig, Henry thought. He stripped him of his watch, cigarette lighter and his shoes.

'Bit of a shame really,' he said looking down at Jardine. 'I already have a watch, don't smoke and your shoes are too big for me. Still, it'll keep you out of mischief until I get back.' He gave a small chuckle.

Chapter Twenty-One

There were four of them in Jardine's office by late afternoon. Bridgnorth, Hendersly and the two Italians, Mario and Dino. Dino sat on a chair tilted against the back wall. His head drooped, the tight pout hung at the corners of his Latin lips. He looked at Bridgnorth. Who didn't look at him at all – he turned instead to Hendersly.

'Jay is dead – here's the evidence.'

Hendersly leaned on the table on an elbow and looked at the photographs. 'Jesus Christ, a bloody tangle.'

'Yeah. So whoever has Jardine, it isn't him. Killed last night.'

'Henry?'

'Like I said.'

'*Again?*' Hendersly said, his eyebrows topping his forehead.

'Whaddaya mean?' asked Bridgnorth.

'They killed him the night before, as well, only the bodies turned out to be those of Chambers and Vine.' He smiled sarcastically at Bridgnorth.

Bridgnorth's lips shook. '*You* set him up by giving me the girl's car number. *I* arranged for the tag to be placed on him. And what you see is *how* they did it.'

Hendersly did not relish the thought. He stared towards him for a while, then sank back into the chair and put his head against the upholstery. Then he squeezed his eyes tightly together. It made no difference to his foggy head.

The phone rang. Bridgnorth pounced on it before the high-pitched purr had a chance to annoy him.

'Yeah?'

His feet levitated onto the desk with some difficulty. He grunted with effort, holding the phone close to his ear, looking intolerant. He cupped his hands over the receiver when he had done listening and spoke to Hendersly.

'Why are you routing calls through here?'

'I still have a section to run. Important business only, I told them.'

Hendersly jerked his knees clear of the desk, weaved to his feet and snatched the telephone receiver.

'Yes?' He listened with amazement at the voice.

'The communication of the dead is tongued with fire. Here Bridgnorth, speak to Jay.'

He thrust the telephone at Bridgnorth, smiled smoothly, deliberately, with great 'I told you so' satisfaction. Bridgnorth's mouth dropped, like a side-show clown. He held the receiver just above the desk and gesticulated to Dino to pick up the extension. The Italian cocked his hat back, took a fat, unfiltered cigarette from a flash case and lit it. The smoke curled from the sides of his mouth. Slowly he drew upright and took the extension. Bridgnorth glowered.

Henry spoke: 'I don't want to waste words. I've got Jardine. I intend to kill him. Afterwards, I shall go to the police. There may be a chance I'll stay alive long enough to do some damage to whatever he's been involved in, and to you, I doubt it. But I'm doing this for my wife. You must know about her – after all, you killed her last night. Remember?'

'Listen – listen very carefully, Henry, and don't put the phone down. Your wife is still alive. Do you get that? They missed her last night. Somebody else died instead. That chap, Tomkins. You hear that. Your wife . . .' Bridgnorth snapped his fingers at Hendersly for the name.

'Anne,' Hendersly mouthed.

' . . . Anne is still alive.'

Henry wiped the sweat from his brow with the hand holding his gun and said nothing for a while.

'Where is she?' he asked softly.

'She spent last night in that hen-coop on wheels you call a caravan in Wales. We thought she'd have flown there and checked the place out. No sign of her though. We're still looking. How about a deal – her for Jardine? Straight swap.'

Henry was silent, his soft breathing was the only sign he was still there. Bridgnorth continued.

'We'll get her first – don't fret. It's not amateur hour any more,' he said looking at Hendersly pointedly, 'or a bunch of bloody foreigners. Me this end, you that end. You buy that?'

Another long pause.

Henry set the phone down.

'I'll see.'

The line went dead. Bridgnorth slammed down the receiver and glared at the sun on the carpet. Hendersly was busy peering down a ventilating shaft in the corner. He jerked his head up when the call ended.

'What's the deal?'

'No fucking deal, that's what,' Bridgnorth fulminated.

'Shrewder than I thought, then.'

'What?'

'Jay – playing cat and mouse with you,' said Hendersly.

'He'll wait until he thinks you've found Anne and then negotiate.'

'If he hasn't killed Jardine by then,' fumed Bridgnorth.

'Is that what he said?'

'Sure as hell did.'

'Extraordinary,' oozed Hendersly as he straightened up and moved towards Bridgnorth. 'By the way, don't you feel you're suffering some sort of conflict of loyalties?'

'With regard to what?'

'I've never heard you refer to your little Italian friends as anything but bloody foreigners and I don't think it's part of the Bridgnorth rough charm – yet you're securing this deal for them.'

Bridgnorth snarled at him. 'Do I hate the Henderslys of this world? You know why you've turned out so good at this? You're not just ice, you're a bleedin' perma-frost. The perfect Permanent Under Secretary material.'

'You think my career will get over the wiggle in the snakey line you've been responsible for?'

'You're working on it,' snarled Bridgnorth.

'I've no choice but to stay in with you lot, to the death, however many more deaths there have to be.'

Bridgnorth looked at him coldly. 'You're the sort who presided over our decline, Hendersly, to the point where it's entirely feasible now that the people who'll build that monster project you've been picking at in the corner for real, can hijack virtually the whole country. You're the sort who's gone along with every death this country has suffered since the war, the sort who's kept his job intact, kept his cool, kept the ice-water in your blood and bladder.'

'And *you've* been fighting imaginary battles at our expense,' exploded Hendersly, his eyes blazing.

'Fighting very real battles,' said Bridgnorth evenly.

'To protect people whose incompetence and aloof neglect have got us in this mess.'

Hendersly snorted with disgust. 'And now you're fighting on the side of those you once fought against.'

'*Because* I believe in what this can do for *us*. Not just us as Jardine's men, sub-contracted through Rome, but the national us. That's the honey-pot. Without that channel link the decline continues. Grass grows on the airport runways. We'll be a rumour of a thing that's died. You'll be able to hear them say: "Didn't there used to be a country once, called England",' he broke off and looked at Hendersly. Then at the two Italians. Dino sat, picking at his ear, rolling the wax into a small ball between his thumb and index finger and flicking it lazily at Mario. Who didn't seem to notice, or, if he did, care.

'Right, action,' said Bridgnorth, slapping the desk. 'We'll

need a list of places where Jay's wife could be. Relatives, work-mates, neighbours. Start digging. I'll be here the rest of the day.'

The phone rang. Dino leapt to his feet, grabbed the receiver from Bridgnorth and glared. He spoke rapidly in Italian, his free hand making wide gestures in the air. Bridgnorth looked rattled.

'Oh, Christ, here goes,' he said to no one in particular. 'Some explaining to Rome to do, as well.'

Chapter Twenty-Two

His footsteps echoed across the warehouse – fifty-three, fifty-four, he counted them. Jardine was curled up on the rug in the corner of the room, a fuzzy outline in the murky light.

'Untie these frigging knots will you?' he said when Henry entered. 'They're killing me.'

'More's the pity they won't,' replied Henry curtly. 'You can wait for a few minutes.'

He moved with elaborate slowness towards the gas lamp, lit it and peered down at Jardine. He laid down his gun on one of the packing cases and dipped his hand into one of the brown paper bags he had brought back from town. He unwrapped and devoured a mammoth salt-beef sandwich, followed it off with a chocolate eclair which oozed cream down his fingers. When he had finished licking his fingers, he crunched the paper into a tight ball, threw it against the wall and looked at Jardine. The man was doing his best to look nonchalant, but Henry could tell his torture had worked. Jardine was as hungry as hell. He stuffed the gun in his pocket and ambled over to Jardine, picked away at the knots until they were free of their charge. Jardine stood up. He stretched his stiff limbs and rubbed his wrists.

'Is this necessary?'

Henry stood up, leaned against a large crate, watching.

'Such an elementary question, Mr Jardine. I'm surprised you had to ask it. You don't mind if I don't answer it, do you?'

Jardine stared back. 'Bloody uncomfortable, and damned humiliating, lying there bound up on the concrete floor. Does nothing for one's posture, you know.' It was an attempt at a joke.

'This is not the Ritz. And none of your friends are likely to pop by to see you in your "humiliating" predicament – not if I can help it,' Henry remarked grimly.

'Just trying to ease the tensions a bit, that was all,' said Jardine hoisting himself shakily off the floor onto one of the crates, 'Look, why don't we come to an arrangement?'

'You've already suggested that.'

'Well?'

'I'm thinking about it. Seems like a bad idea to me.'

'I could work some deal – you could benefit too.'

'I'd be digging my own grave if I listened to you. Just get used to the idea will you that *I'm* running the show now.'

'I think you are making a grave error,' said Jardine.

'You would.'

It was the middle of the night and Jardine was snoring, raucous and adenoidal sounds that disturbed Henry, made him despise Jardine even more. He felt no remorse at all when he'd tied Jardine up just after nightfall. And he had been slightly put out at the ease with which Jardine was now sleeping, his body curled up on the make-shift bed.

Henry tip-toed across the concrete in his socks, more out of ill-ease than courtesy towards Jardine. The small torch squirted light ahead of him as he made his way to the pit. A rustling sound a few yards to his right made his heart jump. He turned the torch in the direction of the noise – a large rat was clawing at some straw in a packing case. It froze, its beady eyes fixed hypnotically on Henry. 'Pssssss' he threatened it. The rat darted off into the darkness. When

Henry had finished tinkling into the pit he slunk quietly back into his sleeping bag. The rat had spooked him.

He awoke next morning feeling heavy and sore, as if he'd been running in his sleep. Jardine was writhing beneath the blanket, struggling against the nylon rope around his arms and legs, mumbling incoherently. Henry rolled up his sleeping bag, gave Jardine a gentle kick in the ribs. Jardine grunted, parted his eye-lids and squeezed them together tightly. Henry kicked him again, this time harder.

'Wakey, wakey. Rise and shine!' he cooed mockingly.

Jardine moaned. 'What's the time?'

'Morning,' said Henry uninformatively.

Jardine rolled over onto his back, his eyes sprang open. He saw Henry, sitting on a wooden box by the door, ploughing his way through a mountain of cornflakes. He watched him set down the empty bowl, lick his lips, then move towards him. Henry untied Jardine, returned to his perch, smoothed his hand over the gun in silent warning. Jardine sat up and yawned.

'Mind if I take a pee?'

'You know where it is,' said Henry. 'No monkey business.'

He stood at the foot of the rickety stairs and watched Jardine at the pit. He was taking no chances with his prize catch. When Jardine returned, Henry began twiddling with the knobs of a small transistor, tuned it to LBC, to the news.

'... the biggest single rise in unemployment in three months ... Scotland Yard's anti-terrorist squad are still searching for Hugo Jardine, European Member of Parliament. He disappeared yesterday. Mr Jardine was expected at a meeting with British and French Ministers at the House of Commons to finalise details on the Channel Tunnel project, but he failed to arrive. A spokesman for Scotland Yard told IRN they fear he may have been kidnapped. As yet, no one has claimed responsibility. Terrorist groups have not been ruled out. Fifty-seven-year-old Mr Jardine is a leading British businessman. He is chairman of Frost Engineering International and holds major share stakes and directorships in several large companies. For over ten years, Mr Jardine has spearheaded a campaign to construct a tunnel between France and England. He saw the realisation of this one hundred-and-eighty-year-old dream earlier this year when a British consortium got the go-ahead from the Government. Frost's shares slid by five pence to close at ninety-eight on the Stock Exchange . . . the rift in the Labour Party widened further yesterday as . . .'

Jardine listened impassionately.

'Nice to know I'm missed,' he said without any emotion in his voice.

Henry didn't say a word. He watched Jardine push back the quicks of his nails. The broadcast had put the wind up Jardine. It certainly unnerved him, too, a bit.

'Let's make a deal,' Henry said.

Jardine's shoulders dropped visibly. He smiled, looked gratified.

'Let's start with Rome,' Jardine said.

An hour later they were still talking.

'The West is turning to bandit country, Henry. Private armies. Industrial baronies. Political baronies. Criminal baronies. You've proved the state of things by what you've done in taking me.'

'I was forced into this. Nothing to do with your theory at all,' said Henry.

'Forced. Interesting word. Imposed, inflicted, made compulsory. This chap, Bridgnorth, might say he was left no alternative but to accept the offer of working for me here. I might say that for the greater good I was forced to raise cash wherever I could; no matter what the strings were . . . you're raising a file?' his last sentence came abruptly.

'Correct. I know some of the details of your scheme. But I need the rest.'

Jardine shifted his weight, and said, 'You're quite remarkable, really. We are sitting here, God only knows where *here* is. But here we are. Important people in London and dangerous and important people in Rome, Brussels, other centres of Europe for that matter, are trying to find out what's happened to me. The police are now in on the act.

And you are prepared to raise a file.' He shook his head in mild disbelief.

'Please!' Henry cut in. 'I have to have something apart from your body to bargain with.'

'My body?' Jardine's eyes narrowed.

'These places are cold and damp. You aren't young. You might have any number of conditions worsened by staying here, especially without food or drink.' Jardine raised his eyebrows.

'No. Not until my file is completed.'

'And then?'

'Not until my wife is returned to me, unharmed.'

'You told me she was dead. That I had murdered her.'

'New evidence,' said Henry, his eyes fixed stubbornly on Jardine. 'She escaped the bomb blast which wrecked our house. Instead, you managed to kill one of my colleagues. A man who had nothing to do with you or your perfidious chums.'

'I see.'

'I wouldn't bet on that.' Henry bared his teeth.

'How long is this going to take?'

Henry shrugged.

'Days?'

'Or weeks,' said Henry. 'I mean to get the truth from you at any cost to you, Jardine.'

The shrivelled guard shook his head.

'Flat thirty-three's closed till further notice . . . orders, see.'

'But . . .'

'Just leave it at that, madam. Go and ask the wally outside why. The one who's standing over that bloody great hole in the road. I'm definitely not taking that parcel of yours, either.' He looked down his nose at the large envelope in Anne's arms and shook his head again.

'It's all right. I'll look after that for you, Anne.'

She swung around, looked. In the doorway stood Hendersly, smiling treacherously, she thought.

He said, quoting, '"I think we are in rats alley, where the dead men lost their bones" . . . Rochelle would have been no assistance to you. They killed her here the other night. Didn't the porter tell you?'

'No,' she whispered, staring miserably at him.

'But Henry's still alive.'

She nodded, greatly relieved. Then her lips curled downwards and she said, 'And so are you, I see.'

'I'm a good all-rounder, in line with the best traditions of the service, Anne,' he said digging his hands into his pockets. 'One has to be prepared to do what's best for whichever master one is answerable to.'

'And who have you sold yourself to now?'

He stood in the entrance of the building next to her, stared ahead, said nothing.

'I said . . . who is your master now?'

He was about to answer when Bridgnorth appeared, on foot, his face like putty. Dino and Mario were right behind.

'Car's just here, Hendersly,' said Bridgnorth. 'Get in, both of you. Mrs Jay, in the front.'

They got in. Bridgnorth sat in the driver's seat, made no attempt to drive off. He glared at Hendersly in the rear vision mirror. 'Good at the desk, but a lousy legman, Hendersly. You've got to start a lot younger.'

'I'd have brought her in straight away. You didn't give me a chance.'

'Or maybe you'd have taken her and the file to Henry? Or tried to do a deal for yourself.'

Bridgnorth leaned forward and turned on the radio, loud.

Hendersly looked at Dino on his left, then at Mario on his right. Both had flick knives clutched in their thick hands, threatening. Hendersly looked at Bridgnorth's eyes reflected in the mirror.

'I've done my best for you Mr Bridgnorth. I've always done my best. I've not just done as I've been told. I've thought ahead, tried to anticipate. I've been a good number two. I didn't ask for explanation I just got on with cover-up after cover-up. I never complained when time after time it went wrong because you couldn't handle Jay.' His lips white and dry, his eyes fear-crazed, 'This isn't fair . . .'

He didn't stand a chance. They plunged their knives deep into his side, again into his chest. He slumped forward and hit his head on the upholstery. Blood oozed, spread across his shirt. Anne let out a scream. Bridgnorth threw his hand over her mouth. The music bellowed out.

'Is he dead?' said Bridgnorth.

'Good as,' replied Dino.

'Most unfortunate,' said Bridgnorth. 'Tragic, that he tried to double-cross us. Just tragic.' His voice changed, became hard. He snapped, 'Now get him out of here. Find his keys. Put him in his own contraption – the Vauxhall just in front of us. And be discreet will you?'

They wrapped the car rug around his body, propped him between them and walked slowly to the car in front. Hardly anyone noticed.

'A glass of water at least?' Jardine pestered. He'd been talking for what seemed like hours without a break. His throat and mouth were dry, his lips white. Henry didn't look up, continued to write trying to keep pace with Jardine's speech.

He said, 'Now, the precise arrangement by which your bid for the contract came to be the one accepted by the British, the French and the EEC.'

Jardine shrugged, defeated. 'Funding was difficult, it's taken years of behind-the-scenes talks, it's still going on. The EEC's agreed to cough up with a fifth of the money. Five hundred million or so from the transport infrastructure fund, the same again from the European Investment Bank – we achieved that despite a lack of guarantee from the British Government. It's been tricky since the change of Government in France. But we've pulled together a package. Other sources include public issues and private placement of long-term, fixed rate bonds in various international capital markets. Mainly the UK – it's the only place interested which could provide us with sufficiently big chunks of money for up to twenty-five years. The rest of the money would come from British pension funds and clearing banks, the banks working a syndicated loan system.'

Jardine paused while Henry skated his pen across paper. Then he resumed his explanation.

'These investors wouldn't regard the project as entirely free of political influence and therefore not a true equity situation. We were to have agreed a hefty compensation system should the British or French decide for one reason or another to pull the plug. But it would be unlikely.'

'Why?'

'One of the deals I arranged – one of the reasons why I was successful in getting this project off the ground was that the British and French did a deal with the EEC – we got the go-ahead and the money as a way of compensating Britain for its allegedly disproportionate contributions, to help with the agricultural fund. Also, to ensure that Britain didn't pull out of the Common Market. They're locked in there now, with quite a nice package, regardless of whether any musical chairs take place in Westminster at the next general election. Their hands are tied. Of course, the whole deal was really cemented, not just by me.'

'Who else then? One of the top dogs in Le Pouvoir?'

'No. Our power lies in controlling the institutions, controlling the cash flow in and out during the construction period – and afterwards. Tolls should pay for the running of the Tunnel. The man who really pulled the deal off as far as we were concerned is British and backed by Le Pouvoir. He coerced the banks and institutions with a nod and a wink, a few sherries. Let's just say the Bank of England was more than useful in pulling off the deal.'

Henry puffed his cheeks, exhaled. 'That's pulling power indeed.'

For several more hours, Jardine continued his monologue while Henry transcribed copiously, stopping him when he became bogged down by the welter of information, making him repeat, explain certain things.

Jardine veered off the subject, said wearily, 'I do see the

faces of you people, going to your offices, seated at your desks. I've often envied you. For me, it's Strasbourg one day, Brussels the next, a meeting in London, Paris, Geneva for dinner. I've been tired, ill. I seem to be nauseous most of the time. Stress I'm told. Often, I think how nice it would be to be the person opening the door, handing over the telephone, rather than having to chair or sit through one more meeting, arrange a further pay-off, debt, credit. You go home at five, half-five, whenever. I'm eating plastic food somewhere above Europe, sat at one of a dozen desks, wondering sometimes how I cope with it all.'

'Let's face it, Jardine. There are advantages in owning and controlling things. Massive benefits, I would have thought.'

'I'm a legal fiction. A paper fabrication. If I didn't exist, company accountants would have to invent me. I'm a great go-between, recognised City figure. But what do I *really* control. Not even my own physical security.' He stopped, put his hand on his forehead. 'Henry?' Jardine jerked his head towards him. 'What I looked like surprised you, didn't it? I wasn't quite what you expected, was I? Am I right?'

Henry scraped his teeth over his bottom lip, pensively.

'I suppose.'

Jardine nodded, reassured.

Henry ploughed on. 'Let's get back to the file, shall we? Your link with the Italbank fraud?'

'Simply that Vacheron threatened to blackmail me into helping him. His girlfriend in the Commission's legal department had read something in the files that tied me in with the Italians. I think that was it. Some person came to explain. It's hard to remember.'

'And Vacheron was killed.'

'So you tell me.'

Jardine gave a weary sigh. He tried to focus on Henry and found his vision blurred. He was hungry, his body was uncleaned, smelly. And he had given Henry Jay details of a scheme which only a handful of top people knew about. He felt lousy.

Chapter Twenty-Three

She got out of the car and allowed him to push her up the steps into the building, a run-down Georgian house converted into an office, like so many in that part of North London. She stared red-eyed, her face was gaunt, her body limp with shock. They walked into a small room. Bridgnorth flicked the light switch. The fluorescent tube sputtered and cracked. He bent down and turned on what appeared to be an office copier.

He tried to make conversation. She only half-listened to what he had to say. Her eyes were fixed on the machine, it was a paper shredder. As Bridgnorth talked he fed in Henry's file, page by page. The machine spewed them out the other side in long, thin strips into a rubbish bin.

'Never underestimate your underlings, they're the people your back's turned to. That's what I try to get across to the trainees.' He seemed to be giving her a lecture. She tried to fathom the reason, but her mind had closed.

'Never under-claim expenses and never assume it's not an accident you've got where you are, because somewhere in the centre of the office is a Jay, a Tomkins, a Hendersly, just waiting their chance.' He paused, fed a few more sheets into the machine and continued: 'Hendersly . . . bumbled into something he didn't understand. Tomkins. Too sheer bloody persistent wanting to do his job right. Henry . . .'

The last sheet of Henry's computer fraud file cascaded in ribbons into the bin. Bridgnorth looked up triumphantly. Smiled. She stared blankly. He spoke again.

'There's something extraordinary about everyone, don't you think? Think hard enough about everyone you know, there's something unexpected in there somewhere. Henry's persistence. Hendersly suddenly finding the guts to double-cross me.'

She found her voice. 'You don't know what he was going to do. He might have wanted to surprise you, bring me back, bring Henry's file as his bonus catch; prove his competence.'

Privately, she thought it unlikely. Hendersly had lacked the moral fibre. Even when he had wanted to help Henry he had lacked the guts to deliver the file and, by a cruel twist of fate, Tomkins had been murdered. And for what? She gazed down at the great mound of shredded paper.

'Let's go,' Bridgnorth said, grabbing her arm. He led her along the dingy hallway into a large, well-lit room. The two Italians were there. She stared sullenly at them; noted their expressions; arrogant, bored. Their treacherous occupation was given away by their faces; they might have once been good-looking, a long time ago, she thought, but now their eyes and lips were cruel, beyond caring.

'Why did you decide to use this place?' Bridgnorth's eyes wandered over the spartan room and fixed on Dino.

'Because Jardine's office is hot. Fuzz all over the place.'

'And how the hell do we keep in touch with Jay and does Rome know where we are?'

'It's all been arranged, don't you worry,' he smiled, as if it hurt.

'We've got Jay coming on – wants to hear the dulcet, happy tones of his wife to make sure she's okay. And we're waiting for a call from Rome to give the green light to the swap.'

Dino put out a nicotine-stained finger. 'Stop fussing, me and Mario have things under control.' It was more a threat than a gesture of comfort.

The four of them sat there. Anne looked lost, bewildered, Bridgnorth twitched impatiently, Mario and Dino gabbled softly in words only they could understand. You could cut the atmosphere with a knife.

The phone rang.

'I'll get it,' Bridgnorth cautioned Dino who had reached across to lift the receiver. 'It's probably Rome.' Dino shrugged, lit a cigarette and blew the smoke at the ceiling, watched Bridgnorth dash across the room.

Bridgnorth picked up the receiver, listened.

'Henry, she's here. We've got Anne with us . . . hang on a minute, I'll put her on.' He cupped his hand over the mouthpiece, hissed, 'Nice and cheerful like – or we'll have you go the same place as Hendersly.' He gave her the phone.

She trembled and continued to tremble. 'Darling, it's me . . . yes, I'm fine . . . yes, they're treating me all right . . . you? Are you well? What's happening . . . what are they going to do?'

Bridgnorth snatched the receiver from her hands and spoke. 'See, the little woman's in good hands and in one piece, just as I promised. We're still waiting for Rome to call to okay the swap . . . You've already spoken to Rome?'

He heaved his body to the edge of his seat, his voice raised. As he spoke the other phone let out a sharp ring. Dino got up, walked sleepily to the other side of the room, answered.

'Hold it a minute, Henry, the other phone's just gone . . . could be Rome now. Is it?' he turned towards Dino.

The Italian nodded, put the phone on the desk, perched himself on the window-sill and stubbed out his cigarette.

'They want me?' asked Bridgnorth.

'Mario,' said Dino lazily.

The conversation was short, Mario said little, nodded a lot and then set the phone down. He spoke rapidly in Italian to Dino.

'It checks. Rome says "yes".'

It was a quarter to eight in the morning and Henry was already up and dressed and brooding over *Private Eye* in the gloomy light of the warehouse. He used to enjoy his fortnightly fix of caustic wit and scandal and turned the pages with great relish to find subterranean comment on Cabinet Ministers he knew, on the aristocracy he didn't. But this morning he had other things on his mind and the magazine which normally soaked up his attention now seemed tawdry and crude. He flung it aside. Jardine was awake but not moving from his make-shift bed. In less than two hours Henry would be negotiating an exchange with Bridgnorth. He should have felt elated. Instead, he felt utter dread. Henry stood and pulled his jersey down over his hips, fiddled with the broken zip on the suitcase. Didn't know what else to do. He had been up since dawn, shaved, washed – though the water was cold and stung his face. His clothes were fresh but slightly crumpled from lying too long in the suitcase. He had packed almost everything neatly into the boxes he had brought nearly a week before. It never occurred to Henry how ludicrous it all was. That in less than two hours it wouldn't matter; that his life would hopefully return to some semblance of normality. He had been concerned with getting the stuff out. Just as he had predicted, the Daimler had been nicked a couple of days after he left it unlocked on the dirt track. He hadn't considered his escape route. Madness, he muttered under his breath. Total madness.

Jardine picked at the corners of his sleep-clogged eyes and looked up.

'So, it really is to happen today then, not just something I dreamed last night?' His face was pale, eye-lids puffed and lips cracked. His hair was frizzed and wiry. His arms hung loose by his side.

Henry looked at him almost pityingly. 'Yes,' he said. 'In a couple of hours' time you'll be free.'

'I don't know that "free" is exactly the word I would have used. Still, take your point, old man. They're handing your wife over then?'

'Yes.'

'And making a few concessions besides?'

'Of course.'

'Amazing they trusted you overnight. I'd have thought they would want to exchange your wife for me immediately to be on the safe side. They must have believed you wouldn't pull the wool over their eyes.'

'Precisely the opposite, as a matter of fact. When I wouldn't tell them where we were, insisted they met me somewhere and that I would direct them to the warehouse they became cagey, thought, nightfall, Jay knows the lay of the land – could be a trap. This way, they figured daylight, instant swap. I phone them an hour before with the location, they come on down, do it, that's it.'

Jardine smiled, said, 'Well, I can't say I'll be sorry to leave this place – get something inside my belly. Any chance of getting something to eat, now that you've got all the information you want from me and you've decided not to kill me?'

Henry looked at him, his eyes wide with surprise.

'Yes, I knew you wanted to kill me,' said Jardine softly.

'You could have fooled me, you were so calm. Weren't you afraid?'

'Shitting bricks, actually. Years of training at disguising my thoughts, feelings, helped. And I thought that if I struck a deal with you, I might get out of here alive. God only knows what I'll go onto now. My guts go watery thinking about it. I'll probably be blackballed by everyone, even my wife – until now, she's valued the perks of marriage too strongly to leave me. One whiff of public scandal, she'll be off. You don't know how bloody lucky you are to have a wife like Anne who's stood behind you through all this.'

'It isn't over yet. Who knows what she'll do once I'm back. Things have changed so much. I've changed, that will be the hardest thing for her to take.'

'Could be the best thing that's ever happened to your marriage. You never know.'

Henry pried himself from the packing case, walked up and down the small space, then said, 'You know it's strange, the power and adaptability of the mind – I wanted to see you suffer, wanted you dead. I hated you for what you had done to my wife, my friends and colleagues. I wanted revenge. Now those feelings have gone, irretrievably, locked in the back of my mind, like pain. Now I feel sad, wish that all of this had never happened. But it couldn't be stopped, could it? Not by anyone. Not really. Even now, it will go on, won't it?'

'In one shape or another,' said Jardine.

'To think that in different circumstances you wouldn't have even spoken to me at all.'

Jardine nodded, eyes down. 'Probably not,' he replied honestly. 'What are you going to do after all this is over, Henry?'

'All I want, all I've ever wanted, is to get back to my desk. I don't suppose Hendersly – that's my boss – will allow that. I was going for promotion, I suppose I could still get it, now that my competition's been so crudely removed. Get back to being boring, plodding, meticulous old Henry with a new twist, I suppose.'

Anne looked at Bridgnorth with cool disdain. As they drove along, heading towards Woolwich, Bridgnorth could feel her great dark eyes examining his profile, as if the outline of his face might hold a clue to his mind inside.

'Henry know this area well?' asked Bridgnorth staring at the road ahead, his hands clamped to the steering wheel.

'Pretty well,' replied Anne non-committedly . She felt terrified. While fear paralysed her mind, made her seem unconcerned. Which was far from true.

'Sure we're going in the right direction, we seem to be headed for a shopping centre?' Bridgnorth said craning his neck to check with Dino in the rear-vision mirror.

'Just keep driving straight through. That's what he said,' Dino glared.

The Vauxhall turned off the main road and began to bump down the dirt track. Mario heaved up in the seat and peered between Bridgnorth and Anne, said something in Italian.

'Just here will do,' translated Dino. It had started to rain, light drops fell on the windscreen.

Anne pulled her coat around her and asked in a composed voice, 'What's supposed to happen now?'

'Ask no questions and we will not tell no lies,' said Dino.

She overlooked his double negative reply, waited, as Bridgnorth turned off the ignition. He put his hands on his knees and stared across towards the warehouse. Where the dirt track ended there was dead brown grass with a few low bushes scattered about. Apart from that there was nothing between the car and the warehouse.

Dino and Mario got out of the car, looked across at the warehouse, had a few quiet words with each other and turned back towards the car.

'Let's go, Bridgnorth,' said Dino, holding a sawn-off shotgun waist high. Anne got out, stumbled over some rubble by the side of the track. Bridgnorth grabbed her arm sharply and continued to hold onto her as they walked across the dry grass.

They got to the warehouse. Dino kicked open the door, it swung back a few feet, then shuddered to a halt.

'Okay, you first,' he said pointing the gun at Anne.

She was shaking uncontrollably now and couldn't move. Her wet hair clung to her face, her eyes were glassy with fear. Bridgnorth jerked her forward and they stepped inside, Dino and Mario right behind them, guns raised.

They could barely see. A weak sunlight filtered through the sky-lights on the side, beaming up specks of dust.

Mario muttered something, pointing to Anne.

Dino spoke to her. 'He wants you to stand there, to the left . . . no further over.' He pushed her roughly. 'Please.'

She turned her head round to face Bridgnorth, and said in a quivering voice: 'They don't mean to let Henry away, do they? It's a trap.'

'Co-operate, woman. You have no choice,' he told her gruffly.

Mario turned to Bridgnorth, spoke in Italian.

'Him. The middle. Slowly.'

Dino translated. 'He wants you along there.'

He shoved the gun in Bridgnorth's back and pushed him to the right. Then took cover behind a sheet of corrugated iron. He looked around to see if they had missed anything, nodded approvingly, smiled without parting his lips.

They didn't wait long. From the darkened corner on the far side, Henry emerged, clutching a file in one hand. He stepped forward, slowly, deliberately. His face was grave.

Anne gasped when she saw him. Henry stopped walking, stared at Anne. She opened her mouth to say something but caught Dino's warning eye and caught her breath.

'Please,' he said. 'There is nothing you can do now.' She nodded and pinned her eyes on Henry. He began walking towards them. Bridgnorth moved forward. They met in the middle of the vast room, stood side-by-side; if anything should go wrong, Bridgnorth wanted to make certain there was a clear line of fire to Henry. He spoke without any tone in his voice. 'Jardine?' Henry jerked back his head, his eyes fixed on Bridgnorth's face. Bridgnorth squinted into the dark corner, saw Jardine's figure blurred in the dim light, his arms behind him, presumably bound. But he was alive.

He turned back and yelled. 'It's okay, he's here.'

The sound rippled around the room, Bridgnorth watched Dino and Mario leave their cover, crouched as if ready to fire. They didn't move. Something had gone wrong. The plan was for one of them to ease in and grab Jardine while the other pinned his gun on Henry. His face was red and sweaty, his throat tight. The two guns swivelled. He heard the hammer click on Mario's shotgun. The slug from the gun knocked him forward. He staggered back, the puzzled frown still etched across his forehead as he was falling. His putty face was whiter than Henry had ever seen before. Then he slumped onto the hard floor, like a half-filled sand-bag, blood oozing out from under him.

Jardine darted forwards, struggling with the knots binding his wrists. It was a fatal mistake. Dino raised his gun and took aim. The gun jumped. Jardine hit the floor with his face, writhed for a few seconds, then went limp. It was a clean kill.

Henry stood there, the file still clasped in his hand. The pistol lay dormant in his pocket. He stepped around Bridgnorth's body, barely glancing at him and made his way towards Anne. She collapsed into his arms, weeping. He kissed her hair gently, held her firmly in his arms

'Time to go home,' he said a little unsteadily.

They stopped walking and leaned on the railings, looking down into the water. Behind them was the Greenwich Observatory. The mild, wet autumn morning had collapsed into a muggy afternoon. Henry and Anne had walked for miles, saying little to each other. Now he linked his arm through hers, began talking. He explained everything; his days in the bedsit, Brussels with Hannah, Rochelle, all about

Jardine. She was crying now. He brushed the tears from her face with his fingers and drew her close. There were few people around, it felt like a Sunday. No one paid any attention to them.

Henry felt as if he had descended in an extremely fast lift; his stomach was somewhere high in his chest, his throat was tight. Anne looked up at him and smiled weakly. She stopped crying and blew her nose loudly on Henry's crinkled handkerchief.

'It's strange, how I was always the strong one, you were the one who panicked, but when I saw you standing there, those Italians with their guns pointing at you . . . it seemed as if everything had changed . . . you were so certain and I felt utterly . . .' her voice petered out.

He stroked her hair softly.

'I was petrified,' he admitted. 'I almost ran. Then I realised, if I did, I'd wreck their plans completely.'

'You mean, you knew they were going to kill Jardine and Bridgnorth?'

He nodded at the ground.

'Rome decided the operation was in danger of collapse with Jardine alive to talk – and he would have, eventually. He was too close to them, he'd have been a sitting duck, the press, they'd have had a field day on him. Besides, he'd done most of the work on the Channel scheme they needed him for.'

'What about Bridgnorth?'

'Too ambitious, too mediocre, I suppose. One thing I've come to learn since this blew up in my face, they wouldn't go in for any indulgent liquidations.'

'You have to be joking – Chambers, Vine, Richardson, Tomkins, to name a few – all ruthlessly murdered.'

'Necessary.' He paused. 'Of course, Tomkins got in the way. It was a grotesque error.'

They lapsed into silence for a while. Then, she said: 'So what's the problem stopping them from going ahead now?'

'Me,' he said heavily. 'I raised a file, got enough information to hang them all.'

'That file's easily disposed of too, you know.'

'Too?'

'Bridgnorth's finest hour was spent gloating over a shredding machine out of which poured a very mangled computer fraud file.'

'So, the bastards got their hands on it after all.'He spoke slowly, bitterly. 'They won't mince this file. And it wouldn't do them any good if they did. I broke through to Rochelle's office, fed everything into the Government's computer network. Unless I'm alive to code in a counter-instruction every month, hundreds of civil servants throughout the country in over two hundred and fifty computer centres will get an eyeful of extraordinary information. The details are in my report – Appendix Fifteen. Only no one ever reads a report properly though, do they?'

He suddenly felt very tired and everything seemed to drift past him without making contact.

Anne squeezed his hand.

'Henry Jay. I do love you so much.'

'And I love you.'

'Where to from here?' she asked, her voice barely above a whisper.

'Let's stay in a hotel, treat ourselves.'

'Just where do we get that kind of money?' she turned her gaze full at him. 'The insurance people will take forever to cough up.'

'Everything's taken care of. Rome's picked up the tab, they'll see us through. Let's forget all that, let's forget everything. We'll have a few drinks and then . . . we'll go to bed.'

Epilogue

Henry opened the door, nervous. There was nobody in the office. Bolder now, he walked across to his old desk and sat down. He swivelled round the chair and stared at the wall ahead. The same old postcards, yellowing memorandums on the noticeboard. The pot-plants were still on the window ledge. Just as before. He stared down at his desk, bare and recently polished. Tomkins' desk was the same, except for a flutter of papers in the two trays marked 'in' and 'out'.

The typing pool girls would soon start trickling through the door. He wondered how much they knew. Not much, he supposed. He got up and began walking around the office, whistling softly to himself a tune he'd heard on the radio as he left the hotel. He didn't hear the door open, see anyone walk in. His back was turned. A voice said:

'Back early I see, Henry, from special leave to face the music, eh?'

Henry swung around towards the voice to confront a weasel-faced man in his forties with slate-grey eyes piercing him.

'What do you mean?'

A stab of fear punctured his stomach. He hadn't expected confrontation so early in the morning, least of all from Richard Potter, A Higher Executive Officer in the department. He didn't like Potter much, never had. Potter gave him a toothy smile.

'You were supposed to read a paper on the history of the watermark at the Philately Society on Thursday – remember?'

Henry choked back a smile of relief and said, 'Of course. I'll have to make my apologies. It completely slipped my mind.'

He grinned now, apologetically, he hoped. Potter probably hadn't a clue what had been going on behind the scenes. Whatever had happened over the past few weeks had been smothered by the highest officials. Henry wondered just how long it would stay that way. He flipped casually through the pages of a file on one of the cabinets. He exuded an aura of cool superiority. Neither of them said anything for a while. When the pause had made its impact, Henry spoke.

'So, what's been happening while I've had my feet up?'

Potter dug his hands into his pockets, spoke conspiratorially.

'There's definitely something up. Don't know what, though. There are new security procedures – odd-bods popping up to interview people, files being called for from all over the shop. I'm sort of filling Anthony Chambers' shoes in the meantime, and I can tell you this much, you've been well out of it all.'

'Sounds it,' said Henry, shifting his thoughts.

He moved back and sat down at his desk.

'Not that desk,' said Potter abruptly. 'Take a look at this.'

He pulled a memo from the orange in-tray on one of the typists' desks and gave it to Henry. It was obvious he had already plundered the trays before Henry arrived. His eyes drifted down the page, told him that Hendersly had been promoted to the Ministry of Agriculture, Food and Fisheries. Tomkins had been 'promoted' to Principal Scientific Officer, deputy, Manchester.

Potter leered. 'You've done all right out of it, haven't you?'

Henry ignored him, continued to read the memo. He sucked in the words with pleasure: he'd got Hendersly's job! He read on. Temporarily, until such time that the post can be filled on a full-time basis.

'You must be mighty pleased,' Potter continued.

Henry shrugged. He collected up his briefcase and files and walked out of the office, brushing past Potter. Imbued with growing confidence he walked into Hendersly's office, stepped behind the desk, sat down and placed his feet under the desk. Potter had followed him into the room. He was still wittering on.

'You must have some good friends in high places, Henry, making themselves busy for you, eh?'

Henry despised Potter, loathed him. He stared at him

without saying a word. Potter continued his snide remarks.

'Everyone thought Tomkins was going to get the job you know. But as you see, he's gone to Manchester.'

That was one way of putting it, Henry thought.

Potter was patently jealous. His prose was unexpurgated, his voice was nasal and irritating.

'Do you think you'll be able to manage then, till they get a proper replacement for Hendersly, eh?' he asked using sarcasm with all the subtlety of a cosh.

Henry dropped a pile of forms onto the desk, clasped his hands together and stared long enough to send Potter's gaze off in another direction round the room.

'I think I should be able to cope, Potter,' he said, feeling relaxed and in total command. 'Yes, I should cope quite nicely.'

The best thing about the future, Henry remembered, is that it comes only one day at a time.